A is for Amish

SHELLEY SHEPARD GRAY

A is for Amish

KENSINGTON
PUBLISHING CORP.

www.kensingtonbooks.com

KENSINGTON BOOKS are published by

Kensington Publishing Corp.
900 Third Ave.
New York, NY 10022

All Kensington titles, imprints, and distributed lines are available at special quantity discounts for bulk purchases for sales promotion, premiums, fund-raising, educational, or institutional use. Special book excerpts or customized printings can also be created to fit specific needs. For details, write or phone the office of the Kensington Special Sales Manager: Attn. Special Sales Department, Kensington Publishing Corp., 900 Third Avenue, New York, NY 10022. Phone: 1-800-221-2647.

Library of Congress Control Number: 2024932254

ISBN: 978-1-4967-4884-3
First Kensington Hardcover Edition: July 2024

ISBN: 978-1-4967-4885-0 (trade)

ISBN: 978-1-4967-4886-7 (ebook)

10 9 8 7 6 5 4 3 2 1

Printed in the United States of America

He renews my strength. He guides me along the right paths,
bringing honor to his name–Psalm 23:3

A happy home is not merely having a roof over your head
but having a foundation under your feet—Amish proverb

Chapter 1

August

It had been a while since they'd all been in one car together. Because each of his siblings lived in different suburbs and hamlets around the Cleveland area, whenever the four of them got together, it was easier to simply meet at a restaurant for a quick bite to eat.

Today was different, though.

Even though Martin was the oldest brother and the one driving, he felt just as nervous as his twenty-year-old brother, Jonny. He had the steering wheel in a death grip and every worst-case scenario was running through his head.

What in the world were they actually thinking about doing? Had they lost their ever-loving minds?

"You okay up there, Martin?" Kelsey asked.

"Yeah, why?"

"Oh, I don't know. Maybe because you've been wearing a permanent frown for the last ten miles."

Kelsey, all curly blond hair and blue eyes, was his favorite sibling. From the time she'd been born, he'd looked after her. Even though she was now twenty-two years old, she still sometimes looked to him for guidance.

That was fine with him. He was used to looking after himself and the rest of them. Even though Beth was just two years younger than he at twenty-five and could take care of herself, he still felt protective of her.

"Have I been frowning? I didn't realize it."

"Sure you did," Jonny said. "And the reason she noticed is because I've been frowning just as much. Guys, I can't believe we're actually thinking about doing this."

Even though he'd just been thinking the very same thing, Martin felt obligated to calm his brother's worries. "Remember, all we're doing is thinking about it. Don't forget, if we change our minds this afternoon, no one will even know. Especially not Mommi and Dawdi."

"They know something's up with us," Beth chimed in from the passenger seat next to him. "Mommi sounded pretty skeptical when I told her that the four of us want to pay them a visit because we haven't seen them in a while."

"Has it really been that long since any of us went to visit?" Kelsey asked.

"I saw them around Easter," Beth said. "None of you could make it." Just as it usually did when they were all in elementary school, her voice carried a hint of criticism.

Martin groaned. "Don't act like I blew our grandparents off for no reason. I told you that I was stuck going to Cara's parents' house with her."

"I didn't say you blew them off, Martin." Her voice softened. "I am sorry you two broke up."

"I thought she broke up with you, Martin," Jonny said.

She had. He hadn't tried to persuade her otherwise, though. He'd met Cara at work and had thought her snarky comments behind their customers' backs meant that she was fun. He'd soon found out that she was simply mean.

Pushing thoughts of Cara aside, Martin said, "I called our grandparents just last month. They were doing well."

"I'm not going to lie," Kelsey said. "I haven't seen either Mommi or Dawdi in almost a year. In fact, the last time Mommi called and left a message, I forgot to call her back."

"You were graduating and looking for a job. She understood."

"I know, but that's hardly an excuse. What about you, Jonny?"

"Um, well, I drove down to see them last month. I needed a break from school."

"You never told me that," Beth said.

"Why did you need to know?" His tone was a little defensive. Martin wondered why.

Beth didn't seem to notice, though. "Don't keep us in suspense. How were they?"

"The same as Mommi and Dawdi always are. They're good."

"You mean 'wonderful-*gut*,'" Kelsey teased.

Jonny chuckled. "Yeah. Anyway, we had a super time together. I drove them to a farmers market in Berlin and then we cooked out in the backyard. It was awesome."

"Did you spend the night?"

"Yep. I wasn't planning on it, but I started thinking that I would rather be with my grandparents than with my three roommates."

"Your friends are crazy," Kelsey chided. "I can't think of anyone who would rather be with them in that gross apartment than with Mommi and Dawdi."

"It isn't that gross."

"It's not that clean."

He chuckled. "I can't argue with you there, but would

you expect any different? All of us are working and going to school."

"And going out."

"That's true. But anyway, I can't deny that it was good to sleep at their house. The sheets smelled so fresh, and Grandma made cornmeal cakes, eggs, and bacon."

Martin's mouth watered. "Did she serve hot maple syrup with the corn cakes?"

"You know she did."

"So . . . you liked being there?" Beth asked.

"Of course." He cleared his throat. "It was as good as it always is. All I'm saying is that no one would pass up a chance to stay at their house if they could help it."

"Except for Mom and Dad," Kelsey said.

Glad he was approaching a stoplight, Martin groaned. "Kelsey, why did you bring them up?"

"How could I not? I mean, aren't you thinking about Mom and Dad-and wondering how each of them is going to react if we actually go through with this plan?"

"Actually?" Beth turned around to look at their sister. "I thought we were all on the same page. I thought we were all going to Walden today to tell our grandparents that we want to be Amish. Just like them."

"I think we're thinking about it . . . but who even knows?" Kelsey asked.

"Kels is right," Jonny said. "Mommi and Dawdi might put the brakes on this idea before we do anything besides talk about it."

"I hope not," Kelsey said. "I've always kind of wanted to be Amish. If I back out now, I think I'm always going to regret it."

"It's one thing to think about becoming Amish. It's another to actually go ahead and start the process," Martin said.

"We all know that, Martin," Jonny said. "Don't act as if we don't."

"Sorry. I guess that did sound condescending. The truth is, I'm sort of freaking out."

"You should pull the car over," Beth said.

"Why? Are you afraid I can't drive while I'm freaking out?"

"Maybe we don't want to be stuck in the back seat while your head is obviously not on the road," Kelsey said.

"I'm fine."

"Actually, I was thinking more along the lines of your pulling over so we can talk this through again," Beth said.

Jonny groaned. "All we've done is talk through it all. We Zoomed together three different nights this past week. What else do we really have to say?"

Martin pulled off to the side in an empty parking lot. "Let's get out for a minute."

For once, none of them argued or questioned. They just unbuckled their seat belts and got out.

And then, there they were. Standing together.

It brought back so many memories. Of them all standing together before church on Sundays. Getting ready to ride the bus to school together.

Wondering when their mother was coming home.

They all had their father's and grandfather's dark blue eyes. Jonny and Beth had their father's lanky build, Kelsey favored their mom, and Martin seemed to follow in their mom's brother's footsteps. Their uncle was a football player in college and was huge.

Beth crossed her arms over her chest. "I think we should be honest with one another. Each of us should share as a percentage how much they're seriously thinking about becoming Amish."

This was a classic Beth move. Making a pronouncement and expecting the three of them to go along—then being shocked when they didn't follow her lead immediately.

When Martin noticed Kelsey and Jonny exchange looks . . . and that Beth wasn't volunteering to go first, he sighed.

She noticed. "What?"

Martin bit back the worst of the snarky comments running through his head. "Beth, really? We're suddenly supposed to say how much we want to be Amish?"

"I think it's a perfectly good idea."

"Fine. You go first."

She looked away. "How about you?"

"No. It was your idea. Go."

Her eyes darted to Jonny and Kelsey. Without looking their way, Martin knew they were gazing at her with the same expression he was.

She sighed. "Fine. I'm sixty percent."

"That's it?" Jonny asked.

"Leaving everything is going to be really hard. I'm not a hundred percent sure I want to do it. And don't get mad because I'm being honest."

Jonny lifted his chin. "I'm ninety."

Martin was floored. Jonny was not only the youngest sibling, he also led the most English life. "Kels?"

"I'm somewhere in between. I guess seventy-five percent? What about you, Martin?"

"I don't know for sure. It fluctuates. Some days, when everything is going fine, I don't want to be Amish at all. Other times, something will happen or I'll get overwhelmed . . . and I'll be almost a hundred percent."

"That's unhelpful."

"I know. I'm a mental mess right now. My brain feels scrambled."

Beth worried her bottom lip. "Maybe we should have waited until we were sure about what we wanted to do before going to see Mommi and Dawdi."

"I want to see them," Kelsey said. "Don't you?"

"Of course. I'm just saying . . ." Her voice drifted off. "I'm just trying to be honest here."

"There's nothing wrong with that," Martin said. "If we can't be honest with one another, we're never going to be okay."

"That's what this is all about anyway, right?" Jonny asked. "Don't we all just want to be okay?"

No one replied as they got back into the car, but no one really needed to.

That statement, at least, was something all of them could agree upon.

Chapter 2

Patti Coblentz had never seen her sweet neighbor in such a state. Yesterday, when they'd crossed paths at the farmers market, she'd known within seconds that something was bothering Sylvia Schrock. She'd been staring at a container of berries as if the decision about whether to purchase them was a matter of life and death. That had been so out of character for the easygoing woman, Patti had reached out to her.

She'd never imagined that Sylvia and her husband, Josiah, were getting ready for a visit from their four English grandchildren. It was obvious that the young folks' appearance wasn't a usual occurrence. Patti was eager to lend a hand, so she had volunteered to come over that morning and help Sylvia make the luncheon and mop the floor.

Now, looking at the clock, she saw it was time to leave. Her neighbors' guests would be arriving soon.

"I think that's everything, Sylvia," she said as she headed to the front door. "Enjoy your visit."

Sylvia's look of panic was almost comical. "Wait. Don'tcha want to stay here for a spell? You could meet them. They're all near your age."

"That's kind of you, but I'm afraid I'd be in the way."

"Not at all. They'd be happy to meet *ya*," she added in a rush.

"Perhaps." Or perhaps not. If she'd been so blessed as to have grandparents like Sylvia and Josiah, she would not have wanted their long-awaited reunion marred by a stranger.

"Please stay long enough to say hello."

Concerned about how stressed Sylvia's expression appeared, Patti relented. Even though she had several things to do at her own house—and still didn't think it was wise to intrude on this family moment, she never could say no to the woman. "All right, but don't make me feel bad when I say it's time for me to leave."

Sylvia's golden-brown eyes lit with relief. "I'd never do that."

"I wasn't born yesterday, Sylvia."

"That's true, but you aren't as tough and world-weary as you like to act, dear. You're only twenty-five."

"I feel like I'm twenty-five going on fifty."

"That's simply your nature." Moving one of the ties of her *kapp* away from her face, she added, "But that ain't a bad thing, true?"

Patti wasn't sure about that. She'd cared for her great-aunt until she died two years ago. Now Patti had inherited a four-bedroom house and a full acre of land to take care of while most other women her age were focused on eligible men and a wide-open future.

She sometimes found herself wishing that she didn't already feel as if she'd lived a lifetime.

"Chin up, child. There's nothing wrong with having your head firmly placed on your shoulders. The Lord gave you the maturity to handle everything He's thrown at you. That's a blessing, ain't so?"

"*Jah*. It is." Just as she was about to offer Sylvia a cup of her own coffee, a car pulled up. "They're here."

Looking a little shaky, Sylvia got to her feet. "I guess I'm as ready as I'll ever be."

"Where's Josiah?"

"He's out in one of the fields. He'll come in soon."

"Do you want me to try to find him?"

"*Nee*. I think he's a little nervous about seeing the grands as well. It sounds awful, but they're a mite overwhelming when they're all together." She grimaced. "They talk a lot."

"Sylvia!"

"It's true! Anyways, no worries about Josiah. He'll join us when he's ready."

Patti nodded her understanding, but the truth was that Sylvia's words didn't make a bit of sense. As far as she knew, both Sylvia and Josiah got along with their grandchildren just fine. It was only their son, Mark, who they sometimes had issues with. Though she might have imagined that, Patti realized. She didn't recall either of them ever saying a bad word about any of their family members.

Opening the front door, she gestured for Sylvia to go on out. It didn't escape her notice that the gesture would be more appropriately made to a young child than an older woman. "Come on, dear," she coaxed. "I'm sure they're wondering where you are."

Whether it had been the gesture, her smile, or the reminder that her beloved grandchildren were outside, Sylvia's expression eased.

"You're right." After quickly squeezing her hand, Sylvia walked out the front door with a big smile on her face. "Hallo, *kinner*!"

All four turned around.

"Mommi!" a willowy blonde said as she rushed forward. "I'm so happy to see *ya*."

"No happier than I feel seeing you." Raising her chin, she added, "And you, too, Jonny dear. And Beth and Martin."

"It's been too long, Mommi. I'm sorry for that."

"You are busy. That's how it's supposed to be," she said as the others took their turn to hug Sylvia tight.

After the oldest-the one who Patti was fairly sure was named Martin-hugged Sylvia, he seemed to notice Patti standing in the doorway of the house, watching them.

Meeting her gaze directly, Martin seemed to take in everything she was in one fell swoop.

Patti felt her face heat. She no longer thought much about her looks until someone like Martin came around. That was when she remembered that the port-wine stain on the side of her neck was dark and obvious. And-contrary to what her mother said-ugly. That was when all the teasing she'd endured returned tenfold and she was once again trying to blend in with the scenery. Anything to avoid being noticed.

"Who are you?" he asked.

Well, she had to give him credit for asking her directly instead of going to his grandmother.

"I'm your grandmother's next-door neighbor."

"I see." He didn't move or make any effort to introduce himself.

Which, in her opinion, was pretty rude.

Who did he think he was anyway? One of the girls, the willowy blonde, stepped closer. "Hi. Please ignore my *bruder* Martin. He's standoffish with nearly everyone. We haven't met, have we? I'm Kelsey."

Sylvia glanced her way. "Close the door, Patti. You're letting in flies."

She closed it. "Sorry."

Kelsey was still wearing a friendly smile and standing by her side. She fairly oozed goodness. "Your name is Patti?"

"Yes. Patti Coblentz."

"Well, as you know, I'm Kelsey, and my rude brother is Martin. Then there's Beth and Jonny." She winked. "He's the baby of the family, but don't tell him I said so."

"I heard *ya*, Kels," Jonny said as he held out his hand for her to shake. His smile was slightly bashful. "I'm real glad to finally meet *ya*, Patti. Gram talks about you all the time."

"She talks about you, too."

"Me?"

"Well, I mean all of you." She waved a hand in the air, obviously trying to encompass all of them.

Walking with Sylvia, Beth said, "Gram just told me that you've been helping her prepare the house for our visit. That was really nice of you."

"It was my pleasure. She does a lot for me. She and Josiah both do." Glad that Sylvia looked like her usual self again, Patti added, "I'm going to be on my way now, Sylvia. See you later."

"Are you sure you don't want to stay, dear?"

"*Danke*, but I've got some things I need to do at home."

"Oh, of course you do. I kept you here all morning."

Thinking it was strange that Sylvia's husband still hadn't made an appearance, she added, "Do you want me to find Josiah for you on my way out?"

"There's no need for that. I'll do it," Martin said.

Once again, she felt him studying her intently—and had the unfortunate feeling that he found her wanting. Eager to remove herself from his scrutiny, she pasted a smile on her face. "It was nice to finally meet you all! Goodbye!"

"Bye, Patti," Jonny called out. "Thanks for sticking around to say hi."

Patti smiled at him before walking back to her property. Then she realized that she wasn't alone. "Martin, do you need something?"

"No. I just thought I'd walk with you to see if my grandfather's in the barn. It's on the way to your house, right?"

"*Jah.*"

Feeling even more self-conscious, she continued to stare straight ahead. At least that way she wouldn't feel as if he was staring at the mark on her neck.

"So, it's really nice of you to help out my grandmother so much. Do you do that a lot?"

She shrugged. "I'm not sure what 'a lot' is to you. We like to help each other out when we can."

"What about your family?"

"What about what?" Really, she had had enough of his questions.

"I mean your parents. Your siblings. What are they like?"

"They are nonexistent. I live on my own."

"They've all gone to Heaven?"

"Martin, forgive me, but you're asking me a lot of personal questions that aren't any of your business."

He looked taken aback. "I don't see how asking about your parents is all that personal. You are on my grandparents' property. I have every right to know more about you."

Patti's temper flared as she felt his too-pretty eyes focus directly on her. Against her will, she squirmed under his regard.

Inside, though, she was fuming. Had she ever met a man so full of himself? She certainly didn't think so. What she needed to do was finish the conversation before she said something she would likely regret.

Pulling herself together, Patti stopped at the entrance to the barn. "That might be your opinion, but it sure ain't mine."

"It ain't?" He raised an eyebrow.

Patti wasn't one for violence, but she wished she was the type for just a second. Removing his smirk would feel awfully good.

Praying for patience, she folded her hands over her chest. "I'd rather not answer any more of your questions right now, Martin. I might be on your grandparents' land, but I don't know you at all. As far as I'm concerned, you're a stranger."

"Fine."

"And just in case you're wondering, your grandfather is likely in the very back," she added, pointing to the barn's entrance. "He enjoys his workshop."

"I know where his workshop is."

"Then it seems you have everything taken care of. Enjoy your visit. It's been a while, so I'm sure you'll find it *gut* to be here." She started walking before he had a chance to say another word.

Yes, she was being rude, but there was something about him that she found very aggravating. No, *everything* about him was aggravating.

And disconcerting.

And . . . he was far too handsome for his own good.

Picking up her pace, Patti hurried home. She needed to get some space between her and Martin Schrock. No doubt he and his brother and two sisters would be gone very soon. Given their track record, they probably wouldn't return for months. She wouldn't see him again for a long time.

She only hoped it would be just as easy to get him out of her mind.

Chapter 3

Martin could hear his grandfather's laughter all the way to where he was standing at the front of the barn.

As his irritation with Patti faded, he realized that his grandfather had just heard most—if not all—of their exchange.

He felt like sinking into the floor.

"*Ach*, Martin, she got you gut," Dawdi called out. "I didn't know Patti's tongue could be so biting. I'm surprised your clothes ain't on fire."

He was surprised, too.

"Hey." Peeking in through the doorway, he spied Dawdi walking toward him with the spry gait that a man twenty years younger would be pleased to have.

"Hey right back."

"So, it sounds like you overheard Patti give me what for?"

"*Ach*, indeed I did," Dawdi said as he gripped Martin in a warm hug. After slapping him twice on the back, he pulled away and continued. "Not that I was spying on you two or anything. I was simply taking my time coming out."

Martin didn't blame him. The way he and Patti were ex-changing words had been rather intense. He would've stayed out of the way as well. "Sorry you had to listen to us."

"I didn't mind. Besides, I wasn't only avoiding you two."

"Oh?"

"Your grandmother has been in such a tizzy about your visit, I wanted to give her a moment to settle down before I jumped in."

There was that reminder again. He, Beth, Kelsey, and Jonny were grown up and had always been loving and re-spectful to their grandparents, so he didn't understand his grandma's anxiety. "Why was Mommi so worried about us being here? Was this bad timing or something? Did she not want us to visit after all?"

"It weren't that. It was *all* of you coming at once."

"I never would've thought that would bother her."

His grandfather waved a hand. "She might have misread things, but she's had a feeling that the lot of you coming to-gether was no coincidence." He raised an eyebrow. "Was it?"

"*Nee.* We did plan it. The four of us wanted to talk to you and Mommi about something at the same time."

Dawdi stared hard at him. "Well, now I'm starting to think that maybe my wife was right to be concerned about this visit." He turned and started toward the door. "Come on, son. Let's go get whatever you grands have on your minds out in the open."

Martin might resent the way his grandfather made him feel like an awkward teenager, but he was beginning to think that was the case. Since when did he sidestep the truth as he was doing at the moment?

Since never.

"It's nothing bad," he added quickly. "But I'm afraid it has to do with all of us. I need to wait until I'm with the oth-ers and Mommi before I tell you what's on my mind."

"I understand." He paused, then added, "I'm pleased to

hear that you and your siblings have remained so close. That's important, I think."

"I think so, too."

Beside him, his grandfather kept walking, though his shoulders eased and his spirits seemed to lift. "Don't forget to eat hearty. Your grandmother and Patti have been cooking up a storm for two days."

And . . . there was yet another reminder that nothing about this impromptu visit had been easy for his grandparents. "She didn't have to go to so much trouble."

"She don't have to care about you, either. But she does." Slanting him a meaningful look, he added, "Which means you'll eat, *jah*?"

"Yes, Dawdi."

"*Gut*."

As they continued to stroll toward the house, Martin said, "By the way, Mommi sure seems close to Patti."

"That's because she is."

"Patti wouldn't tell me much about her family. She acted like they're not around, though." Suddenly he realized that he'd been an idiot. No wonder she'd been offended when he'd asked where her parents were. She was Amish and likely very sheltered. A lot of Amish girls still married young. She'd probably left her parents' home several years ago. "Have you met her husband?"

Looking thoughtful, Dawdi shook his head. "*Nee*. Not yet."

"Really? Why not?" If he were Patti's husband, he'd want to make sure he knew who his wife was spending so much time with. He had a feeling that he was going to have a protective streak a mile wide when it came to his future bride, especially if she was a pretty woman like Patti.

After waiting another second, his grandfather burst into laughter. "I haven't met Patti's husband because she ain't married yet, Martin."

"She's single?"

"Very much so." He chuckled as he swung open the back door. "I got *ya* good."

"That you did."

"Martin? Josiah? Is that you?" Mommi called out.

His grandfather winked at him. "*Jah*, Sylvia. Martin found me. We'll wash up and then it's time I saw my other three grands."

"We're waiting on you, Dawdi!" Kelsey said.

Exchanging a look with Martin, he winked. "I expected nothing less."

As always, his grandmother had made too much food, though Martin knew he would never complain about that. Mommi had barbecued chicken cooked in the oven, roasted potatoes, broccoli salad, fresh rolls, corn, and Cherries on a Cloud, a combination of pie filling, Cool Whip, cream cheese, and gelatin that was somehow considered a salad. Last but not least were peanut butter bars and a coconut cake.

Martin would've been embarrassed about how much he consumed except for the fact that Jonny, Kelsey, and even Beth had cleaned their heaping plates.

Then it was time to wash dishes and put it all away. Dawdi went into the living room to rest while the four of them helped their grandmother clean, just as they had back when they were little kids living there in the summer.

"This brings back memories," he mused.

"I was just thinking the same thing," Beth said. "Look at us. I think we're all in our usual spots, too."

Kelsey held up her dishcloth. "Yep. Once again, no one wants me to wash, only dry."

Jonny, who'd been drying dishes, too, frowned. "I don't remember what I used to do when I was here. What chores did I do when all four of us came at once, Grandma?"

"Pretty much what you're doing now, child. Talking instead of working."

It felt good to chuckle at the joke. Especially when his insides were churning. They were now minutes from breaking the big news, and Martin had no idea how his grandparents were going to take it.

He also had no idea how they were going to broach the subject. They should've practiced that, he realized. They really should have talked about this a whole lot more than they had.

"I think we've done as much as we need to do for now," Mommi said. "Let's go sit down and finally have our chat."

Beth tensed. "Are you sure you don't want us to help you put all this away? I don't want to make more work for you."

"It's no trouble, Beth. I am sure." Reaching out, she cupped Beth's cheek. "Don't worry, child. Everything is going to be just fine."

"You sound so sure."

"I am. The Lord is with us, right? With Him, all things are possible."

"Yes, Mommi," Beth said.

If Beth didn't sound completely certain about that, Martin knew she wasn't the only one.

Chapter 4

Kelsey was getting antsy. The six of them had been sitting in the living room for ten minutes and the tension between their grandparents and themselves was getting worse and worse. She wished that wasn't so.

Their grandfather looked as if he was trying to decide whether to start pacing or finally fall asleep in his chair. When she glanced at Martin, he didn't meet her eye.

He was chickening out, too.

It seemed that one of them had to get the ball rolling. It might as well be her.

"Mommi, Dawdi, we have some news."

Mommi raised her eyebrows. "We know. I also know that you aren't too eager to tell it to us."

"Is it about your parents?" Dawdi asked. When the four of them gaped at him, he grunted. "What have they done now?"

"Has Mark finally gone off and gotten married?"

"I don't think so, Dawdi."

"Did Helen?" Mommi asked.

Dawdi gave their grandmother the sweetest smile. "I'm pretty sure Helen is still working and traveling, Sylvia."

"She is," Beth said. "I talked to Mom a couple of days ago."

"You did?" That was news to her, though she supposed she shouldn't have been surprised. Beth always had gotten along better with their mother than she had.

"If it ain't your parents, it must be the four of you. And by the way you four are dancing around the reason you're here, I'm guessin' it's not good news," Dawdi continued. He took a deep breath and then stared at Kelsey so intently that she felt her cheeks turn pink. "It's time, child. Whatever it is will be all right. Come out and say it."

"Please, dear," Mommi said.

Kelsey knew they were right. Plus, their grandmother was clenching her hands so tightly, her knuckles seemed to be turning white.

It was time to deliver the news. "All right. Beth, Martin, Jonny, and I have been thinking about becoming Amish and we want the two of you to help us."

Their grandparents froze.

Beth inhaled sharply. "Kelsey, that's the best you could do?"

"What's wrong with that?" She raised her voice. "I waited and waited for one of you to step in."

"Still . . ."

"You could've done this, Beth. Unfortunately, you didn't say a word."

Beth, usually so calm and collected, blurted out, "That's because I was waiting for Martin."

"Me? You're the oldest."

"So? You drove."

"What does that have to do with anything?" he fired back.

"You two should stop arguing," Jonny intervened. "What's done is done."

"Like a bull running through a china shop," Beth bit out.

"Oh, stop. They're fine." Realizing that their grandparents were still silent, Kelsey glanced their way again. "Are you two okay?"

"We're both just fine," Dawdi said.

He wasn't smiling, though.

Mommi raised an eyebrow. "At least one of you finally told us what was on your minds."

Unfortunately, Mommi didn't look all that excited about their plan.

Suddenly rethinking everything, Kelsey wondered if they'd just made a huge mistake.

Oh, not with their plans. But maybe they should've written Mommi and Dawdi a note first? Done something to ease the shock of their news? She glanced at their grandparents again.

Neither looked any better. Actually, both looked irritated with them. Displeased.

For some reason, that hurt her feelings. Didn't their grandparents realize how difficult this announcement was to make?

"Mommi, Dawdi, I wasn't joking."

"I figured that out, child," Dawdi said. "But come now. You have to admit that this whim of yours is silly."

"No, it's not."

Beth nodded. "Kelsey's right. The four of us have been talking about leaving everything behind and becoming Amish for a while now."

"Yet this is the first time you told us?" Mommi asked.

"We didn't want to tell you until we were certain," Martin said.

"Why not?"

"Well, we didn't want to get your hopes up."

"Is that how you thought we'd react, son? That your grandmother and I would be very pleased to have four new Amish members of the family and we'd all be Amish and live happily ever after?"

Kelsey was offended. Plus, she'd never realized that their grandmother even knew how to sound so snippy. Mommi was gentle and good. She was Amish! Didn't that mean she was above such things? "You don't need to sound so sarcastic. We're serious."

"I can see that."

She didn't act like she did, though. Actually, Mommi looked as if she was trying not to laugh. Becoming more hurt by the second, Kelsey leaned forward. Just as she was about to tell Mommi and Dawdi exactly what she thought of their attitude, Jonny pressed a hand on her arm. "Let me."

She leaned back in her chair, more than happy to let him have a chance to make their grandparents understand just how serious they were.

Dawdi leaned back and crossed his legs. "Is it now your turn to try to convince us that this foolish idea has merit?"

Jonny shook his head. "No. I can't speak for Beth or Martin or Kelsey. All I can say is that I'm certain about this. I don't want to live an English life. I want to change the way I live. I want to be Amish. And it isn't something Beth or Martin brought up and I decided to go along with. I've been thinking about it for years."

For the first time, their grandfather looked as if he was taking them seriously. "Why did you never say anything?"

"Because I didn't think it was allowed."

"Allowed? Who did you think would tell you it wasn't?" Mommi asked. "Josiah and me? Or the bishop?" She paused. "Or your parents?"

Kelsey inhaled. Josiah and Sylvia never talked about their parents. Never more than in passing.

Jonny seemed just as surprised by the question, but he gathered his wits together quickly. "Yes."

"Yes to what?" Martin asked.

Jonny glanced back at their brother, paused to meet her eye and Beth's, then turned to face their grandparents again. "Yes to all of it. I figured everyone I knew, whether it was my parents or you two or Martin and my sisters or even my friends, would tell me I was foolish and that I didn't know my own mind."

"You were worried that we'd react like we just did, weren't you, child?" Mommi asked in a soft tone.

"Yes."

She swallowed, seeming to come to terms with what they were proposing at last. "Becoming Amish isn't easy. Living Amish for the rest of your life is even harder."

"We know that," Kelsey said.

"I'm sorry, but you really don't. Sure, you know a few words of Deutsch and you've learned how to care for a horse and use a kerosene lamp. But that ain't all there is to living this way—and adopting our beliefs whole-heartedly."

"What else do we need to do?" Beth asked.

"That, child, is not something I'm prepared to answer tonight. You've caught me off guard, and if the four of you are serious, I want to give you a serious answer."

"I understand."

"I hope so."

Dawdi leaned forward, resting his elbows on his thighs. "Here is what I suggest: We all go to sleep and rest and in the morning have breakfast together, and then you all get on your way. But if all four of you are serious, decide which one of you is going to undertake this journey first. Then that sibling will need to live with us for a year as Amish."

"Why only one of us?"

"We're older, and we don't suddenly want a household of six people. Plus, you aren't small *kinner*. You're used to your jobs and your friends and your electronics and your noise. And maybe one another. God is going to be needing a lot of your attention."

Mommi nodded. "Only one of you at a time. No more than two, if you're determined."

Dawdi stood up, signaling that the conversation was over, whether they wanted it to be or not. "And one last thing. I don't know if birth order is going to have much to do with who goes first." Looking at Beth, he said, "This time, I think it should be the one who is most ready to abandon his or her English life. Pray on it, but don't decide tonight. Understood?"

They all nodded.

"*Gut.*" Turning to Mommi, he said, "I'm off to shower."

"I'll be right behind you." Getting to her feet, she said, "Don't forget to take flashlights, children. You know where everything is. *Gut nacht.* I love you."

"I love you, too, Mommi," Kelsey said.

The others echoed her words, and then the four of them sat in silence for a moment when they were alone again.

"What should we do?" Jonny asked at last.

"Exactly what Dawdi said," Martin replied. "Let's grab our flashlights, go to our rooms, and get ready for bed."

"I was sure we'd be leaving tonight," Beth said. "I have work tomorrow."

"You know how life is here. The sun will shine through the curtains and you'll be up at dawn, whether you planned on it or not. After breakfast we'll head home."

Beth nodded reluctantly, though Kelsey privately thought she was being a bit silly. They hadn't been given much of a choice.

And she was also sure that the conversation they'd just had was just a taste of what the next year would be like for one of them.

She wondered who was going to be the first to take the plunge.

Hopefully, God would let them know real soon.

Chapter 5

The best thing about late August was that she had time to sit on the front porch with her coffee. She'd finished working on the books for all of her clients for the month and was able to concentrate on her home. That was a blessing.

Closing her eyes for a moment, she enjoyed the slight hint of cooler air on the breeze. Fall was around the corner, but not yet.

At this moment, with the birds chirping in the distance, the scent of fresh grass in the air, and the sight of her flowers in full bloom, Patti knew there was no better place for her to be.

She might wish for things to be different from time to time, but she was certainly grateful for every brand-new day.

The sharp snap of a twig opened her eyes, but it was the sight of the approaching man that made her spill her coffee down the front of her dress. She'd just poured the cup a few minutes before and it was scalding hot. The liquid soaked through the thin fabric of her dress as if it was a thin cheesecloth instead of sturdy cotton.

Wincing at the heat, she jumped to her feet. If she didn't have company, Patti reckoned she would already be pulling out the pins that held the front of her dress in place.

"Are you all right?" the man called out as he rushed forward.

No. No, she wasn't all right, but she wasn't going to say that out loud. Now that the coffee had cooled a bit, the spill was slightly more bearable.

He was now just a couple of feet away. "I'm sorry for scaring you. I should've called out to you, but I didn't want to disturb your prayers."

It was Martin. The older Schrock grandson. He was also handsome, with his serious expression, blue eyes, thick blond hair, and one perfect dimple that appeared when he grinned.

He was the last person she wanted to see. Of course, he had on his English clothes, too. A snug-fitting T-shirt and a pair of faded jeans. How did a man get a pair of jeans to fit him like a glove?

Embarrassed at noticing such a thing, Patti averted her eyes. Pretended the bright red cardinal in a nearby tree was half as interesting to look at as her guest.

It wasn't. Not even close.

"I wasn't praying," she blurted out. Embarrassing herself again. Because she sounded as awkward as she felt.

"Oh. You had your eyes closed."

"I know. I was enjoying the morning's quiet." She grimaced as the heat from the coffee dissipated, making her just feel wet. If she wasn't mistaken, chill bumps had appeared on her arms. Her first thought was that now he was seeing her not only in her worn-out, faded chore dress but in stained clothing.

Irritated that any of this was crossing her mind—because he'd come over uninvited and caused her to almost burn herself—she picked up her fallen cup. "What may I help you with?"

Martin looked taken aback. "Nothing. I was out for a morning walk and noticed you here. I only came over to say hello."

"Oh."

He was studying her as if she was an unusual creature he'd never seen before. "Ah, do you want to go change your dress?"

She might have been offended, or maybe even felt as if she should put him in his place—after all, no decent man should be saying things like that to a relative stranger. But the wet fabric against her front was very uncomfortable.

"It will take me a few moments to change," she warned.

His lips curved up. "I have two sisters. I know all about waiting for a woman to change her clothes."

She was tempted to point out that his sisters were English but stopped herself just in time. That would've sounded snippy and a bit full of herself, too.

There was also the simple truth of Martin's situation, which was that he had Amish grandparents. He knew all about straight pins holding a dress together.

She realized as well that he wasn't staring at her birthmark. It looked as if he didn't even notice it. It was a sad commentary on her state of mind, but she found that appealing.

"Would you care to have a cup of *kaffi* in the kitchen while I change?"

"I'd love a cup of coffee, but maybe after I pour myself a cup, I'll wait out here?"

She was curious whether it was his manners or his simple preference that prompted the suggestion, but Patti figured it didn't matter.

"That sounds *gut*. Come on, then."

He strode forward quickly and pulled open the door for her. She felt like rolling her eyes—after all, this was her house not his—but she murmured her thanks before walking in. "The kitchen is straight ahead," she said. "The percolator is on the stove and the cups are hanging on the pegs nearby. Cream is in the refrigerator."

"I drink it black, but thank you. I'll see you outside."

"I won't be long."

"It's early. I've got time."

As she walked down to her bedroom, she wondered what he meant by that. When she removed the pins and grabbed a washcloth to wipe the coffee residue from her skin, she winced. There were several bright red marks on both her chest and thighs. Her pale skin didn't look in danger of blistering, but it had been marked. No wonder she'd wanted to tear off that dress.

The warm washcloth felt good against her tender skin, but she barely had time to appreciate the soothing touch before pulling another dress from a hook in her bathroom.

It was a dark pink, one she'd worn as an attendant at a friend's wedding, and she usually only wore it around the house. It was a vain thought, but the color made her feel self-conscious, especially when a child at Bethany's wedding had innocently pointed out that the color of the dress was almost the same color as the mark on her skin.

Reminding herself that Martin was no one to her beyond her sweet neighbor's grandson, Patti jabbed the pins through the fabric of the dress and hurried back outside.

Martin had bypassed the pair of chairs on her front porch and was sitting on the top wooden step. He turned when the screen door opened.

Then, to her shock, he smiled.

"What?" she asked. Was it that she was wearing a bright pink dress that was too fancy for morning chores? The fact that it matched the port-wine stain on her neck or that she looked breathless?

"Your toenails are polished."

She'd forgotten to slip back on her old white Keds.

It felt as if someone had smashed her insides into a thousand particles. She felt sick as panic engulfed her. "Please don't tell anyone," she whispered.

All the amusement in his eyes vanished in a split second. "Patti, do you think I'm judging you?"

"*Nee.*"

When he continued to stare at her in concern, she shrugged. "Maybe. I don't know."

"I know we're strangers, but I'm telling you now, I'm not that kind of man. I don't care if you paint your toenails or not."

This was mortifying. "I know I shouldn't have painted them in the first place."

He shrugged, as if it didn't matter to him.

And maybe it didn't. But in spite of that, Patti felt the urge to explain herself. "I have an English friend named Tori. We exchanged gifts at Christmas. The nail polish was in her package for me."

"Why would she give you such a thing?"

"I . . . because I'm always commenting about the colors she paints her nails. They're bright colors—fuchsia, green, red, even black. Sometimes she paints each fingernail a different color. She gave me the bottle as a joke, I think."

Martin was still looking at her intently. "Maybe. Or maybe she thought you might like to try it out?"

"I did, at that," she admitted. Feeling as though she had swallowed some truth serum—because there was no reason on earth why she should keep talking about her toenails— she added, "I painted them on New Year's Day, just as a whim." And because she was lonely and bored. "But I soon realized I didn't have any nail polish remover. When I couldn't get it off, I put another coat on because no one would see it anyway. And then I grew to like it."

He chuckled.

"You're laughing at me."

"No . . . well, kind of."

"That's not very nice."

"Oh, stop. I mean, I guess I am, but it's not because I'm shocked. Look at me, Patti. Obviously, I haven't been living Amish. Half the girls I went to school with painted their nails." He grinned again. "Heck, I even know some guys who paint their nails occasionally."

"Truly?" When he nodded, she blurted out, "Why would they do such a thing?"

"I don't know." He shrugged. "Maybe for the same reason you painted your toes. Because they felt like it." Standing up, he said, "What I'm trying to say is that I'm not shocked, and I'm certainly not going to report you to my grandparents. Though, to be honest, I don't think either of them would be all that shocked either."

"Of course they would. They are upstanding members of the community."

"Maybe they're upstanding because they worry more about what's inside people's hearts and their actions than how Plain they look in the privacy of their own homes."

"Maybe so."

He handed her his cup. "Thank you for the coffee. It was excellent. It was kind of you to offer me some, especially because I have a feeling you lost most of yours when I arrived."

"You are welcome." Gathering her courage, she said, "If you are up early tomorrow, stop by and I'll pour you another cup."

"Thanks, but the four of us are leaving pretty soon. Beth needs to get back for work. Plus, I think my grandparents need a break from us."

"Already? I doubt that."

"We kind of gave them some news last night that was a shock. They weren't all that happy with us, if you want to know the truth."

"Is everything okay?"

"Yes. I mean, I think it will be. They gave us a lot to think about." Looking into the distance, he murmured, "Josiah and Sylvia are two of the smartest people I've ever met. They're some of the best, too. They say more in five minutes than some people say in five hours."

"I'm blessed to live near them."

"I'm pretty sure they feel the same way about you, Patti." He stuffed his hands in his pockets as he turned. "Have a good day."

"You too. You take care of yourself in the city."

"Thanks, though I might not be there for much longer." He smiled at her again before walking away.

Leaving her to wonder what he'd meant by that.

It was only later that she realized Martin hadn't seemed to notice the mark on her neck at all. It was as if it didn't even exist.

Chapter 6

The mood in the car was one hundred and eighty degrees from what it had been just twenty-four hours before. The four of them were sure a lot quieter. Martin didn't mind that. His mind kept jumping from one conversation to the next. First, he'd think of something one of his siblings said, then he'd focus on a piece of advice from their grandparents.

And then he'd think of Patti Coblentz, and he'd feel more confused than ever. She'd been sweet but had a bit of a backbone to her. She was accommodating but not a pushover.

And so pretty, but not in the polished, fussy way that so many of the girls he dated were. No, her beauty was unassuming and quiet. Like the first rays of sunshine at dawn.

First rays at dawn? He rolled his eyes. Since when did he wax poetic about anything? How could one forty-minute visit with a shy, almost awkward neighbor of his grandparents be one of the highlights of his time in Walden?

"Did anyone get any sleep last night?" Jonny asked after another ten minutes had passed.

"You know I didn't," Martin said. They'd shared a room,

and each of them had tossed and turned so much, he'd been tempted to ask his brother if he'd brought along a deck of cards. Even playing hearts by flashlight would have been better than lying in the dark, wishing for sleep.

"Yeah, I know. But who can blame you? Those twin bed mattresses feel like. they're made of concrete," Jonny said. "Girls, how about you?"

"My bed was comfortable enough, but I couldn't relax," Kelsey replied. "I kept looking around the room and imagining it being my room for the next year."

"I did the same thing," Beth said. "But I also kept thinking about when we were little and used to come up for a month at a time. I thought the rooms were bigger." She chuckled. "And yes, that the beds were more comfortable."

"It was sure easier to share one bathroom when we were younger," Jonny said. "Kels, you take forever in there in the morning."

"He's not wrong," Martin quipped.

"Sorry, I'm used to having my own."

"We all are," Beth said. "I can't believe you had to wash your hair."

"I can't believe I forgot Mommi wouldn't have a blow-dryer," Kelsey said with a moan. "I look like I stuck my finger in a light socket."

"I'm surprised you even got a good look at yourself," Beth said. "The bathroom mirror is so small."

"That's because the bathroom is so small," Jonny said. "I ran into the door in the middle of the night."

Martin grinned but couldn't ignore the fact that their tiny gripes did have some seeds of truth—and signaled some problems each of them would encounter when they became Amish.

"When we were small, I thought having a flashlight in the

bathroom was fun," he mused. "Now it just feels like a royal pain."

"I used to like listening to the birds," Jonny said. "Last night all I kept thinking about was that I'd trade a couple of robins for a ceiling fan."

"Is it bad that I was kind of hoping all those birds would shut up?" Beth asked.

Kelsey laughed. "All of our complaints mean that we've gotten spoiled, don't they?"

"Maybe. Or maybe they simply mean that we need to think about this dream of ours a little more seriously," Beth said. "Spending the night at Josiah and Sylvia's house was a reality check."

"I've been thinking about it pretty seriously all along," Martin said. "Haven't all of you?"

"I have," Beth replied. "But it's obvious that I've conveniently forgotten a lot of the details about Amish life."

"Such as faith and living Plain?" Jonny asked.

"No, things like horses and hay and flies." He really hated the flies that seemed to sneak in through every screened window.

"Did any of you think that our grandparents seemed a little distant this morning?" Beth asked about thirty minutes into the drive back to Cleveland.

"I didn't notice anything," Martin said. Though he privately thought that even if they had been acting distant, he might not have noticed. He hadn't been able to stop thinking about Patti.

"I didn't either," said Jonny.

"Neither of you noticed that something felt off this morning? Remember when we offered to do the dishes? Didn't you think it was strange that Mommi didn't take us up on our offer to help her?"

"Not really, because you made quite a point last night of

letting us know that you had to leave early for work," Jonny shot back.

"If we'd stayed to do the dishes, we'd have gotten an even later start than we already did," Kelsey added. "I think you're worrying about nothing. Our grandparents have never been shy about saying something if they think there's a problem. If they were upset, we'd know."

"Maybe." Beth pursed her lips. "I don't know, though. I still think something was off. I kept seeing Mommi and Dawdi exchange glances when we told them our idea. It was like they were having a whole private conversation in front of us."

"I noticed it, too, Beth," Jonny said. "I thought it was me, though. Come on, Kels. Didn't you think something was different about them? And be honest."

"Well . . . I didn't think they were acting distant as much as irritated."

Martin was surprised. "You think they're irritated with us?"

"Yes. I think we took them off guard and they don't like surprises."

"Our grandparents probably thought we came for a visit because we missed them," Jonny said. "Then what do we do? We say we want to be their houseguests for a year."

"And have them teach us a new language," Kelsey added.

"You're right about that, but what can we do? We had to be honest." Half thinking out loud, Martin added, "It's better to be up-front and honest with them."

"About that. I started thinking that Mommi and Dawdi might have a point," Jonny said.

"What?"

"I think it might be best if all four of us didn't descend on them at the same time."

"All four of us are thinking about becoming Amish,

though," Kelsey pointed out. "We were going to do this to-gether."

"I get that," Jonny said. "But I don't know if all four of us are feeling the same sense of urgency."

This was news to Martin. Glancing at Jonny in the rearview mirror, Martin noticed he was looking pensive. "Maybe you should tell me what you mean. Have you changed your mind?"

"No, but I'm also aware that I'm only twenty years old. I just started my junior year at Baldwin Wallace. If I drop out in the middle of the semester, I'm going to lose that money and the credits for my classes."

"You're right," Beth said. "That's a good point."

Sounding more stressed, Jonny added, "Plus, everything in my life is going to change. I know I've said it's what I want, but last night I started thinking that maybe it would be a good idea to wait a spell. Don't be mad, Martin."

Before he knew it, Martin was back in his parental role. "I'm not mad. Don't ever think I don't want to hear what you have to say."

"All right. Then I think it might be easier if I wait a little bit. Besides, it ain't like our grandparents' house is all that big."

"There is just that one bathroom," Kelsey teased.

"I think Jonny is making a good point," Beth added. "Some of us should wait. Who wants to go first?"

"Some of us?" Martin really wished he wasn't on the free-way so he could get a better look at everyone's faces. "Bethy, if you've decided you don't want to be Amish after all, you should say so instead of pushing it off."

"I'm not saying that, Martin."

Martin didn't want to argue with her, but he knew Beth well enough to realize when she was saying something be-tween the lines. She was having second thoughts and using Jonny's words as an excuse.

But who was to say that was wrong?

"What do you think, Kelsey?" he asked gently.

"Sorry, but I haven't been weighing any pros or cons. I know what I want to do."

"You sound so sure," Beth said.

"I am. I don't have any doubts. I've made up my mind. Ever since Mom and Dad got divorced, everything in my life has felt like it was tossed on its side. I don't know how all of you felt, but I was always feeling like I either needed to please Mom or Dad or stay out of their way. The only place I ever felt completely at ease was with our grandparents."

"Are you sure that wasn't because they were happy and Mom and Dad weren't?" Jonny asked.

"Mommi and Dawdi were happy, but it was more than that. It seemed as if I fit in when I was in Walden. I felt like I fit in with the Amish. I want to change my life. Honestly, I can't wait to live the next year with our grandparents."

"I want to go, too," Martin said.

"Let's do it, then," Kelsey said. "Martin and I will spend the next year with Mommi and Dawdi and become Amish. Then you two can follow. Next year you can choose to live either with them or with me or Martin."

Beth chuckled. "Kelsey, can you imagine that? Jonny or me living with you to become Amish?"

Beside him, Kelsey didn't even crack a smile. "I can imagine it real well. After all, I'll be Amish and you won't. Someone is going to have to teach you everything you need to know."

"Martin, do you hear her?" Beth asked.

"Yep, and she makes a lot of sense. I'll call our grandparents and leave a message on their answering service about our new plan. As soon as I hear back from them, I'll report back to the three of you."

"And then?" Jonny asked.

"And then? Well, I guess we'll see what happens a year from now."

"We'll either be Amish or not," Kelsey said.

"*Jah*," Jonny said, just before they all returned to their thoughts for the rest of the trip.

Chapter 7

October

"Have *ya* heard the news, Patti?" Marge asked as they—and several other women—were helping Sylvia Schrock finish setting up the food for lunch after church service.

"What news are you talking about?"

"Two of Josiah and Sylvia's grandchildren are moving in with them on Tuesday."

Marge had kind of whispered the news, but her voice—just like the gossip she was sharing—carried far.

Patti didn't know how to respond. Though she knew about Martin and Kelsey's upcoming move, she had no desire to encourage Marge's gossip. Or provide fodder for everyone's eager ears. But she didn't want to be rude to dear Marge either. Honestly, the prospect of Englishers hoping to enter their ranks was news. No doubt about that!

"I have heard," she said at last.

"From Sylvia or someone else?"

"Sylvia."

"Yes. You two are fast friends, ain't so?"

"We are friends indeed."

Looking for Sylvia but not catching sight of her, Marge leaned close. "I'm worried about her," she said in a low tone. "Aren't you?"

"*Nee.*"

"Really."

Though she didn't want to encourage Marge's gossipy ways, Patti feared she was missing something. "Why should I be worried?"

"Because these *kinner* likely have no idea what they are getting into. Too many folks think that being Amish means wearing a dress and *kapp*, eating noodles, and saying '*Gut*' every now and then."

Patti couldn't resist chuckling. She wasn't sure if outsiders thought there was more to their lives or not, but there did seem to be a perception that things like living without electricity were the most important parts of the Amish way of life.

Anyone who was Amish knew the truth—that it was faith that mattered. Faithfulness to Him all the time. No matter what. His will created a clean heart. Patti believed that to be true.

It wasn't always easy, though.

Even now, when she was gossiping with Marge.

Wanting to try to get the conversation on a better foot, she said, "I feel certain that Martin and Kelsey know there's more to being Amish than that."

"You know their names?"

"I live next door to Sylvia and Josiah, Marge."

"I didn't think Sylvia would talk to you too much about them."

Then why had she asked Patti what she knew?

Before she could stop herself, she blurted out, "I met Martin. We talked for a spell. He seemed nice."

"Not wild?"

"*Nee*. Not wild at all."

"What about the girl? What is—"

Sylvia stepped forward. "Marge, if you are so interested in my grandchildren, you should stop by later this week and meet them instead of pestering poor Patti. It's a wonder she doesn't have her hands up in an attempt to shield herself from your constant questions."

"Forgive me, Sylvia. I shouldn't have been talking about your news. And, uh, sorry, Patti, if I made you uncomfortable."

Sylvia patted Marge's arm. "No worries, dear. If no one was talking about Martin and Kelsey coming to live with Josiah and me, I would think it very strange indeed. The children's arrival seems to be all that Josiah and I can think about." Frowning slightly, she added, "Day and night."

Marge nibbled on her bottom lip, then blurted out, "Living Amish for a year is a long time."

"It is."

"Do you think they'll last?"

"Yes."

Patti couldn't resist commenting on that. "You sound so certain."

"I am. Josiah and I feel that we need to be positive for their sakes." She waved a hand in the air. "In any case, I think they have a good chance. None of the four are fanciful people, but of them all, Martin seems to be the steadiest. Once he sets his mind to something, it never changes. For better or worse."

"What about Kelsey?"

"To be honest, I wouldn't have imagined Kelsey coming with him, but she's always been the most independent."

"You don't think she's following him?"

"*Nee*. She made up her mind and would've been here no matter what. Also, we must remember that living with us for a whole year is just a recommendation. Both Kelsey and

Martin know some Deutsch and a lot about our lifestyle already. One of them might be ready to be baptized before the year is over."

"I guess we'll see what they think, and Preacher Richard," Patti added.

Sylvia smiled. "*Jah*, I think Preacher Richard is especially looking forward to being of assistance."

"I'll look forward to meeting them," Marge said.

"They'll be at church in two Sundays. I'm sure you'll meet them then." Sylvia's eyes widened. "At your house, Patti."

She hadn't forgotten. "It's coming up quick." Remembering herself, she added, "I'll look forward to hosting Martin's and Kelsey's first Sunday service as members."

"Almost members," Sylvia corrected.

"It's fitting, ain't so? After all, they'll be almost Amish."

Sylvia's eyes lit up just seconds before she started chuckling. "Indeed, Marge."

Patti had stayed at the Schrocks' house for several hours after the last buggy drove down the drive and all the benches had been carefully returned to the wagon in preparation for services at her house.

She'd used the excuse that she'd be happy to help Sylvia make pillowcases for the bedrooms, but really she wanted to be sure to give her friend some emotional support. It was apparent that no matter how much Sylvia might act as though having Martin and Kelsey live with them full time for the next year was no problem, Patti knew her well enough to realize she was worried.

"It's going to be really different around here."

"I agree."

"Is Josiah their sponsor?"

"Technically, *jah*. But everyone knows that both he and I will be working hard to help Martin and Kelsey."

"It's going to be a challenge to make big meals again."

"I think so."

"More money, too?

"*Jah*, though the children already said that they'd pay the food bills."

"Are you going to let them?"

"I reckon I will. They're grown adults and hard workers." Looking down at the pale pink pillowcase on her lap, she picked up her embroidery floss and began to stitch delicate daisy designs along the top seam of the case. "There's a part of me that feels like jumping up and down, I'm so excited, Patti. I always wished Mark hadn't turned away from our faith so easily."

"Of course you must think that."

"I miss him."

"I know you do."

"I've always liked his wife and know that Helen did her best to raise the four."

Patti knew there was more to the story than what she was saying. "I'm glad they spent so much time here with you and Josiah."

"Me too. Of course I hated the reason—which was that their parents were either fighting or they wanted a break from parenting—but I was thankful to build such a close relationship with my grandchildren."

"Martin told me that his memories here with you and Josiah were some of the happiest of his childhood."

"I'm glad to hear it. I'm sad that they don't have other good memories, of course, but I am thankful that they found happiness here." She smiled softly. "That might make me a prideful fool. But if I am, I don't mind."

Returning to her stitching, which was a far simpler scalloped design on the blue pillowcase, Patti smiled. "What made you get pink and blue pillowcases for your grown grandchildren, Sylvia? And decide to embroider designs on them, too?"

"Martin and Kelsey might be grown-ups to the rest of the world. To me, though, they'll always be two little ones looking for cookies, hugs, and acceptance."

She was surprised by that but had heard the censure in Sylvia's voice. Boy, it seemed as if she was continually sticking her foot in her mouth where her friend's grandchildren were concerned.

Wanting to respect Sylvia's point of view but also being honest, Patti weighed her next words carefully. "I know I didn't spend much time with them, but all four seemed to be capable people."

"Oh, they are capable, for sure and for certain. But that don't mean each of them hasn't had their fair share of trials."

"Even Martin?"

Sylvia's golden eyes glinted. "*Jah*, child. Even Martin."

"Sorry, I was being rude." Again.

"I gather that he didn't make a very favorable impression on you."

Why had she said a single word? "He was fine."

Her eyes back on the embroidery, Sylvia chuckled. "Don't sound so frightened! I'm not offended. I stopped taking responsibility for members of my family a long time ago."

"I'm not frightened. I just didn't mean anything."

"I know you are too kind to pry, but one thing you might want to know about Martin, Beth, Jonny, and Kelsey is that they are very close to one another but each has traveled their own path. Martin, being the oldest boy, has taken a lot of responsibility for the others."

"What about their parents? Their father is your son, yes?"

"*Jah*. His name is Mark." She exhaled. "Our relationship with him is mighty strained, I'm afraid."

"I know he jumped the fence."

"He did, but we accepted that." She paused, seeming to debate whether to add any more information. Finally, she said, "We love Mark and we loved his wife, Helen, too. Unfortunately, after deciding to have four children, they decided they weren't too happy with each other and got divorced."

"Which had to be disappointing."

"That is putting it mildly." Her golden eyes filled with tears. "I always thought they should have tried harder to work things out. That's what counselors and preachers are for, *jah*?"

Patti nodded.

"Mark said they tried counseling, but it was too late. By then their minds were already made up." She lowered her voice. "And that's when everything with the children fell apart. Though Mark and Helen shared custody, neither of them seemed inclined to devote time to their children's needs. More and more, my grands told us about being home alone or being picked up or dropped off late."

"Those poor kids."

"*Jah*. Josiah and I had a terrible time watching everything unfold. From what I understand, Craig and Cindy—Helen's parents—felt the same way. But no matter how much the four of us tried to intervene, we were each told in one way or another that it wasn't our place. But the problem wasn't that we couldn't help—it was that neither Helen nor Mark changed. They still argued, and they still put their own desires ahead of their *kinners'* needs.

"Oh, Sylvia. I guess Martin and the others were aware that all of this was going on?"

"To be sure. I have a feeling their teachers, their neighbors, and even all their friends were aware of how much their lives changed after the divorce." Poking the needle through the fabric again, she added, "It was all very sad and frustrating—for the *kinner*, for all us grandparents, and for Mark and Helen, too."

"I suppose." Patti didn't want to be mean, but she couldn't

help but feel that someone should've given Mark and Helen a good talking to.

"I know my son and Helen love their children, and I know my grandchildren love their parents. But that experience changed them."

"It would've changed anyone." She smiled softly. "But they found comfort with you."

"They did. And I'm grateful that Josiah and I have been their steady support system for most of their lives." Looking contemplative, Sylvia smoothed the fabric of the pillowcase. "I worry, though."

"About what?"

"I fear the *kinner* are confusing the peace they found here with us with the Amish way of life. I worry they're so desperate for stability and belonging that they aren't seeing what's right in front of their eyes."

"You and Josiah will always be there for them, no matter what."

Folding the pillowcase into a neat rectangle, she nodded. "I don't know how to tell them that, though."

"What does Josiah think?"

"He thinks the Lord is working through all of us, and that we need to let our grandchildren enact this plan of theirs. He's afraid if I intervene too much, I might make things harder for them in the long run."

Patti wasn't so sure about that, but her family circumstances were very different. "I might be wrong, but I have a feeling that Martin, Kelsey, and the others are determined to see this plan through. And who even knows if it's wrong or right? I've met several people who feel that if they move to a new house or a new city or take a new job, a lot of their problems will go away. Sometimes that even happens. Why wouldn't it be the same with a new way of life?"

Sylvia nodded. "Change can be a good thing, but change

can't fix what's wrong or work miracles. I'm worried that Martin and the others are going to get here, unplug, start living Amish . . . and suddenly realize they still have the same problems they came here with."

"They just don't have electricity anymore," Patti finished.

The smile they shared told her everything she needed to know. No matter what happened with Sylvia's family, she and Patti were going to remain close friends. That was a blessing indeed.

Chapter 8

When Martin realized he'd have to hire a driver to take him and Kelsey to his grandparents' *haus* in Walden, he knew his dream of eventually living a Plain life was about to become a reality.

As the clock ticked forward, each minute bringing him closer and closer to making such a big change, Martin made another tour of his place. He told himself he just wanted to make sure that the electronics were unplugged and everything was put away. But really, he needed a moment to say goodbye to his stuff. He shouldn't feel nostalgic for his big-screen television, his closet of suits, or his expensive coffee maker that made excellent cappuccino, but he would be lying if he tried to tell himself otherwise. So many of the possessions in the apartment were symbols of his promotions and bonuses. Yes, his reliance on "stuff" to make him happy was part of his problem, but there certainly had been moments when he was happy in this life. He'd worked hard in high school to earn scholarships to college and worked even harder in college to land a good job. His salary had helped his younger siblings, too.

Even though their parents liked to believe they were still involved in their children's lives, Martin felt the opposite. By the time he was a freshman in high school, each of them had seemed more interested in dating than parenting.

Time and again, he'd felt obligated to make sure Kelsey and Jonny had everything needed for school or whatever sports or club they were involved in at school. Beth had been the same way. She'd been the one who had taken Kelsey shopping for homecoming dresses and had sat through Jonny's sports banquets.

Though he'd been awarded scholarships to a couple of universities out of state, he'd elected to stay nearby. So had Beth. Though they'd never actually sat down and discussed it, the two of them had tried to be the stability in their younger siblings' lives.

All four of them had turned out okay, but they'd each felt the loss of their parents' attention. It was obvious that their parents had already moved on emotionally.

Annoyed with the direction in which his thoughts had gone, he stood back in the entryway of his well-equipped apartment.

Kelsey was talking to one of her girlfriends on her cell phone. The cell phone she'd promised to leave behind but so far hadn't stayed off long enough to do more than hug him hello and ask for his help with her three suitcases.

She'd ignored his judgmental look, too. All she'd done was shrug, as if packing her favorite pillow, robe, slippers, and face cream wasn't a big deal.

He was pretty sure it was.

But whatever. Glancing at his watch, he saw that their ride should be there within ten minutes. No way was he going to give Kelsey a hard time about using her available technology one last time. The two of them—as well as Beth and Jonny—had all agreed that giving up their English life and becoming

Amish was not something that could be done lightly or according to another person's wishes.

He was not going to be the one to tell his younger sister what to do—even if he thought she'd actually listen to him.

Martin did wish she'd finish up and come wait with him, though. Not because he was lonely but because he wanted to have a private conversation with her before they got in the driver's car.

As if she read his mind, he heard her call out a tearful goodbye to her friend and run into the bathroom.

"Sorry about that," she said as she moved to his side. "That was Diana."

They might not see each other too much anymore, but he knew that Diana was Kelsey's best friend from college. "Was she trying to get you to see reason?"

"What? Oh, no. She thinks I'm doing the right thing."

"Really?"

Kelsey nodded. "She knows I've been feeling out of sorts ever since we graduated. She said spending the next year becoming Amish feels like the right decision."

"Wow, I'm impressed."

"Why? What have your friends said about our plan?"

"I haven't told them."

Her eyes widened. "Martin, what are they going to think when you don't answer their texts or phone calls or emails?"

"That I'm busy."

"Yeah. They will . . . until three months go by and you still are out of touch."

He hadn't thought of that. "Hopefully they'll reach out to Beth or Jonny."

"Mm-hmm."

Yeah, that was a little hard to believe, too.

She blew out a sigh. "I guess you're just going to have to write them a letter."

"What are you talking about?"

Kelsey raised her eyebrows. "You know, do that thing where you pick up a pen and write down your thoughts on a sheet of paper, fold it up, and then stick it in an envelope."

"Kels . . ."

"And then you need to either put the letter in a mailbox or go to the post office?"

"Sarcasm doesn't look well on you."

"I could say the same about denial and you, brother."

"I'm not in denial."

"Are you sure about that?"

"Look, I haven't told anyone because I didn't want to hear what they'd have to say about my choice. . . ."

"And?" she asked softly.

"Or listen to them say 'I told you so' when I change my mind." There, he'd said it.

And . . . there was what he'd feared he'd see when he admitted his awful truth. Hurt in her blue eyes.

"You're doubting yourself?"

Unable to meet her eyes, he turned his head. "Yes."

"Why, Martin?"

"I don't know if I'm strong enough." When she began to smile, he lowered his voice. "I'm serious, Kels. What if all these dreams I have about living happily ever Amish are wrong?" Taking a breath, he started talking faster. "What if I discover that I'm no happier living Plain than I am living in this nice apartment and going to work every day?"

"Are you sure you're not overthinking everything?"

"Maybe I am; I don't know. All I do know is that I am worried. Really worried."

"Now I understand. You're not afraid of giving up your life . . . you're afraid that even after doing all this, you still won't be happy."

That was it. Absolutely. He'd been searching for happiness his whole life. First during his early childhood, when he'd been longing for just an hour of his parents' attention but instead always felt they just wanted him to help care for all the other kids. Then, when he was in school and nothing held his interest. Not any particular sport or musical instrument or subject.

Even his job had never left him completely satisfied. Though his work in the finance department afforded him a nice apartment, car, and lifestyle, it brought little joy. Those things made his life comfortable, but he was hardly home enough to enjoy them.

At first he'd believed his dissatisfaction at work stemmed from the fact that he spent most of his days surrounded by three cream-colored cubicle walls. But now, even though he'd learned he was about to get a raise and an office of his own, he was still unhappy.

In a lot of ways, Martin realized he was still as pessimistic about his future as he'd been when he was small.

"Martin, am I right?" she prodded.

"Yeah." He braced himself, mentally preparing to hear a whole host of happy platitudes about his blessings.

But his sister, always so full of surprises, did nothing like that.

Instead, she nodded. "That means you really do have a lot to work on. You're going to be busy, Martin."

"Yeah," he said again as the downstairs buzzer rang. His pulse shot up as he pressed the intercom.

"Dennis Car Service."

"Thanks. We'll be right down."

"Take your time. Hey, do you need any assistance with your luggage?"

His sister had three suitcases, but he only had one. "I think we're good."

"Gotcha," the driver said before disconnecting.

The sudden silence was yet another sign that things were getting very real, very fast.

He turned to Kelsey. "Are you ready?"

The determined gleam in her eye was adorable. "As ready as I'll ever be."

He nodded. "All right, then." Grabbing his duffel and his sister's heaviest-looking suitcase, he headed for the door. "Let's do this."

Behind him, Kelsey grabbed both handles of her wheelie bags and pulled them out into the hall. Seconds later, the door was locked and the key was in his pocket. Worried about his future, he'd elected to keep his apartment for a while longer.

Just in case he changed his mind.

When the elevator door opened, Kelsey led the way in, moving to one side so he and the bags would fit. Finally, the doors closed and the elevator started its journey to the lobby of the thirty-floor apartment building.

For once, Kelsey didn't say a word, just stood in front of the doors with a blank expression on her face.

He couldn't fault her for that.

At the moment, there wasn't much to say.

Or, perhaps, there was actually far too much to share.

Chapter 9

Kelsey knew enough from conversations with her parents and past visits to her grandparents that no two drivers acted in the same way. Some were naturally chatty, others so quiet that they seemed almost rude, and then there were all the ones who either drove too fast, played annoying music, talked on their phones, or were so conscientious that they almost made passengers nervous.

Although Art Dennis had been hired by Martin and had never driven around any Amish in Holmes County before, Kelsey couldn't help but wish he did. He was reserved but cordial, helpful but distant, and an extremely competent driver. She knew that Sylvia would appreciate his attributes very much.

As the miles passed and their trip south on I71 continued to take them farther away from Cleveland's city streets and closer and closer to the country roads around Holmes and Wayne counties, the reality of what they were doing was finally setting in.

Maybe it was the fact that she was sitting in a car without

holding either her phone or her Kindle for the first time in, well, *ever*, but her stomach was beginning to tie itself up in knots.

She really wished Martin was a chattier sort of person.

"What are you thinking about so hard?" she whispered.

He jumped before pulling himself back together. "Hmm?"

"Sorry if I startled you, but what's going on?"

"Nothing. I just . . ." His mind drifted off while he obviously tried to put together the right words to express his thoughts. "I guess I've just been thinking about Beth and Jonny. And Mom and Dad."

She'd been thinking of them all, too. "Are you worried that we'll drift apart from them?"

"From Beth and Jonny? No, of course not. The four of us will always be close, no matter what."

"You sound so certain." She wanted to believe that the four of them would always be as close as they were right now, but if all four of them didn't become Amish, she didn't see how that was possible. One or two of them would have their feet planted firmly in the outside world while the others would be entrenched in the Amish community.

"Family is family, Kels," Martin said with such great certainty in his voice that she would've started to believe the same thing if she didn't already.

"I know."

"I know you do." Smiling at her gently, he added, "I'll always look out for you, no matter what happens this year."

"I'm a grown woman. That isn't necessary."

"I can't help it. Old habits die hard." Just as she was rolling her eyes, he murmured, "I'd say the same thing to Jonny or Beth."

"I can see that."

He narrowed his eyes. "What do you mean by that?"

"Nothing. Nothing other than the fact that you've always looked out for the rest of us. Especially Jonny and me."

"I looked out for you because I wanted to, not because you've needed my help."

She sure had agreed with that sentiment when she was in her early teens. She'd very much resented him showing up at her high school when she'd started dating Charlie. Even though Martin was right and Charlie was a jerk, she sure hadn't wanted him interfering with her love life.

"I've always appreciated you."

Martin shrugged. "That's nice to hear, but you don't have to say it."

"No?"

"I knew you loved me. That was enough."

"Of course I loved you. You're my big brother." She winked. "Plus, we're compatible."

"True, that. Beth is . . ."

"Too bossy. While Jonny is —"

"Too unpredictable," he finished.

They traded smiles. Finally, she mentioned the one topic neither of them had broached. "What did Mom and Dad say when you told them the news?"

"Nothing."

"Martin, I know that's not true. Both of them went nuts when I called." She glared at him. "How come they didn't do the same to you?" Just as he opened his mouth to reply, she blurted out, "Wait, is it because you're older and a boy?"

His lips twitched. "I am both."

"That's so wrong." Feeling fired up even though she should've seen it coming, she waved a hand. "You know, they need to get with the times if —"

"Kels, I didn't tell them."

Kelsey didn't know if she was more dismayed by the fact that he could go on and on about how he was "going to look out for her" but let her be the one to tell their parents news that was guaranteed to make them angry . . . or dismayed that he hadn't been able to tell their parents about his choice to join the Old Order.

Was he really so estranged from them that he didn't think they needed to know?

Or was he really so unsure about sticking it out?

Not wanting to tackle either of those conversations in front of anyone else, she tapped her foot and made sure Martin knew that he could have saved her a lot of pain if he'd at least given her a heads-up.

"That's why they went ballistic? Because they had no clue?"

"I guess so."

Art exited the highway and headed to a smaller, two-lane road. It looked familiar, but Kelsey didn't pay too much attention to the exact route their driver opted to take.

"Hey, look at that," Art said. "The Amish are already starting to prepare some of the fields for winter."

Looking at the team of four Belgian draft horses pulling a plow, with a guy about her age expertly managing the leads as the team went back and forth through the field, Martin nodded. "It is late August, after all."

"Sounds like you know something about farming."

"Not really."

"Oh? Huh. What brings you two out this way anyway? Is this place a vacation resort or something?"

"No," Kelsey replied. "It's our grandparents' home. We're going to stay with them for a while." She grinned to herself. Their driver was probably thinking that they needed every convenience known to man because they'd packed so heavily.

"This vehicle has USB connections back there in between the front seats. Do you see them?"

"I do."

"You might want to charge up your phones and such. The Amish don't have electricity in their houses."

"Thanks, but we're good," Martin said.

"Oh, all right, then."

Art remained silent for the rest of the trip. Kelsey didn't blame him. Their actions and comments were probably confusing him.

Forty-five minutes later, they pulled into the gravel drive of their grandparents' farm. The moment she opened the Suburban's door, she was inundated with hot air that smelled of dirt, grass, horse, and home. Gathering her things, she realized that Art's vehicle was likely the last source of air-conditioning she'd come in contact with for a while. Sure, her grandparents frequented some stores—such as Walnut Creek Cheese—that had air-conditioning for the comfort of their customers. But otherwise, her body was going to have to get used to being warm until the air turned cooler with the change of seasons.

For the first time since they'd begun their crazy discussions, Kelsey had serious doubts. Maybe she wasn't equipped to handle such an extreme change in lifestyle. Sure, she was probably a whole lot more used to living in an Amish home than a woman her age who'd grown up in Los Angeles or some other big city far away from a Plain community, but she'd always known in the back of her mind that she could go home and have all her stuff.

No, her normal way of life.

Maybe Martin was right to keep their plans to himself. Maybe it was inevitable that all her good intentions were going to evaporate once reality hit.

Maybe she was so full of pride that it was only natural she'd fall now. The Lord had simply been waiting for her to realize that she wasn't strong enough to completely flip her life upside down. He'd been waiting to remind her that she shouldn't have taken all her blessings for granted.

"Kelsey! Martin!" Her grandmother's voice rang loud

and clear over the hum of the Suburban's idling engine and the chaotic monologue in her mind.

She turned. Saw Mommi's lovely face and open arms. Spied her grandfather just behind her shoulder, waiting for his turn to welcome her back. To welcome her home.

And that was when she knew: Everything might not be easy, but it would be right.

This was right where she belonged. The Lord knew it, too. She could feel it in her bones.

Chapter 10

October 12

Martin and Kelsey Schrock had been living at their grandparents' house for three days. Everyone in Walden was talking about the two new members of their community. Speculation about how easily the two very English twentysomethings were going to assimilate into Plain living was rampant.

Patti couldn't even call everyone's focus on Sylvia and Josiah's grands gossip either. Sylvia would be the first to say that such curiosity was only natural.

Patti was glad of that because she couldn't seem to stop thinking about her new neighbors herself. Though her thoughts and prayers were usually centered upon the grandparents rather than the grandchildren. She was worried that they might be struggling. Even if Martin and Kelsey were Amish, their move to their grandparents' house was bound to cause a disruption. It was inevitable.

Every couple of hours, she found an excuse to walk outside and peek in the Schrocks' direction. Patti knew it wasn't likely, but she was hoping to catch sight of something going on over there.

Unfortunately, she hadn't heard or seen a thing.

Maybe it was because she lived alone and had too much time on her hands. Or maybe it was because she was concerned about Sylvia and Josiah and hoped the stress of their grandchildren's arrival hadn't been too much for them to take.

Or maybe it was because she was simply too curious for her own good. Or jealous that Sylvia was probably now far too busy to sit and chat for a spell with her young neighbor.

But whatever the real reason for her decision to visit her neighbors next door, Patti knew she couldn't help herself. Armed with a still-warm coffee cake covered in a fresh-from-the-line dishcloth, she walked in between the row of pear trees that her grandparents had planted when they were newlyweds and headed to the Schrocks' home.

The morning sun was shining and the sky only contained a few wispy clouds. It was going to be a beautiful fall day. The faint hum of crickets buzzed, the noise mixing in with the occasional call from birds, the squawking from the Schrocks' hens, and the usual rustle and movement inside their old wooden barn.

But then she heard it.

Laughter coming from the front porch, interspersed with barely discernable, lively conversation. It sounded as bright and happy as the day.

It was also far from commonplace . . . and stopped her in her tracks.

But it was too late. All three people sitting on the front porch looked her way when she approached. No, not three people: Sylvia, Kelsey, and Martin.

It was obvious she'd interrupted them. They'd been relaxing and enjoying their cups of morning coffee together. Why they were sitting on the front porch at ten in the morning she didn't know.

Then Gus, the Schrocks' old sheepdog, shuffled forward, his blue eyes as sweet and welcoming as always.

While Patti's brain went walking and she searched for something to say, Gus barked.

Feeling foolish, she finally spoke. "Hiya. I brought over a coffee cake."

Sylvia gestured her forward with the hand that wasn't holding onto her coffee cup. "Come on over here, child. Don't be shy."

Just as she was sure her face was turning the color of one of the tomatoes in her garden, Kelsey jumped to her feet. "It's good you're used to Mommi's humor. Otherwise I'd be afraid you were in danger of getting your feelings hurt."

Peering at her over the top of her glasses, Sylvia said, "What brings you over, child?"

"Oh, I don't know. I felt like baking this morning. Then, of course, I realized that I didn't need to eat a whole coffee cake." She bit her lip. Even to her ears, the excuse sounded made up.

"It smells *gut*," Martin said. "What kind is it?"

"Cinnamon with pecans and sour cream."

Kelsey grinned. "It sounds amazing and it smells that way, too."

"*Danke*."

She got to her feet. "Mommi, would you like me to bring out plates and forks?"

"*Jah*. Bring a knife and some napkins, too."

Kelsey was gone before Patti had gathered herself together enough to offer to get everything for her. "Do you think she needs help?" she asked Sylvia in Pennsylvania Dutch.

"*Nee.*"

"What did you say?" Martin asked.

She'd been rude. "Forgive me. I spoke out of habit. I asked Sylvia if she thought your sister needed help. She said no."

"I got the 'no' part." He frowned.

"Martin, it's like Josiah told you: A year is a mighty long time. There is no need for you to be in such a hurry to speak Deutsch fluently."

"I'm going to need to learn it, though."

"This is true."

"I'll be glad to help you with any words you'd like to know," Patti said. "I can't imagine trying to learn a new language at my age."

"It's been more difficult than I thought, that's for sure."

"Like I said, I'll be glad to help. Both of you."

"*Danke.*"

Martin looked determined not to meet her eyes. She didn't have to wonder why. Obviously he was sensitive about the topic and didn't want a stranger eavesdropping.

Not that she actually *had* been eavesdropping.

"Patti?" Sylvia said.

"I'm sorry, yes?"

"I asked what you thought about Martin taking his time."

Darting a look his way but only finding a stoic expression, she said the first thing she thought of. "I think it's good advice, though I can understand Martin's frustration. I'm so used to living in our community and taking for granted that everyone is fluent in both languages that I didn't even think about what language I was speaking before I opened my mouth. The words just came. If our places were reversed, I would hate not knowing what people were saying."

"Umm." Sylvia shrugged.

Her expression looked rather cryptic. Patti wasn't sure what she was thinking.

Kelsey's appearance at the door was the perfect excuse for Patti to hurry to her side to help. "I'll take the knife and spatula."

"*Danke.*"

Patti tucked her head so Kelsey wouldn't see her smile. Kelsey's pronunciation wasn't wrong exactly. It was more like it was so deliberately said that the "thank you" was woefully mismatched to her true sentiment.

"Who would like to slice?" she asked.

"You should, Patti," said Sylvia. "After all, it is your cake."

"All right, then." With three sets of eyes upon her, she carefully sliced four pieces, set each on a plate, then handed out the treats with the napkins and forks that Kelsey had provided. Grateful that there were so many rocking chairs on the porch, she took the closest vacant one and perched on the edge, one hand holding her plate on her lap, the other holding her fork and napkin.

She was waiting to try her slice until the others had sampled theirs. Then she bit into hers and smiled. It was tasty and moist. Not dry at all.

"It's mighty *gut,*" Martin said with a smile. "Wonderful-*gut.*"

"*Danke.*"

The four of them dug in and ate in silence. The slight reprieve in conversation seemed to ease her nerves.

"Patti, my grandmother said that you live by yourself in your aunt's house," Kelsey said.

"Yes, that's true."

"Where are your parents?"

"They've both passed on."

Martin's eyes filled with sympathy. "They must have been young. I'm so sorry."

"They were rather young, though my father was in his sixties and my mother in her fifties."

"But you can only be . . ."

"I'm twenty-seven. My father was thirty-eight when I was born. So, young to go to heaven, but not too old to have a child."

Martin exhaled. "I bet you think I'm the nosiest person you've ever met."

"Not at all. You two aren't the first people to wonder about our ages. It's normal to be curious, I think."

"We've already gone down this path, so how did you end up with your great-aunt's house?" Kelsey asked.

"That is, if you don't mind telling us about it. If you'd rather not, we understand," Martin added.

"It's not a secret either. Basically, no one else in my family wanted the house, so my aunt Frieda called me to her deathbed and offered it to me in front of everyone gathered. All my life I've been yearning for a home. A real, permanent place to settle. I accepted right away."

Both Kelsey's and Martin's eyes were wide. Patti didn't blame them for being shocked. Her story did sound like something out of a dark, gothic novel. All that was missing was a thunderstorm and mysterious footsteps lurking outside the door.

"Of course you did, Patti," Sylvia said in that sweet tone of hers. "Anyone would've done the same thing."

She wasn't sure if anyone would have done the same or not, but she supposed it didn't matter. All she knew was that she'd never regretted her decision.

After taking another bite of coffee cake, Martin set his plate on the railing that ran across the front of the porch. "No one in your extended family had hard feelings about it?"

"If they did, they didn't make them known."

"Wow."

Kelsey glared at her brother. "You have no call to judge or comment, Martin. This is Patti's story and life. Not yours."

Patti had never looked at her situation in quite that way before, but she couldn't help but think that Kelsey might have just made a valid point. She was in the middle of her own story. So far, each chapter had ended on something of a cliffhanger, but she'd persevered and moved forward with as much dignity and grace as she'd been able to muster. And because of that, she was still standing.

No, she was doing more than that. She was standing on her own two feet and continuing to get up in the morning with a feeling of hope. While it was true that she didn't know what lay in her future, she was in good company. The Lord provided for each of them but also held the ending to each life's book in His hands. It was up to Him to decide what was going to happen in her future. Not her.

"I didn't take either your comments or your questions the wrong way," Patti told Martin at last. "I'm really not all that sensitive about my past." She shrugged. "After all, it's not like I can change it."

"Put that way, I see your point."

"It's the only way to see it," Sylvia said without a thread of doubt in her tone. "You must keep looking forward, Patti."

"I know."

"If you don't mind me asking, what were you all laughing about when I walked up?" At their blank stares, she realized they'd probably already forgotten about whatever had struck their funny bones.

"Oh!" Kelsey exclaimed. "We were laughing about my story this morning. I was mentioning to Mommi that I'd forgotten just how unruly my hair is."

Kelsey had dark golden hair the color of honey in the sun. When Patti met her the first time, it was hanging loosely down her back, the ends grazing her shoulder blades. It had looked like thick strands of silk. Today, though she didn't have on a *howe*, it was pulled back from her face. Only now did Patti notice that it wasn't near as smooth or shiny as before. "What happened?"

"I can't use my flat iron." At Patti's look of confusion, she added, "It's a tool to straighten hair."

"She'd just asked Mommi if a battery-operated flat iron was permissible."

Patti wasn't sure if it was or wasn't. "Now I'm curious, too. What did you tell her, Sylvia?"

"First, that worrying about having smooth strands of hair tucked under one's prayer covering doesn't seem like taking being Plain to heart."

"And then Josiah popped out on the porch and said Kelsey should remember to ask the bishop when we meet with him before church on Sunday."

Patti just about spat out the sip of coffee she'd taken. She loved Bishop Frank. He was in his seventies but never seemed old-fashioned or stodgy. Actually, he often seemed more open to new ideas than a lot of other people.

But even so, she couldn't imagine talking to him about hairstyling. "Are you really going to ask Bishop Frank about styling your hair?"

"Of course not," Kelsey blurted out.

"But she's tempted," Martin said with a grin.

When Patti turned to her again, she noticed that Kelsey's cheeks were pink.

"I know I shouldn't worry about my looks, but it's hard to come to terms with this 'new me' I see in the mirror. I'm used to makeup and straight hair. I bet you think I'm being ridiculous, huh?"

Patti knew Kelsey hadn't meant anything cruel by her comment, but the question did remind her just how different her looks were from this very pretty woman. "I don't. I don't think there's anything wrong with wishing one's appearance could be different." Touching the dark mark on her neck, she shrugged. "I simply had to stop wishing for things that were never going to happen."

Kelsey's eyes widened. "If you think I meant anything about your birthmark, please know it was the furthest thing from my mind. I was only being foolish and vain."

Uncomfortable now, she stood up. "There's nothing for you to worry about. I didn't take offense. I do need to get going, though."

"*Danke* for the cake and the company, Patti," Sylvia said.

"You are welcome. Good day."

"Patti, hold up," Martin called out as he rushed to join her.

"Yes? Do you need something?"

He nodded. "I need to walk you home."

"There's no need for that."

"I disagree." When she was about to argue, he blurted out, "Yes, yes, I know. You're an adult and a capable woman and know this area and all the people a whole lot better than I do."

"But?"

"But humor me, okay? I want to walk you home. No, I think I need to do this."

"Why?"

"I don't know. I just do."

For better or worse, his answer made complete sense to her.

Chapter 11

Walking next to shy Patti Coblentz, in her short-sleeved, violet-colored dress, faded blue cardigan, and worn canvas sneakers made Martin feel as if he'd entered a portal into another world. Like the kids must have felt when they went through the cupboard and entered Narnia.

Though he hadn't seriously dated anyone in months, he'd been on plenty of dates. Those events had usually happened at night, in a noisy restaurant or in a bar with a group of friends, and they'd been full of joking, laughter, and light flirting.

Although he and Patti weren't on anything close to an actual date, he'd be lying if he didn't admit—to himself at least—that there was a new tension between them. He noticed every shy glance his way. Every blush and smile. It was all so chaste but felt so right.

And because of that, he wasn't sure how to act. All the women he'd dated had been far more outgoing and confident. Some had been more experienced and worldly than he. He was torn between flirting with Patti and keeping her at a distance. After all, he wasn't Amish, so nothing should be happening between them. But he couldn't seem to stay away.

Hence, the Narnia comparison.

No, that was not a good comparison. Perhaps it was more like he was walking in a different country where everyone was pleasant enough but had different norms and language. He could get along just fine, but he couldn't let his guard down. Out of fear that he would do something so foolish that he would inadvertently offend the other person when that was the last thing he wanted.

He really didn't want to do anything to spook Patti. Not that he had experience dating a ton of women, but all of them had the same background that he had. High school. College. Commutes and apartments. They were comfortable in the city. Comfortable with themselves.

Patti didn't seem to be any of that.

Martin wished it was cold enough to stuff his hands in his coat pockets. Then, at the very least, he would have something to do with them. Unfortunately, the weather had not changed in the five minutes that had passed between the time he'd told Patti that he wanted to walk her home and the present.

They were currently almost at the dividing line of pear trees, each of the five standing tall and proud, like soldiers in front of a grand palace.

In their shadows, he and Patti paused. He was wishing he had something meaningful to say. And, unfortunately, still wondering where to put his hands. At the moment, they were by his side—which would be the normal way to have them . . . except that he was fighting an overwhelming urge to wrap an arm around Patti's slim shoulders or reach for her small hand and link their fingers together.

He wasn't sure why he needed to touch her. Maybe It was

the wistful look in her eyes that he'd spied just seconds before she'd blinked, quietly erasing the moment of vulnera-
bility that he was beginning to see was always lurking
underneath the brave smile she presented to the rest of the
world.

Slipping between the trees, Patti cleared her throat. "So,
we're almost at *mei haus* now."

"I can see that."

"There's no reason for you to walk me any farther."

"I disagree." He reached out a hand, reminded himself
that he still should not grip her elbow or hand, and dropped
it quickly yet again.

She noticed.

And seemed to pull into herself even more.

Why was he messing this up? "Sorry," he mumbled.

"For what?"

He supposed he might as well just say the words. "I keep
wanting to reach for your hand. I know it's not proper,
though. But that's why I dropped my hand. It has nothing to
do with you."

"You don't want to hold my hand?"

"Of course not," he blurted out. And then he realized just
how rude he'd sounded. Yep, just when he'd thought he
couldn't mess things up any worse, he had managed to do it.
"Patti, that came out wrong. I meant to say that I do want to
hold your hand, but I shouldn't. Do you understand what I
mean?"

She studied his face. "I'm sorry, but no."

Great. Now he was going to have to spell out the obvious.
"Come on. We hardly know each other. We're practically
strangers. And strangers don't go around holding hands."
And . . . now he sounded like he was in elementary school or
something. Why couldn't he keep his mouth shut?

Patti looked down at her feet. "Hmm."

Hmm? What did that mean? Against his better judgment, he started talking again. "Plus, it ain't like we're courting. People might talk."

"*Jah*. I can see that they might. If, you know, there were people around to see us and comment." She was still looking down at her feet, but he was pretty sure that her lips had just twitched.

Martin wasn't sure if it was because she was hurt, she was mad, or she thought he was being ridiculous because he was English and had no real inkling about courting in an Amish community.

He was really starting to wish he'd taken her hand the way he'd wanted to in the first place.

It was official. He was three times the fool. But the hole he'd dug was already so deep, he didn't know how to backtrack. "I promise, you don't want anyone to gossip about you. There's nothing worse than knowing you're the focus of a bunch of rumors and speculation." Just thinking about the way so many kids and even their parents had treated him and his siblings after their parents had divorced and become consumed with their own lives made him cringe.

"You're right." In a span of seconds, Patti's expression turned from honest confusion to a blank canvas. All her feelings were bottled up again.

For some reason, that made Martin feel guilty. It made no sense, because he knew he was in the right. She was sheltered and very Amish. He was . . . well, he didn't know what he was anymore. Maybe just someone so confused by his life that he was fumbling through it all.

"We should talk about something else."

"Such as? And don't say the weather."

"I wasn't going to talk about the weather." But what was a suitable conversation? Half the time he talked to women about the new series they were watching on TV or their jobs or their commutes. Patti didn't have any of that. "Do you have a pet?" he blurted out.

"*Nee.*"

"You should. Pets make a house a home."

"How do you know that? Do you have a pet?"

"No." Once again feeling that he sounded like an idiot, he blurted out, "I've been thinking about a guinea pig. Well, two."

"You want two guinea pigs?"

"You can't have just one, you know."

"No, I didn't. Why not?"

"Guinea pigs like friends."

"So they're like you and me."

He couldn't help but grin. "I suppose they are."

"What would you do if I wasn't Amish?"

His mind went blank. He'd thought they were talking about the preferred social interactions of rodents. "I'm sorry, you lost me. What do you mean? Are we back to discussing holding hands?"

"Obviously."

"Hmm." All things considered, he would've been happy to discuss pets some more.

She made an impatient sound. "What would you do if I was an Englishwoman you met through a work friend or something? Would you hold my hand, then?"

"Nope."

"I see."

"No, you don't. I'm not describing this right. Patti, if we were at work or met somewhere after work . . ."

"Where would we meet?"

"I don't know. Like a sports bar or a pub or something . . ."

"I didn't know you drank alcohol."

"I don't drink. I mean, not really. I've had a beer from time to time."

"Oh?"

Martin wasn't sure if she was shocked by the thought of him having a beer while watching a ball game, or if she was simply giving him a hard time. Deciding not to risk offending her either way, he said nothing. Only shrugged.

A few steps later, she peeked at him again. "If we had met in a sports bar—whatever that is—what would I have ordered?"

Martin didn't know whether to laugh or cover his face in embarrassment. This woman! She pushed all his buttons. But instead of turning him off, her audacity somehow made her more attractive. "I have no idea. You tell me."

"I don't know my choices. Obviously I've never sat in one of those places."

"It's nothing bad, Patti. Imagine a place where there's about six televisions attached to the walls, each playing a different sports game. There are tables and a bar, like at a restaurant, and they serve beer and soda and water and probably something like chicken wings."

She looked slightly disappointed. "Is that it?"

"Um, no. Other stuff, too. Chips and salsa. Ah . . . pretzels, maybe? Fried pickles, too." He was just making things up now.

She giggled. "Martin. Fried pickles?"

"They're good." Loving the light in her eyes, he playfully nudged her. "Now that I think about it, if we met there, I'm fairly sure you'd have a Coke and some pretzels."

She paused. Her expression flitted from wonder to appreciation to dismay. "Huh."

"Huh?"

"I'm just saying . . . I don't sound like a very exciting woman."

"What's wrong with ordering a Coke and pretzels?"

"I don't know. I think I'd order something more interesting, like Dr. Pepper at the very least."

He couldn't help it. He cracked up. "You're the type of girl to live on the edge, hmm?"

"To be sure. I . . . I might even order sliders, too." She lifted her chin slightly. "If I wanted to be really shocking."

Martin loved this side of her. Loved how quick she was. Loved how she might be shy, but she didn't back away from him. "If you did that, I'm sure I would ask you out."

"Yeah, right." She shook her head with a wry laugh. "I'm not even sure how we got onto this silly conversation."

He knew. It had all started with him being attracted to her and attempting not to hold her hand. "For the record, I don't even notice your birthmark anymore."

All of the mirth faded as skepticism filled her eyes. "Are you being serious?"

"Of course I'm being serious. I wouldn't joke about that. I'm sorry I brought it up again, but I wanted you to know that I could care less about a small mark on your neck."

"You're telling the truth, aren't you?"

He nodded. "I wouldn't lie about that, Patti."

"*Mei* Aunt Frieda used to say that I made too much of my flaws."

"I don't know what your flaws are, but that mark isn't one."

"No?"

"No. Not at all. I kind of like it. It's unusual and makes you different." When she looked ready to argue, he said, "I promise, different is good."

Patti stared at him for another moment, then smiled. "You might be right. Being different can be a really good thing."

Unable to stop himself, he reached for her hand and tugged her closer.

Patti didn't protest one bit. Actually, she seemed pleased that he'd finally taken her hand.

It made the already gorgeous day that much brighter.

Chapter 12

Mommi was quiet for a spell after Martin left to walk Patti home. A few minutes after they'd left, Kelsey brought their dishes inside and washed them. Then, she found two stainless-steel bowls in a cupboard and carried them back out to the front porch. Along with a bag of dried pinto beans.

After reminding Kelsey to look for pebbles when she sorted the beans, Mommi kept gazing into the distance, as if she was attempting to locate Martin on the horizon.

It was obvious that her grandmother was worried. Kelsey wondered if she was more concerned about Patti or Martin.

"Everything okay?" Kelsey asked after fishing out three tiny stones and placing the beans in one of the bowls.

Her grandmother started. "Hmm? I was . . . I was just thinking about your brother. And Patti."

"And?"

"And I could be wrong, but I think something is blooming between them."

Well, that was not what Kelsey had supposed her grandmother was thinking about. "Are you serious?"

"Oh, *jah*." Still looking at the empty path, she murmured, "When I watched them walk away, I started thinking how maybe they aren't as different as I'd first thought. As a matter of fact, from a distance, they don't seem like a poor match at all."

Match, as in a courting couple? Kelsey was kind of shocked. Who knew her grandmother could be such a romantic? Not her! "I don't know about that, Mommi."

"Really?"

Putting the beans to one side, Kelsey chose her words with care. "Grandma, I think Martin was just being nice," she said. "You haven't seen him in social situations, but he's usually a pretty popular guy. He's handsome and easygoing. I mean, he's easygoing on the outside."

"He is handsome. I am pretty sure that Patti noticed his looks, too."

"I bet she did. Most girls do. That said, Martin and Patti are very different."

"Do you really think so?"

"Yes. I mean, not only is he not Amish but Martin is a protector. He not only looked out for all of us when we were growing up, he's always looking out for people now. For example, even though most women Martin knows probably are used to doing whatever they want, he doesn't think it's safe for women to walk around by themselves at night. He's always the first person to offer to walk a woman to her car, even if he doesn't know her well."

"So you're thinking that's why he walked Patti home. To keep her safe."

That did sound like a stretch—but she still didn't think his action meant that Martin was flirting with Patti. "You know what I mean, Mommi. Martin has good manners."

"To be sure he does."

Her grandmother's comment seemed particularly vague. "That's a good thing, right?"

"*Jah*. It is."

"Why do you look upset, then?"

"I'm not upset," she snapped.

"Okay." Kelsey looked down at her feet. Whatever was going on with her grandmother was obviously a private thing.

"Ack. I'm sorry for snapping at ya', child." She took a deep breath. "The truth is that I am a little upset, but it isn't your fault." Finally turning away from the empty path, her grandmother added, "I'm simply being a little foolish and letting my imagination get the best of me. Don't mind me." Anything Mommi might have added was cut off when a man riding a gas-powered bicycle pedaled up the drive. "Well, look at that. It's Richard."

Kelsey glanced at the newcomer, then did a double take. She'd expected Richard to be an older man, an old friend of her grandparents.

He was far from that. This Richard was fit and trim and had short, dark hair with a hint of curl. He was tan and had a fluid way about him that spoke of confidence. She also noticed that he was clean-shaven. That was a pretty good indication that he wasn't married.

Unable to stop herself, Kelsey got to her feet.

"Hiya, Sylvia," he called out as he approached. "How are you today?"

"I'm good, Preacher Richard. I'm enjoying the morning with my granddaughter Kelsey."

This man was their preacher?

As Preacher Richard got closer, Kelsey noticed that his eyes were dark and his teeth a bright white.

She knew about those perfect teeth because he was smiling at her. He also smelled good.

She couldn't believe she'd noticed how a preacher smelled!

"Kelsey," he murmured in a low tone that held a hint of a drawl. "At last we meet."

"At last?" She looked at her grandmother. What had she been telling Richard about her?

He noticed the curious look she sent Mommi. "Sylvia and I might have had one or two conversations about you and your brothers and sister."

"Nothing bad, dear," Mommi said in a rush. "Don't look so worried. It was just normal talk in passing."

"Hmm."

He grinned as he held out a hand. "What I'm trying to say—in a poor way, I fear—is that I'm mighty pleased to meet you."

She smiled back at him as she shook his hand. It was warm and solid and perfect. The hand of a man who wasn't afraid to work. The opposite of the last guy she dated, who acted as if putting gas in his vehicle was a big deal. "I'm pleased to meet you, too," she replied in what might or might not have been a breathless tone.

And now, what should have been a simple hello had taken several minutes. And . . . they were still holding hands.

Mommi noticed.

She cleared her throat. "I was hoping you'd be able to stop by the house, Richard. Do you have time to join us for lunch? Or at least sit a spell?"

"I might. What time is it?"

She looked up at the sky. "Um, noon, or thereabouts. We'll be sitting down to eat pretty soon. It's cream of broccoli soup, roast beef sandwiches, and fruit ambrosia. Oh, and coconut cream pie." She winked. "Kelsey made the pie."

Kelsey knew she was also blushing. "It's just a pie, Mommi."

"You worked hard on it, though. I'm sure it is going to be tasty."

"I never turn away coconut cream pie," Richard said.

"I can't promise it's as good as my grandmother thinks it is."

"If it's half as good, I bet it will be fantastic."

Just as she was drinking in his blinding smile like the foolish girl she'd just turned into, Richard added, "I could stay for lunch if you really don't mind. And if you have enough to spare."

"I don't mind."

"What do you think, child?" Mommi asked. "Do you feel we have enough food for Preacher Richard to join us?"

That question took her off guard. Her grandmother had to be up to something. No way would she offer the preacher lunch, then change her mind without a reason.

After a moment, Kelsey realized that she was being given an out. Sure, it would be awkward, but if she really didn't want the preacher's company, she could make up an excuse about the meal.

But there was no way she would do that. Even if she wasn't trying to become Amish, she wouldn't deny a friend of her grandmother's a seat at their table.

"We do," Kelsey said in what she hoped was a gracious tone. "We have more than enough. I, for one, would be delighted if you joined us." Of course the moment she said those words, she wished she could take them back. She sounded like a spinster in the middle of a Jane Austen novel.

What had gotten into her?

Looking like the cat who'd gotten all the cream, her grandmother grinned. "There's your answer, Richard. You'll be joining us for lunch and dessert."

"It seems so." He leaned back in his chair and flashed her another beautifully blinding smile.

Kelsey's heart gave a little jump, signaling that her pleasure at his visit had nothing to do with either her faith or wanting to become Amish.

Oh, she was in so much trouble.

Chapter 13

Sitting in the living room of the Schrocks' home, sipping a glass of apple cider next to Kelsey while her grandmother put the finishing touches on lunch, Richard felt as if he was in the center of a snow globe. Any moment, he expected someone to give the globe a good shake and he'd be back where he thought he should've been in the first place.

But, of course, such a fanciful thing was not going to happen. Instead, he needed to come to terms with what was happening—and how he felt about it. This was definitely an example of reality being far different from one's imagination.

No, Miss Kelsey Schrock, with her curly blond hair, piercing blue eyes, and sweet disposition was completely outside his imaginings. Just as his reaction to his first sight of her had taken him completely off guard.

When Sylvia and Josiah had first spoken to him and Bishop Frank about their four grandchildren becoming Amish, he'd been confused. And, yes, more than a little bit skeptical. Very few people in their midtwenties suddenly decided to become baptized in the Amish faith. If they did, it was usually because they were having a difficult time in a number of areas in their lives, or because they were enchanted by the idea of stepping away from their jobs to live in bucolic splendor. They never considered the sacrifices they would have to make, or the faith in the Lord they would need to have.

Because of that, he'd begun to wonder if these wayward grandchildren of the Schrocks were attempting to pull something over on Sylvia and Josiah. Even though he'd never met them, he'd allowed himself to think all sorts of uncharitable things. Maybe the kids were lazy, or in need of money, or wanted to take advantage of their grandparents' generous hearts.

Of course he'd hardly had much of a conversation with this woman, but common sense was telling him that he'd been completely wrong.

It was obvious that Kelsey was nothing like the confused Englishers he'd had experience with, or the grifters he'd imagined. Though she wasn't dressed Amish, she was dressed conservatively and seemed comfortable in the house. She also seemed to be perfectly at ease with her grandmother's way of life.

To his surprise, he could imagine Kelsey being Amish and fitting right in with their community.

Realizing he'd been staring at her for more than a minute without saying a word, he reached for his glass and took a healthy gulp. "How long have you been here now?"

"Just a few days."

"That's not too long."

"No, it's not. But I've stayed here before. Just not recently."

"I see. So, um, how are things going?"

"Well, I think." Looking at her grandmother, who was

working in the kitchen, Kelsey added, "I've been sleeping better than I have in years. I think I'm using muscles I'd forgotten I had." Her eyes were sparkling.

"I bet you'll get the hang of everything soon."

"Oh, I'm getting the hang of it."

"She's doing a *gut* job, Richard," Sylvia called out.

"Mommi, are you sure you don't need any help?"

"I don't. Not a bit."

"Fine."

"You aren't missing your familiar way of life?"

"Not yet. But like I said, I haven't been here very long." Kelsey's eyes narrowed. "Did you come over to make sure I'm committed to becoming Amish?"

"Not at all." But even to his own ears his comment didn't ring true.

She peeked toward the kitchen. When it was obvious that Sylvia had walked down the hall, Kelsey's tone became more pointed. "Or are you checking to see if I'm sneaking around with my cell phone or something?"

"Not at all. I'm only making conversation."

"Hmm."

So, she was irritated with him. Maybe more than that. "Kelsey, I promise I am being sincere. I wasn't asking questions with a hidden agenda."

"I hope not. Because if that were the case, I think it would be rude."

"Or because I was concerned about you," he pointed out.

"Or my grandparents." She crossed her legs. "I hope you aren't imagining that I would ever do anything to hurt them."

He held up his hands. "I surrender," he joked. "I promise that I don't mean any disrespect to either you or your brothers and sister."

"Kelsey, are you causing trouble again?"

Turning bright red, she closed her eyes. "No," she murmured.

"It sure sounded like it."

Richard looked over his shoulder at the man who had just come into the room. He was obviously her brother. "She's not. We're simply getting to know each other." Standing up, he walked over to shake hands. "I'm Richard Miller. You are Martin, I believe?"

"*Jah*." He shook his hand. "I hear you are staying for lunch?"

"I am. I was invited." Why he added that, he didn't know.

Martin looked confused for a second but recovered quickly. "I'll look forward to getting to know you better." Looking down at his shirt, he frowned. "I should go get cleaned up first."

"Where's Dawdi?"

"He's coming along."

Looking even more agitated, Kelsey got to her feet. "I should go help my grandmother."

"I am fine, Kelsey!" Mommi called out. "You stay there and entertain our guest."

Martin grinned as he went up the stairs.

Sitting back down, Kelsey sighed. "I'm beginning to feel a little bit like a teenage girl with a suitor over."

"I promise, I didn't come calling."

Her eyes widened the same moment he wished he could cut out his tongue. What had possessed him to say something like that? "Not that, ah, I wouldn't want to call on you."

"No?"

"No. I mean, I would, if I was looking for a spouse. Which I am not."

"I'm not looking for a suitor either, Richard."

Ouch. "Of course you aren't."

"I don't know what kind of woman you are used to, but I don't need a man to be happy."

"I didn't suppose that you did. I . . . I only came over to say hello to you and Martin, and to see if you intended to come to church on Sunday."

"We do."

"I'll let Bishop Hershberger know."

"*Danke*, though I believe he is already aware of that fact."

Hoping to put them back on even ground, he asked, "Do you have any questions or concerns I can help you with in the meantime?"

"About being Amish?"

"*Jah.*"

"Not at this time."

"Okay. Well, if you do have questions, feel free to reach out."

"Thank you, Richard. I'll be sure to reach out to you if neither of my grandparents can answer one of my questions."

She was as prickly as a porcupine! "I'll look forward to that. I mean, discussing church things. Not having a personal conversation""

"I can't imagine you wanting to have any other type."

When she gave him another death stare, he started praying for guidance. "I'm sorry, Kelsey. Everything I'm saying seems to come out wrong. I don't know why."

"Give the preacher a break, Kelsey! *Mei haus* ain't the place to indulge in these verbal acrobatics."

She flinched. "I didn't mean to do that."

"It sure sounded like it to me," Dawdi called out. "Stop it, please. You are giving the poor man fits and we need him in good health. We like our preacher."

"You don't need to worry about me, Josiah," Richard called out.

"Someone's got to."

Looking even more uneasy, Kelsey closed her eyes. "I'm sorry, Dawdi. I'll be better!"

"*Gut!*"

Turning to Richard, she whispered, "I'm the one who should be apologizing to you. I don't know why I was acting so defensive. It wasn't right."

"I'm not offended."

"You should be," she added, leaning toward him. "I've been rude. Here you came over to say hello, and I'm being difficult. Thank you for stopping by and for the kind offer of help."

"You're welcome." Kelsey smelled like cinnamon rolls. Not anything overpowering, just slightly . . . yummy. He was torn between wanting to find a way to lean closer and keeping himself at a respectful distance.

Martin, who'd just joined them, glanced his way, then studied him for a long moment.

This time Richard knew he was the one blushing.

"Let's all go eat now, children," Mommi called out just as Josiah joined them.

Kelsey couldn't get up fast enough. "I'm going to help my grandmother."

He nodded. At this point he didn't care if she was feeding him an obvious lie or not.

"Don't let my sister rattle you too much," Martin said. "Kelsey looks adorable and cute, but she's feisty."

"She's like that with everyone? Not just with me?"

He grinned. "Absolutely not just with you. She's always been a girl who knows her own mind and isn't afraid to let others know it. It used to drive my sister Beth crazy. I wouldn't take it personally."

"Kind of hard not to. I came to offer support but instead I think I only upset her."

"For what it's worth, if she didn't like you, she would

have treated you in a far calmer manner. Only people she likes can get her back up like that."

He smiled before deciding that might not be the best response.

But inside, he was grinning big. He was perfectly fine with Kelsey liking him.

Because as much as he wanted to pretend he hadn't noticed, he had found her to be the prettiest girl he'd ever seen.

Chapter 14

Martin liked Richard right off the bat. He was personable, was a plumber and a handyman full time, had grown up in Indiana, and had been a preacher for two years. If they'd been next-door neighbors growing up, he was sure they would have been friends.

In addition, even though they didn't know each other, Martin already respected him. He knew that even putting one's name into the lot was stressful. Discovering the marked Bible was sometimes seen as both a blessing and a curse. No man accepted this fate easily-especially if he was chosen by the Lord to be a preacher at such a young age.

He also appreciated that Richard was also kind to his grandparents. He had a nice way with them—both easygoing and respectful. Yet he somehow managed to elicit a certain level of respect from Josiah and Sylvia. Martin had a feeling that respect had not come easily but had been built over time.

But all that didn't mean that he liked the way Richard kept eyeing Kelsey as if she was the best thing he'd seen all day.

No, he didn't care for that at all.

"Martin, did you not understand Richard's question?" Dawdi asked.

He'd been so focused on his thoughts, he hadn't even realized that Richard had spoken.

"Sorry, I guess I didn't. Could you repeat that?"

"Certainly. Ah, are you missing your phone and car?"

Across from him, Kelsey grinned.

Martin ignored it. "Actually, I am," he replied truthfully. "But I'm getting used to it."

His grandparents exchanged looks. "I didn't know that," Mommi said.

"It's not important. I'll get by."

"What about you, Kelsey?"

"I am, too, but probably not as much as Martin."

"Why is that?" Richard asked.

"Well, I was in college, so I'm used to walking everywhere on campus. Martin commuted."

"I thought all college students used their phones all the time."

"We do. I mean, I did. But I told everyone who I was going to miss texting and seeing on Instagram and such about my plans." She grinned. "Now I spend about an hour every afternoon writing letters."

"You're adapting."

"Yes. I feel a little bit like one of those ladies in a Jane Austen movie." She groaned. "Which I just realized probably none of you have seen—even Martin."

"I get the gist of it, Kelsey," Mommi said gently. "You feel like an old-fashioned girl."

"Or maybe an Amish girl," Richard said.

"Yes. Or maybe an Amish girl." She chuckled.

"You can still go down the hill and speak on the phone. You know, leave a message or call your friends."

"That feels like it's cheating, though."

"It's not. It's keeping in touch with people who are important to you while respecting our ways."

"I'll do that."

"You should call folks, too, Martin," Richard said.

"I commuted, but I also worked in a cubicle. Everything in my life was regimented and fast. I'm not sure I'm ready to mesh this life with my old one yet."

"What about your brother and sister? How are they doing without the two of you?"

"I don't know," Martin said, suddenly feeling terrible about that. "What have they told you, Kels?"

"Nothing."

"Why haven't you two been in contact with Beth and Jonny?"

"We all agreed to separate," Kelsey said.

"Why? You two are still their siblings," Mommi said.

"Yes, but we knew being apart would be hard," Martin tried to explain.

"Because we told you that we didn't want all four of you here at the same time?"

"No. Because we're all used to talking to one another a lot," Kelsey explained. "They understand."

"I think you should walk down to the phone shanty and call them both," Dawdi said. "And don't say that it will make things hard. You can't do everything alone. You need support."

Richard nodded. "You need to lean on the Lord, too. He's watching, and I feel certain he's been waiting to help you, too."

"I have been praying, Richard, but I feel selfish praying for myself. I mean, what if He gets annoyed with me because I'm doing what I wanted but am still conflicted?"

"He's not going to get annoyed with you, Kelsey," Richard said. "He already knows what's in your heart, ain't so?"

"I suppose."

"You can always talk to me, too."

"You're busy."

"I could come over again. We could take a walk together and talk. How about that?"

"I'd like that. I mean, I would if you have time."

"I have time. I'll come over in two nights' time, if that is all right with you, Josiah?"

Looking bemused, he nodded. "You might want to be asking her older brother about that, though."

"Why?" Kelsey asked.

Martin folded his arms over his chest. "Because it sounds a lot like Richard has found a way to come calling on you without naming it that."

Before Richard had a chance to speak, Kelsey groaned. "Oh, no. We are not going to start playing this game, Martin. We might be almost Amish, but we've got a long way to go before you can start acting like my guardian."

"Obviously I am your guardian."

"You are not."

"Uh, hold on," Richard said. "All I was trying to do was be helpful."

"See?" Kelsey said.

"I'm seeing more than you think," he said. Turning to Richard, he exhaled. "Kelsey is right, though. She's too old for me to start treating her like she doesn't know her own mind."

"Understood."

Mommi stood up. "I think it's time we had dessert," she said.

"I think that's a grand idea," Kelsey said. "I'll help you slice the pie."

When the women were in the kitchen, his grandfather leaned forward. "Tell me how your job is going, Richard. Are you working on any bathroom remodels?"

"I am."

As conversation eased into something far less personal, Martin leaned back in his chair again. Thought about how he used to spend his lunch hour.

And decided, all things considered, he liked it a lot better this way.

Two hours later, he was walking by Kelsey's side to the phone shanty.

After they'd eaten dessert, Richard took his leave. He'd gone into the kitchen and helped Kelsey and their grandmother clean up. Dawdi had looked amused that Martin wanted to chip in, but the habit was too ingrained in him not to help. Both of their parents had always expected the four of them to handle such chores. Even after their divorce, they'd stayed consistent on that.

Besides, he was so used to living on his own, washing his own dishes didn't seem much of a chore, just a way of life.

Once the dishes were done, they'd decided to call Beth and Jonny.

"Are you worried about talking to them?" Kelsey asked.

"No. Are you?"

"A little bit."

"Why?"

"I guess I'm afraid Beth will think I sound different."

"Already? I doubt that."

"I'm actually afraid that one of them will have changed their minds."

"I've worried they might, too, but I think we should be prepared for that."

"You really think it's possible?"

He nodded. "I do. This is a big step. Haven't you second-guessed our decision?"

"Not at all. I love it here. I love helping Mommi, and Patti next door has been so kind. My life seems easier."

"I guess it is for you."

"What do you mean by that?"

"Everyone seems to think you don't need to do any more here than stay at home and help out around the house. I need to have a new occupation."

"That's not true. No one is expecting you to instantly become a successful carpenter or something."

"I know, but I'm definitely not a farmer. I had a good job in the city, but I gave it up." When Kelsey looked as if she was about to argue, he held up a hand. "I'm not saying that I was happy there, because I wasn't."

"You weren't. Don't start reinventing the past."

Her words were pretty harsh. Martin supposed he should've expected her bluntness, but he was still taken off guard. "Is that what you think I've been doing?"

"Maybe."

"Wow."

"Martin, come on. You might be my older brother, but that doesn't mean I don't see what you're struggling with. I know you were unhappy in Cleveland. I also know that you continually look ahead, wondering if your next idea or plan will make you happy."

He didn't think she was wrong, but he didn't like the way she had neatly classified his personality in one sentence.

"You're right. I am trying to be happy, and it isn't always easy for me."

She leaned against him. "It's not always easy for me either. Plus, sometimes I think we were so excited about this new adventure, we forgot that it's not an adventure, it's a complete change of life."

"I've been praying a lot. The Lord doesn't seem to be giving me much guidance, however."

"Maybe He is, but you don't want to hear it. That's happened to me."

He chuckled. "I think you might have a point there." They were standing side by side in the phone shanty now. "Are you ready for this?"

"No, but I think we'd better be."

"Who do you think we should call first?"

"Jonny."

"Really? Why?"

Kelsey smiled. "Because Jonny is going to be more supportive. He really wanted to come here right away."

"Maybe I should've let him."

"He and I talked, and we decided that having both him and me living with our grandparents might be a lot for them to take. We both talk a lot and can be headstrong."

"Pick up the phone and call him," he said. "Let's hear what he has to say."

Taking a deep breath, Kelsey picked up the receiver, punched in the phone number, and visibly held her breath when the call went through.

When Jonny answered, her smile was blinding.

"Hi, Jonny! It's me and Martin."

Martin leaned against the opposite wall and allowed himself to simply listen to their conversation.

Chapter 15

First days had passed since Martin had walked her home. During that time, the siblings had attended church, met with Bishop Frank, and created yet another round of gossip and speculation around Walden.

As for herself, Patti was trying to get used to her new reality, which was that Sylvia now had company at her house and didn't need Patti's companionship too much anymore. It felt selfish, but she was jealous of Kelsey. And for once, it wasn't even the woman's beauty that created that feeling; it was that she'd replaced Patti in Sylvia's life.

Sylvia no longer needed Patti to help her accomplish simple chores or even just to check on her. Kelsey and Martin did that now.

Which meant Patti now had too much time on her hands. Yes, she had her bookkeeping business, but she couldn't sit at the table and add and subtract numbers all day. She was going to have to find something else to do.

That was probably why she'd greeted Connor a bit too enthusiastically when he showed up at her door. Connor was her oldest friend. Their relationship had always ebbed and flowed, depending on whether Connor was courting anyone or not.

Last she'd heard, he'd been about to propose to Violet, but then they got in a fight and were currently not speaking to each other.

So, she'd been happy to see him. Until he'd started pestering her with nosy questions. They were friends, but she wasn't loving his tone. Or the things he was implying.

"You're not actually giving them the time of day, are you?" Connor asked.

Taken off guard, she stopped washing the living room wall and peered down at him. "What is wrong with becoming friends with Martin and Kelsey?"

"They're English, for one."

"That's true, but who cares? We all have good friends who are English."

"Maybe, maybe not."

"Okay, well then, how about this: They're about to become Amish. Soon they'll be just like us."

He scoffed. "Not hardly. You can't trust anything about them, Patti. You know that, too."

"I don't know any such thing. I've gotten to know both of them a bit, and I think they will be good additions to our community."

"Until they leave." He waved a hand. "People like them always do."

"'People like them'? Connor, do you hear yourself?"

"The question should be, do you hear yourself. You're defending them and you hardly know them."

"I know them better than you do. We both know you don't know them at all." Climbing on the step stool, she dunked her sponge back in the warm, sudsy water and began scrubbing the wall in earnest again.

"Aren't you done yet?"

"Obviously not."

"Hmm."

Connor had come over unannounced. When she'd told him that she couldn't go out to lunch because she was in the middle of washing her living room walls, he'd looked aggravated but had told her that he'd hang out with her while she cleaned.

And that was what he'd been doing, too. While she scrubbed, got splattered with stray water drops, and climbed up and down her step stool, he lounged on the couch and watched.

She hadn't exactly expected him to help her, but it seemed that he was going out of his way *not* to help.

She wished he'd leave.

"I think we're going to have to agree to disagree about Martin and Kelsey, Connor."

"I guess so, until you see that I'm right." He grinned.

"Oh, please."

"It's true." It was obvious he was teasing. Well, almost obvious. There was a thread of steel in his voice that only appeared when he was very fired up about something.

When they heard a knock at the door, Connor finally made himself useful and answered it. Tired of going up and down the stepladder, she stayed where she was.

Then she couldn't believe her eyes when she realized that Martin had come over.

After he and Connor exchanged a few words, Martin spied her in the living room.

"Patti, what are you doing up there?"

"Washing the walls."

He strode to her side. "You aren't holding onto anything."

"Sure I am. I've got a sponge in one hand and a bucket of warm water in the other."

"That's what I meant. Come down and let me help you. You could fall."

"So could you."

"Better me than you though, right? Seriously, come down. You could break your neck."

"No. I have a feeling your neck is just as important as mine. Plus, I know what I'm doing. I do this all the time."

"Accidents happen, though." He was still hovering, as if he was afraid she was about to take a wrong step and come crashing down.

"Why are you here anyway?" Connor asked.

Patti inhaled a breath. "Connor, you're being rude."

"I think I'm being direct."

"I came over to deliver a message from my grandparents, but I also wanted to see you."

"Oh? What do Sylvia and Josiah need?"

Smiling up at her, Martin said, "They need you to come over for a bonfire tonight. I want you to come over, too. Jonny and Beth are coming down for the night."

"Who are they?" asked Connor.

"My brother and sister."

"The two who don't want to suddenly become Amish?"

"They actually do, they're just waiting a year so my grandparents aren't overwhelmed."

"I'm sure they already are."

"Connor, stop! You really are being rude."

"What? It's true. We were just talking about that."

"Still."

"I've got this, Patti. Thank you, but there's no need to defend me."

"There's no need for you to get so defensive," Connor blurted out. "There's nothing wrong with Patti, here, being concerned about what's going on next door to her farm."

"What do you think is going on?"

His voice was mellow, but she caught a note of sarcasm in

his tone. And who could blame him? Feeling her cheeks heat, she turned Martin's way. "We weren't talking about you like that," she said.

"It's okay if you were."

She leaned down. "No, I mean—"

"Patti, truly. I am not upset."

Just as she opened her mouth—to say what, she didn't know—the worst happened. She lost her balance and tilted toward Martin.

Right into his arms.

It would have been romantic and sweet . . . if her bucket of dirty water hadn't come crashing down as well—on top of Martin.

In less than five seconds, he was holding her not-insignificant weight and was soaked to the skin.

And, of course, Connor was there to witness the whole debacle.

She wiggled in his arms. "I'm okay."

"*Nee*, I kind of think you aren't." There was a smile in his tone.

That made the lump of tears that was clogging her throat loosen. He wasn't upset with her. "Let me down."

He let go of her legs but held the upper portion of her body. The change slid her next to him. It was all too close. And should have brought her a feeling of extreme embarrassment.

But all she seemed to be able to do was look into his eyes.

"Patti, what has gotten into you?" Connor said.

She felt her cheeks heat. "I don't know what you are talking about."

"Sure you do. Plus, get that man a towel."

Because he was soaking wet.

With dirty water.

"Oh, Martin. You're going to need a shower."

"*Jah*, I likely am."

It was chilly outside today. "Would you like a blanket to cover yourself for your trip home?"

"I walked, so I'll be fine."

"You walked? Connor, you drove your buggy over, didn't you?"

"I did. Why?"

"Could you take Martin home in your buggy?"

"Do you want a ride, English? Are you too chilled to walk?"

"You know what? I think I am. Thank you for offering." Turning to her, he lowered his voice. "I came over to see how you were doing, but all I did was get in your way. I'll come back tomorrow."

"Tomorrow?"

He nodded. "Or you could visit me."

"I'll do that. I'll come over in the morning."

"Sounds good."

Chapter 16

Martin would be the first to admit that he didn't always read people easily. He often missed cues in a person's body language or the nuance in a specific phrase. It had always been like that, even back when he was in school. It had been a long-standing joke among his friends that he was not the one to reach out to if they needed to discuss a personal relationship.

Though Martin had thought he'd improved a bit since his junior high years, he couldn't deny that his friends were right.

He liked numbers. He liked situations to be black or white. Problems that had specific solutions and needed methodical, step-by-step procedures to solve. That was why he'd done so well at his job in finance.

It was also why he'd considered majoring in engineering.

But the Lord seemed to have decided he didn't need other gifts. He'd never been very good at relationships. Sometimes it was difficult for him to tell if someone was upset or irritated.

But he sure didn't have to worry about that with Connor Beachy. The other man was making no bones about the fact that he did not like Martin and did not want to be driving around someone so smelly and wet in his pristine buggy.

If their situations were reversed, Martin imagined he'd feel the same way.

But because they weren't, he decided to make the best of things. Which, for him, meant getting information. "What's going on between you and Patti?"

Connor tensed but immediately appeared to put on a casual attitude. "We are friends. Nothing more."

"Really?"

"What is that supposed to mean?"

"That I'm surprised."

"You don't think it's possible for a man and a woman to be only friends?"

"I do think it's possible. I have plenty of friends who happen to be women. But the two of you seem a little different, somehow." Actually, Martin thought Connor had acted just a bit too territorial over a woman he claimed to only think of as a buddy. "Plus, you two are about the same age and she's single and you're single."

"We are all those things. In addition, we're both Amish. I guess you think all Amish are anxious to marry and have *kinner*."

"I didn't say that."

"You didn't need to. It was obvious you were thinking it."

Martin considered responding with a biting remark, but he decided against it. For some reason, Patti seemed to be fond of the guy. He liked her too much to alienate her friend on purpose.

Even though he absolutely thought she could do better.

"Martin, while I admire your intention to change your life, it's obvious you have a lot to learn about being Amish."

"I won't argue about that. I'm currently failing miserably at learning Pennsylvania Dutch, doing my best to stay away from my grandparents' chickens, and often wish I could sit in front of my computer or a TV for a good hour in the evenings."

"Yet you expect to eventually feel comfortable?"

"I don't know if I will or not. All I do know is that I want to try. I really don't think I'm making a mistake by living here for a while."

"I wish you the best, then."

"Would you also give me your blessing if I eventually decided to court Patti?"

"Are you being serious?"

"I think you know I am. We're both of marriageable age and becoming friends. If you have no claim on her and Patti is open to me, why wouldn't I want to take things a step further?"

"Patti Coblentz is a fine, upstanding woman. But we both know she ain't marriage material."

Martin thought Connor was wrong. Dead wrong. But there was also something in the other man's tone that bothered him even more. "I disagree."

Connor directed his horse to turn onto the driveway and allowed the buggy's pace to slow. "While I admire your intentions, it's just the two of us here. I think we can be completely honest, ain't so?"

"Yeah." He was still genuinely confused about what Connor was dancing around.

"Then I think you should stop acting as if you were blind."

Martin had no idea what he was hinting at. "You're going to have to be clearer, because I have no idea what that means."

Connor exhaled. "I'm talking about Patti's deformity."

The man's words were so distasteful, Martin was tempted to get out of the buggy and never talk to him again.

But he owed it to Patti to at least hear Connor through. She needed to know what Connor was saying behind her back. "You're talking about the port-wine stain on her neck?"

"Of course. It's not only unsightly, it's a sign of the devil. I would never marry a woman who could give my child such a mark."

"You aren't being serious, are you?" If Connor was joking, it was in very poor taste.

"Of course I am."

"The port-wine stain is nothing to worry about."

"I think it is. It's far more than that."

"I don't even notice it."

"Maybe I should be asking you if you are joking, because everyone notices it."

"Why do you think your children would be born with it? I could look it up, but I'm pretty sure it's just a birthmark, not anything that's hereditary."

"She must have bad blood," he said as he drew the horse to a stop. "I'd never marry a woman who was so disfigured."

"We are all imperfect. And even though I don't consider a port-wine stain to be a disfigurement, I can't believe you would hold anyone's disability or handicap against them. It's wrong."

"You can act all high and mighty if you like, but you asked me for the truth. I gave it to you."

"I never imagined it would be so distasteful." Martin climbed out. "Thanks for the ride, but I have to tell you, I hope I never see you again. And I'm going to do everything I can to make sure Patti doesn't see much of you either."

"Just because I don't want to marry her doesn't mean I don't care about her."

"Just because I'm becoming Amish doesn't mean I won't do my best to make you miserable if you hurt her." He turned and walked into the house, trailing Patti's blanket with him.

Kelsey, who'd been sitting on the sofa in the living room, looked up from the letter she was writing. "What happened to you?"

"Patti fell off a step stool, and I caught her and got a bucket of dirty water for the trouble."

Her nose wrinkled as she approached him. "Wow, you really smell."

"I know. I'm freezing, too."

"Did you just walk here?"

"No, Patti's friend, Connor, gave me a lift in his buggy."

"You met Connor?" Mommi asked.

His grandmother's voice held a note of surprise. And—if he wasn't mistaken—a bit of distaste. "Oh, yeah."

Kelsey looked from one to the other of them. "What's the story with him?"

"There isn't one."

"No, I saw the look you and Mommi exchanged. What's he like?"

"I don't know."

"Mommi?"

Their grandmother frowned before carefully clearing her expression. "Connor Beachy is Patti's best friend. She's told me time and again that there was never anything romantic between them, but I've always thought he acted rather possessive of her. Possessive, but not always respectful. I've never understood their friendship, to be honest."

"Okay. But why are you upset with him?" Kelsey asked.

Still seething over the way he'd talked about Patti, Martin debated what to say. He wanted to be honest with his sister, but he also realized that he had no right to feel so protective of Patti. There was also the possibility that their grand-mother would likely not appreciate his disparaging Connor when they barely knew each other. "Other than the fact that he's a jerk? We had words."

"Uh-oh. What did you say?"

"Not much. At least nothing more than needed to be said."

"Oh, dear," Mommi said. "I hope you didn't go too far."

As far as Martin was concerned, he hadn't gone far enough. Part of him had wanted to teach Connor a lesson with a good right hook.

Which, of course, would've been the wrong thing to do because he was doing his best to become Amish.

"I can't believe she's friends with that guy. He's terrible."

"What did he say?" Kelsey asked.

"He said that he would never be more than friends with Patti because of her birthmark. He said it was a mark of the devil."

"That's awful."

Martin nodded. "Then, as if that wasn't bad enough, he had the gall to hint that having a birthmark means that any children she has could be marked, too."

"But that's ridiculous."

"I know that and you know that. But all I could think was that he might have said something similar to Patti. He doesn't deserve to be her friend."

"At least he gave you a ride home in his buggy."

"Patti asked him to. It was obvious he didn't want to, though."

Kelsey groaned. "Somehow that makes him sound even worse. I hate wishy-washy men like that."

"She'd be better off without him. I told him that I was going to keep an eye on him from now on."

"Did you now?" Mommi murmured.

And there went his promise to himself to keep most of his feelings about the guy to himself. "Sorry, Mommi. I guess I'm not only being rude, talking about a man you've known all your life, but being a bad Amish person."

"I wasn't aware that there was such a thing as a bad Amish person."

Her voice was light and her eyes were shining. No doubt she was teasing him. But still, he felt terrible. Not only was he hoping to become Amish, he was also hoping to improve his life. Unfortunately, he still had a long way to go.

"Obviously I have a lot to learn."

"We all do, child. Every day, ain't so?"

Kelsey winked. "Why don't you go shower, brother? You'll likely catch cold if you wait much longer."

Knowing she was right, he handed her the damp blanket and headed upstairs. Only when he was out of sight did he hear his little sister complain.

"What in the world am I supposed to do with this?"

He couldn't help but grin.

Chapter 17

Connor didn't return to her house after dropping Martin off at his grandparents' farm. Patti wasn't sure if she was glad about that or not. On the one hand, she hadn't expected him to return, especially when she hadn't been shy about showing her disapproval of the way he'd treated Martin.

That said, they'd had disagreements in the past and he'd always gotten over them quickly. She'd expected him to stay for at least another hour. They'd been friends for a long time and never seemed to run out of things to talk about.

Of course, now that his attentions seemed of a more possessive nature, their discussions felt very different. Patti honestly didn't know how to act around Connor anymore. He wasn't nearly as easygoing as he used to be—but maybe he'd never been that way and she just hadn't noticed? All Patti did know was that she missed his friendship but didn't like his new, superior attitude.

Then again, maybe some of the problems they were having were her fault. Even though they'd always been just friends, she'd really believed that it was just a matter of time before they took their relationship to another level.

Now she knew that was never going to happen.

As she wandered around her house, straightening things that didn't need to be straightened, Patti reminded herself to focus on her future. A positive, happy future.

Yes. One day she'd find the right person. She'd fall head over heels in love and eventually marry.

Then, with the Lord's blessing, they'd have children. She'd be busy with her bookkeeping job and taking care of the *kinner*, while her husband would farm the fields around their house, just like Aunt Frieda and Uncle Isaiah had. No doubt she'd hardly have time to sit down, let alone be lonely.

Smiling at her thoughts, she closed her eyes.

Then reality returned. Her house seemed even quieter now that both men had left.

After Connor had driven his buggy down the drive, she'd scurried around to put herself back to rights. Although Martin was doused with most of the water, a fair share of it had splashed on her, too.

Wet and uncomfortable, she'd changed into a fresh dress and *kapp*.

She didn't have a large selection of dresses. Only five for the fall and winter. One was reserved for church, another was a dark gray, for funerals and when she was feeling the need to appear older and more businesslike. That left two for cleaning and her favorite one, a lovely shade of forest green that she'd privately thought of as her courting dress. Even though she wasn't receiving any callers, she'd still made it. Lying to herself, she pretended that she wore it for her own enjoyment.

She slipped it on, and when she headed downstairs again, she felt that she looked her best. She put away her step stool and washrags and had just put the kettle on when she heard another knock at her door.

To her surprise, Sylvia and Josiah had arrived.

"Hiya, Patti," Josiah said with a happy grin. "Sylvia and I decided to come over and visit for a spell. Are you up for company?"

She couldn't remember them ever stopping over on the spur of the moment. Especially not in the evening. "Um, sure?"

Sylvia held up a plastic container. "I brought cookies."

Remembering her manners at last, Patti stepped back. "This is a nice surprise. Please, come in." Hearing the kettle whistling in the kitchen, she added, "It's perfect timing, too. I was just about to make some tea. Would you two like some?"

"I would," Sylvia said. "Josiah?"

"Water will do me good."

"I can get you that, too. If you want to sit down in the living room, I'll be there in a moment."

"No need for that, child. We'll come into the kitchen, too," Sylvia said.

As they followed, she noticed them both looking around, Josiah especially. "Do you need anything?" she asked.

"Hmm? Oh, *nee*. It's been a while since I've been over here, Patti. I was just taking a look around."

"Maybe a mite too intently," Sylvia said under her breath.

"Nonsense. Patti knows I mean no disrespect." Turning to her, he clasped her shoulder. "Everything looks nice, child."

Pleased by the compliment, she smiled at him. "*Danke*. I've been decorating a bit." She pointed to the new shades on the windows. Though they were still plain, they were a pleasing cream color instead of tan, and clean and in good repair. A far cry from the torn and stained shades that were there previously.

"They are lovely, dear," Sylvia said. "They make everything seem fresh and new."

"*Danke*."

Ten minutes later, the three of them were seated at her dining room table, each nursing a cup of hot tea and nibbling on a gingersnap. Patti was enjoying their company. She always did.

But it was obvious that they'd come over for a specific reason. After they'd discussed the weather and the pulled muscle in Josiah's side, Sylvia folded her hands together and looked at Patti intently.

"We didn't come over just to catch up on news. We wanted to talk to you about Martin."

"And Cooper, too."

And just like that, the curiosity that she'd been feeling settled into apprehension. "What about them?"

"It seems to me that you have two suitors now," Josiah said.

"She might."

Patti felt her cheeks heat but valiantly pretended she wasn't embarrassed at all. But boy, was she! "I wouldn't call either of them suitors. Connor is my old friend and Martin . . ." Her voice drifted off as she tried to think of the perfect description. She settled on, "I think Martin is feeling very confused about everything."

"You are right, but I think you're also wrong," Josiah said. "Connor is a friend and Martin is confused. But that don't mean they both aren't interested in you as well."

"No one has ever been interested in me, so I think it would be quite a surprise if they were both interested in me now."

"Not as much a surprise as about time," Sylvia said. "If one of them is the right person for you, of course."

As much as she respected her neighbors and appreciated their help, Patti did not think of them as substitute parents. Honestly, it had been so long since she'd sought her parents' guidance, she wasn't even sure if she had been subconsciously looking for it.

All she did know was that their spur-of-the-moment visit was not making her feel any better. "I hate to be blunt, but I don't understand your concern. Are you worried that I might hurt Martin?"

"Of course not," Sylvia said.

Feeling even more confused, she looked from one to the other. "Then what? Are you concerned that Connor might hurt Martin?"

"Oh, child. You really don't see it, do you?" Josiah asked.

"See what?"

"We didn't come over here to check on Martin. We came over to check on you," he said.

"Me?"

"*Jah*. Because we care about you. We're not sure either of these men are good enough for you," Sylvia said. "We are afraid you might get attached and they'll break your heart." Before Patti could respond, she added, "I don't think Martin is one hundred percent sure that he belongs here with us."

"You don't have to worry about my heart."

"Of course I do. I worry about you a lot. We love you, dear.

"He's torn between two worlds," Josiah said. "I know he needs to work through this on his own, but it is difficult because I want to help him."

Sylvia nodded. "Plus, it's so different with Kelsey."

"How so?"

"It was apparent from her first night in our house that Kelsey was more than ready to adopt our way of life," Sylvia explained. "She's eager to learn and seems to absorb both our language and culture like a sponge."

"Even Richard seemed impressed with her manner," Josiah added.

It took Patti a moment to realize who they were talking about. "Preacher Richard?"

"None other."

"But . . . how would you know this?"

"He mentioned a few things when he stopped by."

"Preacher Richard paid you a house call?"

"Don't act as if that is out of the ordinary. Four of our grandchildren are thinking about joining our faith. There's a lot going on at our house."

She couldn't help but smile. "I'm more interested in Preacher Richard's interest in Kelsey."

"I'm sure he's only interested as our preacher," Josiah said, but he exchanged a look with Sylvia.

"Indeed," Sylvia said. Though her sparkling eyes told a different story.

Patti had had enough of all this guessing and thinly veiled innuendo. "I don't suppose it matters whether Preacher Richard is interested in Kelsey Schrock or not. The Lord is in charge of our futures."

Sylvia nodded. "Yes, dear. That's what we've been trying to tell *ya*. Our good Lord is in charge of all our futures. Even when we aren't sure what we want to happen, He already has a plan."

"We mustn't forget that," Josiah said. "Even when times are tough, He hasn't left us, Patti."

Patti simply sipped her tea but privately admitted her neighbors were right. She'd forgotten for a moment that her future was in God's hands. Somehow and some way, He would help her find her path. The right path.

She just needed to remember that truth.

Chapter 18

Kelsey had been majoring in biology in college and was the valedictorian of her high school class. Her principal had once told her that he was sure she was going to achieve great things. He'd listed all kinds of careers in medicine, each one sounding more impressive than the last.

For a time, she'd thought she might be a research scientist or work in a lab in a cancer center. If Martin hadn't been so interested in numbers, she figured he would have done something similar.

But whereas Martin was always a little awkward around other people, she enjoyed conversing with just about everyone.

In addition, though research science was a job to be proud of, sitting in a lab all day over a microscope didn't interest her at all.

Actually, she'd never yearned to do anything special with her smart brain. She'd never even been motivated financially.

What she'd always wanted was stability and peace. Now that she was spending her days living Amish, she was slowly receiving those things. She found comfort in doing the same things every day and was learning so much about herself and being patient when she worked by her grandmother's side in her garden and kitchen.

Sometimes, when Kelsey went to sleep, her body was so tired that she collapsed. Other times, she used the flashlight next to her bed to read a few pages from a library book before a comforting sense of calm surrounded her. It was lovely.

What was not lovely was Anna. Anna was a four-pound hen who was determined to make her mornings miserable.

She was doing a good job of it, too. Every single time she approached her, Anna would ruffle her feathers, fasten her beady eyes on Kelsey, and hiss. Loudly. It was enough to make Kelsey decide never to eat an egg again.

Or at least avoid Anna as much as possible.

Unfortunately, Mommi said that wasn't an option. "Anna knows you fear her, child. You have to show her that you are in charge."

Mommi's words made a lot of sense. Kelsey knew she was right, too. The chicken's role on the farm was to provide eggs and then, when that was no longer a possibility, to provide them with a good Sunday supper. Kelsey approved. However, whenever she entered the henhouse, she felt like an interloper. She wasn't comfortable collecting eggs, and all the hens knew it.

The only hen who didn't seem to mind Kelsey's hand sliding underneath her to collect an egg was Martha, and that was because she was the oldest hen and usually half asleep.

Now, as the dawn broke in the east with a flash of vibrant pink and violet, Kelsey walked across the drive as if she were about to enter a war zone.

Martin, who was heading to the woodworking shop with Toby, one of their grandfather's best friends, grinned at her. "Egg collecting time again?"

"Every morning."

"It's got to get easier."

"Doubt it. I hate going in there." After peeking out to make sure their grandmother wasn't around, she added, "I think this week is going to be even worse than usual. Mommi mentioned something about cleaning the henhouse."

Martin chuckled. "Uh-oh."

"That's all you have to say?"

"It's just some chickens, sister. Stop acting like they merit your fear, go inside, and show them who's boss."

The problem was that Kelsey knew who was boss, and it was a grumpy hen. "Want to come in with me?"

"Sorry, I'm about to be picked up."

"You'll hear the car approach."

"I feel for you, but you're on your own."

"Fine." She walked two steps, then hesitated.

"Kelsey, you know Mommi's going to wonder what's taking you so long."

"I know."

"So . . ." He made a shooing motion with his hands. "Go on, now."

Kelsey frowned at Martin. For a small moment she felt hurt, wondering why he wasn't being more supportive. And by that, she meant why he wasn't volunteering to go into the henhouse with her.

But then reason returned, and she reminded herself that she was a smart, capable woman who should not be afraid of a dozen squawking chickens. Squaring her shoulders, she walked inside.

As always, the smell hit her like a gale force wind. As far as she was concerned, few things smelled as bad as the inside of a henhouse. Yet the smell was only a bit worse than the cloud of dust and feathers and who knew what else that seemed to permeate the air.

You should be wearing a mask, she told herself. Thinking of the two boxes of surgical masks she had at home, remnants of both her college clinical lab classes and the pandemic, she frowned. She should ask Beth or Jonny to bring them down next time they visited.

She paused, wondering if a mask was even allowed. If she was Amish, was she supposed to suddenly find nothing wrong with the inside of a henhouse?

A squawk pulled her out of her musings.

She turned to the culprit. It was none other than Anna herself. As always, she was perched on the top ledge, glaring down as if she were some sort of royal chicken. One didn't have to have a fanciful imagination to know exactly what the hen was thinking: that Kesley was an interloper, and a weak one at that.

"You are just a chicken, Anna," she said.

Anna lifted her head in a very haughty way. Then, right in front of her, adjusted herself on her morning's egg.

She was practically daring Kelsey to come and get it!

You should go over to her first, a small voice inside her head urged. *Go show Anna who's the boss.*

Kelsey stepped forward. Her movement was accompanied by the nervous squawking of eleven hens. Anna remained silent. At the last minute, Kelsey turned away and went directly to Martha.

Martha didn't move when Kelsey reached for her egg, though the hen did seem to have a rather bored air about her. Two others clucked.

The quicker you do this, the faster you can get out of here, she told herself. Motivated by that reward, Kelsey approached each hen and reached for their eggs. None of them acted very pleased to see her, though none of them pecked at her. That was something to celebrate, she figured.

Finally, only Anna remained. Feeling as if she were a cowboy in an old Western, she approached the bird. "I need your egg, Anna. I can't go back to my grandma without it."

"Squawk!"

"Settle down. This happens every morning. You know you have to give it up."

"Hiss!" The low, awful noise was accompanied by rustling feathers again. Somehow the chicken had almost doubled in size. Then she tensed, obviously ready to peck at Kesley's hand.

Those pecks hurt. She actually had a scar on one of her knuckles from that evil bird.

She took another step forward. Realized she was shaking.

Kelsey could admit it: She was afraid of the hen.

Then the henhouse door opened.

"Kelsey, what in the world is keeping you?"

"You know."

Her grandmother sighed. "How many eggs have you gotten?"

"Eleven. I only have Anna left."

Mommi turned to Anna. "Are you enjoying yourself, miss?" she said as she walked toward the hen.

To Kelsey's dismay, the closer her grandmother got to the hen, the meeker Anna became. By the time Mommi reached for the egg, the hen looked as if she was about to hand it over on a silver platter.

It was impressive.

It was also maddening. She was being bullied by a chicken.

"Come along, dear. We have things to do."

"*Jah*, Mommi."

Her grandmother's lips curved up as they walked back outside. "If I didn't know you had just spoken, I would've thought it was an Amish neighbor girl. You are sounding very Amish, Kelsey."

"*Danke*. I've been trying hard."

"I know."

"Hey, Mommi, about those chickens—"

"No need to say anything, child. I know you are having a time with them."

"I don't know what's wrong. I'm intimidated by them, and I'm pretty sure they know it."

"You aren't wrong."

Walking inside, Kelsey toed off her boots and put on her slip-on black tennis shoes. Then she carried the basket to the kitchen sink and began washing the eggs. "I'll get better."

"Perhaps."

Turning to face her, she noticed her grandmother's expression was carefully blank . . . yet there was a telltale look of amusement there.

"Child, turn off the water." When she did, her grandmother continued. "Kelsey, you might not realize it, but your father used to write me long letters about you *kinner*. He found something special in each of you, which was not hard to do."

"Daed is a good man."

"He loves you. Although he was proud of many things about you, he was always proudest of your grades in school. He loved that you were so smart. I must tell you that Dawdi and I were proud of all your success in high school and college, too."

"Really?"

"For sure." She paused, then added, "The Lord gifted you with a big brain and a thirst for knowledge. When your father wrote us to say that you were considering a job in a research hospital so you could cure all sorts of diseases, Josiah and I were proud of you, too. Once, I even whispered to your grandfather that our sweet little Kelsey was one day going to do great things."

"So, you're upset that I won't."

"I didn't say that. What I am trying to tell you is that I'm not too surprised you are having a difficult time with those hens, and are even having a hard time that you aren't succeeding with them. You aren't used to struggling."

"I might have made good grades, but every class didn't come easy."

"I'm sure it didn't. But you know what to do with facts and figures and science things. Ain't so?"

"I suppose."

"It shouldn't come as a surprise to you, then, that a dozen bossy hens are getting the best of you. Nothing in your childhood has given you much experience with them."

"You're right. I've been expecting too much, haven't I?"

"I don't know if you've been expecting too much or simply have forgotten to let everything happen in its own time. You are in such a hurry, child. Don't forget to take some moments to simply enjoy the journey."

"'Enjoy the journey,'" she repeated to herself.

"*Jah*, it bears repeating, for sure and for certain." Looking pleased, Mommi turned to leave the kitchen. But she paused for a moment. "Before I forget to tell *ya*, I think you should chat with Beth and Jonny more often."

"Why?"

"They are your brother and sister, and they care about you. No matter if you decide to wear a bonnet or not, that will not change. I know you and Martin called them a few days ago, but you should stay in touch regularly."

"Is it all right with you if I go to the phone shanty as soon as I finish washing the eggs?"

"Of course, Kelsey. And please, you're not a child, right? You don't need to ask me for permission about such things."

"*Danke*, Mommi."

Her grandmother chuckled as she walked down the hall. Kelsey wondered if she was amused because she'd reverted to her childhood self or because her current state was such a mess of contradictions, there was no telling how she was ever going to straighten herself out. Likely it was a combination of both.

Fifteen minutes later, wearing a warm sweater over her dress and holding a mug of hot tea, Kelsey walked down the road to the phone shanty they shared with Patti. Ever since her grandma had suggested she call Beth or Jonny, she'd been debating which to reach out to. Beth would give her practical advice but might be too guarded to make her feel better. Jonny, on the other hand, would be full of questions, some of which might be too personal.

She also knew they'd both ask her how Martin was doing now that he was not on the call with her. She wasn't sure what she was going to tell them about him. In a lot of ways, Martin had been searching for happiness for years. Kelsey wasn't sure if leaving his life in Cleveland was going to provide the answers he was looking for. Some evenings, he seemed more confused about what he wanted than ever before. Though that might be because she hadn't been around him so much in ages.

Making a decision, she elected to call Jonny again. Beth was wonderful, but her practicality wasn't what Kelsey needed.

"Hello?"

"Hi, it's me."

"Hey, Kel-kel," he murmured, using his childhood name for her. "What's up?"

"Oh, nothing much. I spent the morning trying to get up the nerve to collect eggs from the henhouse."

"What do you mean, getting up the nerve? All you do is shift the hen and pick up the egg."

"Wait, you've collected eggs before?"

"Uh, yeah. I was on the farm all those summers, too."

"I didn't realize you were collecting eggs."

"I was always the first one up. I think Mommi was trying to give me stuff to do so I wouldn't be underfoot."

What had she been doing? She was beginning to think she'd done nothing but sleep, read books, and help her grandmother with the cooking. "I wish you were here. Anna is so mean."

"Who's that?"

"The head hen."

He burst out laughing. "Kelsey, you are too much. I wish I was there, too. But instead of doing what I want to do, I'm about to head to class."

Once again, she felt guilty that she'd been so eager to live on the farm with Martin that Jonny had had to wait for his turn. "I'll let you go."

Her brother's voice softened. "Hey, I was joking, okay? I'm not mad at you for being there."

"Are you sure about that?"

"Positive. I have a feeling God knew what He was doing when He helped us decide who should go first."

"Thanks, Jonny. I think I needed to hear that."

"I'm glad we talked, then."

"I'll call again soon."

"You better. Tell Martin to check in more, too."

"I will. Love you."

"Love you, too, Kel. Bye."

She hung up the phone slowly and imagined Jonny striding across the Baldwin Wallace campus, his pack on his back and his favorite ball cap low on his head.

That was her a couple of months ago.

Did she miss it? No.

But she did miss feeling comfortable. Walking out of the shanty, she thought about her grandmother's advice and her brother's words. He really was wise beyond his years. The Lord did have a plan for all of them.

She needed to worry less and appreciate the moments more.

And, perhaps, beg Martin to go into the henhouse tomorrow for emotional support.

Surely he'd do that for her.

Hopefully Martin would be enjoying his work at the carpenter shop so much that he wouldn't mind giving her a few moments of his time.

Chapter 19

When Neal, the owner of Walden Carpentry, announced that it was time to go, Martin could barely hold back a sigh of relief. He'd been counting down the hours since lunchtime. Every hour at the carpentry shop felt like two days. It wasn't an exaggeration to say that he hated it.

As he swept his area and put away the tools that Neal had lent him, Martin prayed he could adopt a better attitude very soon. He'd been dissatisfied with his office work, imagining he could find something much more fulfilling. But so far, learning carpentry work had been utterly frustrating.

When was he ever going to get the hang of working with wood?

"Martin, are you sure you don't want me to give you a ride home?" Neal asked.

"I'm positive. It's not a long walk. Plus, I'm gonna stop at the phone shanty on the way and call my sister. That might take a while."

"I understand, but it's cold and at least a two-mile walk."

"I'll be all right. Thanks for the offer, though."

"See you tomorrow, then."

Already dreading it, Martin forced himself to nod. "Yeah. See you then."

Two minutes later, he was walking down the sidewalk with his hands stuffed in his pockets. The cool air had a bite to it, but instead of numbing his cheeks, it made him feel rejuvenated and refreshed.

And free.

The thought caught him off guard. So much so, he almost stumbled. What was he going to do? He'd wanted to be Amish. He'd believed that leaving the city and living a simpler life had been the right decision.

Maybe he'd been wrong.

If he was wrong, what then? All his life, he'd tried to look out for Beth, Kelsey, and Jonny. It was in his nature to be a protector, but looking after his siblings had been a necessity, too. Their parents were so focused on their own lives, they'd forgotten that they still had four kids in need of guidance and attention.

When each of them had admitted that they felt more at home with their grandparents than in the outside world, Martin had been all for making a life change.

But he was beginning to worry that he'd been leading them the wrong way.

The wind had picked up, making him realize it was colder than he'd thought. His coat was warm and thick, but it was still going to be a cold walk to the phone shanty.

If he actually did call Beth.

He'd used Beth as an excuse to avoid riding with Neal. He'd needed a few moments to himself before walking into the house and discussing his day with Kelsey and his grandparents at supper. Work had gone well, but he wasn't sure if it was the right fit for him.

"No, you can say it out loud," he said as he forced himself

to go into the shanty. "At least to yourself, while you're standing in a small wooden shack. You are having second thoughts."

He really was. But why, he wasn't exactly sure. He didn't know if it was because he hadn't found the work to be challenging or because he wasn't comfortable being so dependent on others. He didn't like having to ask someone else to give him a lift. He didn't like that a couple of the men in the company had looked at him sideways as it became obvious that he didn't know much about carpentry at all. He was used to being competent. He was used to working hard and accomplishing a lot. He was used to people thinking he was reasonably smart and had a clue.

Irritated with the pity party he couldn't seem to stop, Martin picked up the phone and called Beth.

"Hey," he said when she answered. "It's me."

"I'm really glad you called."

He could practically feel her smiling on the other end of the line. "Oh yeah? Why?"

"I was just in your fancy condo and I have a bunch of questions about your mail."

"There shouldn't be any bills. Are there? The gas, water, and electric are all paid automatically."

"No bills, but you got a couple of magazines and letters from various organizations you belong to. What should I do with them?"

"Do you mind stuffing everything in an envelope and sending it my way?"

She paused before replying. "Not at all. I'll do that by Friday."

"No hurry."

"You sure about that?"

"Yeah, time moves slowly around here. I'll read them whenever they come."

"Hey, you sound a little off. Everything okay?"

He'd called to seek her advice, but old habits die hard. She was doing enough for him. The last thing she needed was to listen to him complain about being confused. "Yeah. It's good."

"What did you do today?"

"I went to work at a carpentry shop."

"You did? How did it go?"

He could practically see her trying not to laugh. "About as well as you would expect."

"Martin, Jonny is the one who is creative and good with tools. You're far more at home managing finances and doing taxes."

"I know, but that doesn't mean I can't learn."

"But why do you want to? You've always been gifted with numbers."

His sister was right. He had been good with numbers, but he'd also used a bunch of computer programs to do that work. That wouldn't be possible in his new life in Walden. "I'm trying to become Amish, remember?"

"I remember. I could be wrong, but I've always believed that becoming Amish has more to do with what is in one's heart than carpentry skills."

He had to smile. "Way to put me in my place."

"Martin, I'm not trying to put you anywhere. All I'm saying is that I think you're being too hard on yourself." After a pause, she added, "And maybe you're trying to rush things a bit."

"What do you mean by that?"

"The bishop suggested you should plan to live Amish in Walden a year before getting baptized, Martin. There's a reason for that. No one expected you to change overnight. No one except you."

She was right. Beth was completely right. "You know, I

hate it when you're right. How come you always know what to do?"

"I don't. I'm struggling with my future as much as you are."

He hoped not. "Enough about me. Tell me what you've been doing."

She chuckled. "Well, as you can imagine, things are really exciting in the insurance world. But . . . there have been some interesting shenanigans going on between two people in the HR department."

Leaning against the wall of the shanty, he grinned. "Don't leave me hanging. What happened?"

He continued to grin as Beth launched into a story about the couple, the woman's relationship with a client, and how someone else had witnessed an obviously private moment in one of the halls.

The story was far-fetched and ridiculous, but it was the way Beth told it that made him grin the most.

Five minutes later, he hung up, feeling lighter than he had in days.

And then he looked out and saw Patti waiting a few feet away. When their eyes met, something warm flickered inside him. "I'm sorry you had to wait for me to get off the phone," he said as he walked out to meet her. "You should have knocked on the door. I would've hung up."

"It's no problem. I was going to call one of my cousins, but it's not urgent. I can call her tomorrow."

"I'm done. You can go on in."

"Well, I would . . . except I don't see a bicycle or anything. How are you getting home?"

"I was going to walk."

"It's dark out. And cold."

"I'll be fine."

She gestured behind her. "How about you let me give you a ride in my buggy?"

Their farms were adjacent to each other. It would be foolish to make her drive him when he could easily walk the last part of the way. "That's a lot of trouble. I'll be fine."

"It's not too much trouble." She started walking toward her house. "Come on, English. If you're nice, I'll even let you hold the reins."

He couldn't help it, he started laughing. Then he followed her to the buggy and climbed inside.

Chapter 20

"I still can't believe how easy you made driving a horse and buggy look," Martin grumbled by her side.

Even though it was dark, Patti still held her smile. It wouldn't do to hurt Martin's feelings; he'd tried so hard to guide her horse along the narrow drive. But honestly, the man was all thumbs when it came to working with animals. Arrow was as patient as a horse could be, but even her gelding acted as if Martin Schrock should stay away from all creatures with four legs. Patti had to agree. He was either too tentative or too forceful with his directions for the horse.

He did get an A for effort, though. It was rather adorable how attentive he'd been to her lesson.

"You'll get the hang of things soon," she finally replied. "Don't forget that I've been hitching horses to buggies and driving them for a very long time. I even had a pony and cart when I was seven."

"You're right. I'm expecting too much too soon, aren't I? Patience seems to be the order of the day."

"Has someone else been saying the same thing to you?"

"Yes. I was speaking to my sister Beth in the shanty when you arrived." Sounding even more disgruntled, he added, "When I started complaining about some things, she ended the call by reminding me that I have a year to figure out if I really do want to be Amish."

"That sounds like a good reminder. Everything takes time."

"I know. I just wish I was adapting to Amish life as easily as I want to." Sounding frustrated, he exhaled. "And here I am, complaining again."

"Ah, Martin, forgive me, but it sounds like you've been forgetting something important."

"What?"

"That the Lord will guide you."

"I haven't forgotten. That's what I meant."

He'd turned defensive. It was obvious that he'd taken her gently worded reminder as criticism. And . . . maybe it was?

She probably shouldn't have corrected him at all. He'd accepted her offer of a ride, not given his consent for her to correct his words. Keeping her eyes firmly in front of her, though Arrow did not need her help in the slightest, she said, "I'm sorry. I shouldn't have said a thing."

Resting a hand on her arm, he shook his head. "No, I'm the one who is sorry. I gave you a difficult time when all you've been doing is trying to help me. I know that."

"I reminded you about the Lord's help because I've been having to lean on him too. You see, I've got my own set of things I need to work on."

"Like what?"

The better question would be, what wasn't she working on? "Like my bookkeeping business. Like the way I've been living in my aunt's *haus* for years but still haven't made it feel like home."

Gathering her courage, she added, "Like the way I sometimes go to sleep at night wishing I didn't have this mark on my neck."

"Patti. I'm sorry."

His voice had been laced with pity, which was something she didn't want. "*Nee, I'm* sorry. I shouldn't have said a thing. Bet you're glad you asked, huh?"

"Actually, I am. You've reminded me that I need to stop being so self-centered. I need to stop thinking about myself so much."

"I'm not sure there's anything wrong with thinking about yourself from time to time. But . . . maybe you should not be so hard on yourself, too?"

"I could offer the same advice to you," he said in a soft tone.

Struck by how sweet he sounded — no, how affectionate — she glanced his way. And met his eyes.

Even in the dim light, she was struck by how blue they were. And how his usually somber expression was transformed when he smiled. His white teeth gleamed, and the dimple in his cheek appeared. He really was so very handsome.

No, she was struck by how everything about Martin was attractive to her. His usual seriousness. The way he cared about his siblings and his grandparents. The way he was willing to try things he was terrible at. The way he was able to care about her even though he had so much on his plate.

The way he was helping her to become a better person, too. "I guess we're both works in progress, huh?"

"Absolutely." He relaxed by her side. "You know, I'm pretty good at all things math and finance. I'd be glad to help you with your bookkeeping business if you'd like."

"Thank you. I've been struggling with how much to charge some of my newer customers."

"Can't you charge them by the hour?"

"I could, but I'm slow," she admitted, letting some of her frustration show. "I double-check everything, and that takes time. I wish I could do my work more quickly."

"I never thought working faster was better. Not when it came to people's finances, at least. Making a mistake with someone else's money can do a lot of harm. I think you should be glad that you're conscientious."

"Perhaps." She shrugged. "But I still need to make some changes. There's nothing wrong with trying to improve my business."

"How about I come over one day and you can show me how you do things? If I can offer any suggestions, I will."

"You wouldn't mind?"

"Of course not." He grinned again. "Like I've told you, I got my degree in finance. I may not be too good at carpentry or driving a horse, but dealing with numbers isn't a problem."

"Thank you, then. I'd appreciate that."

"I'll try to stop by soon. Is it okay if I come over in the morning, like around nine? Is that too early?"

"Of course not." She'd be up for hours by nine. She pulled into his driveway and directed Arrow to a slow stop in front of his house.

"It's a date, then." His eyes widened. "I mean—"

She smiled at him. "I know what you meant. Have a good sleep."

"You too." In the process of climbing out, he paused, bracing both of his hands on each side of the opening. "Hey, Patti?"

"Yes?"

"Are you still seeing Connor?"

"We are still friends." She actually hadn't seen him since the day she'd fallen off the ladder.

"Is he courting you?"

The question caught her off guard. "*Nee*. I don't think he ever was."

"Is anyone courting you right now?"

"*Nee*," she replied before she realized she should have asked why he was asking such a personal question.

"Good." He flashed a smile again.

And with that, he turned around and walked inside. Leaving Patti with a flutter in her insides that was as distracting as the way her mind was skipping around to all sorts of things she had no business thinking about.

After Arrow turned around and got back on the road, they headed to her house. Sitting alone in the buggy, Patti was thankful for the moment. The stars were out, the quarter moon was bright, and Arrow seemed as pleased as she was to have a break from their usual routine.

"I'm glad we gave Martin a ride, Arrow," she said. "And, by the way, you were a very good horse, letting him attach the leads to you."

Arrow blew out a gust of air, making her chuckle.

She supposed he was right. Martin's heart might be in the right place, but becoming Amish wasn't going to be easy for him.

Of course, few things were ever easy. Not for anyone.

Chapter 21

Several days had passed, but Martin hadn't made an appearance at her house. Patti's feelings were hurt until she'd run into Kelsey during a walk, and she had relayed that her brother was working a lot of hours with a carpenter and had come home exhausted every evening.

She could relate to his not having much extra time because she'd ended up having a busy week herself. She'd picked up a new bookkeeping client. Then, the day after that, she had her quarterly visit with Melissa. Melissa Weaver made candles and candy in her kitchen at night and sold the fancily wrapped items in several gift shops around Holmes County. Because she also had a houseful of *kinner*, Patti traveled to her house to work on her books.

Which was why she'd been sorting through Melissa's jumble of receipts when her client hurried in, a baby on her hip.

"Everything okay, Melissa?"

"I'm not sure. There's someone here to see you," she replied.

Never had someone tried to find her while she was working. She couldn't think of anyone who would contact her about an emergency, so she was even more confused.

"Who is it?" she asked as she stood up.

"Connor Beachy. He said he's your beau?" She lowered her voice. "Patti, are you engaged?"

"*Nee*. And he's not my beau either, but I'll go see. I'm so sorry to disrupt your day," she said as she hurried to the door. "I have no idea what Connor wants."

Looking less alarmed now that she knew there wasn't an emergency, Melissa shrugged. "No worries. I have three-year-old triplets. I don't think my day is ever not chaotic."

Patti smiled at her joke. "You give yourself a hard time. I've never seen your house in an uproar."

"Which is a blessing." Lowering her voice, she added, "Listen, if something is wrong, don't hesitate to use our phone. Since we're New Order, we have a phone in the kitchen."

"*Danke*. I'll keep that in mind." She smiled, but she was inwardly a ball of nerves.

What in the world could have brought Connor over in the middle of one of her appointments?

Confused—and more than a little embarrassed because she couldn't think of a reason why he would have come over to the Weavers' house—she hurried to the entryway.

And there was Connor. He had lowered himself to one knee while one of the triplets was showing him a wooden train. Almost against her will, Patti's heart turned to mush. This was the Connor she used to dream about years ago. Back when she still entertained the idea that they could one day be more than friends.

Now that she'd met Martin, Patti realized Connor and she would never have the kind of relationship she needed or wanted. But that didn't mean she couldn't appreciate that he would be a wonderful father one day.

"Hiya, Connor."

Looking up at her, he smiled. "Hi." Getting to his feet, he murmured to the child, "I'm afraid you'll have to play trains with your *bruder* and *schevster* now."

The boy smiled at him before hurrying back to the living room.

Watching him run off, Connor grinned. "That boy talks a mile a minute."

"He's one of a set of triplets. I bet the three of them are always chatting about something."

"I reckon so." Walking toward her, he reached out a hand. "How are you?"

She didn't take it. "At the moment, I'm feeling mighty confused. Why are you here?"

His confident expression faltered before becoming smooth again. "I had some time today to think about you and me. When I learned you were over here, I thought it might be a good moment for us to talk."

Deciding to ignore the fact that he happened to have time to think about the two of them, she focused on his presence. "Why did you want to talk here instead of at my house?"

"You didn't seem too receptive to my visit last time." His expression darkened. "You also seem to be constantly occupied with your new English friends."

"So you decided to bother me while I'm working?"

"Come now. Things *don't need to* be that formal around here. There's *kinner* running around. I think I saw a fluffy dog, too."

"That's Mopsy. She's a sheepdog." Why she'd decided to share that, Patti didn't know.

She cleared her throat. "Connor, I think it's obvious I'm working. I can't talk right now."

"When can you?"

Afraid that they could be overheard, she opened the door. "Let's step outside for a moment."

"How much longer will you be here today?" he asked as soon as he closed the door behind him.

"Another few hours."

He frowned. "That long?"

"I only come to Melissa's a couple of times a year." Stopping herself before she gave him more of an explanation than was necessary, she hardened her voice. "Connor, what is going on? Why are you so determined that we see each other today?"

"I've been thinking about us."

"And?"

"And I started thinking that maybe I've been wrong." He paused for a breath. "I think we should consider changing our relationship."

"In what way?"

He frowned. "Don't play games. You know what I mean. I think we should consider one day being husband and wife."

Patti didn't know whether she wanted to laugh or cry. "Connor, you know that isn't possible."

"You know that it is. We can make this work, Patti." He lowered his voice. "We're already good friends. My father says that's the first step in every good relationship."

"What about my birthmark?"

He looked uncomfortable. "I spoke with the bishop about it. He said he didn't think it had anything to do with the devil, just an unfortunate disfigurement." Brightening, he added, "He and I went over to the library to use the computer and discovered that it is not hereditary. Our future children won't be afflicted."

He'd spoken to Bishop Frank about her port-wine stain. She'd always known that it troubled him, but she had never heard the reasons why. Now he'd shared his concerns about her being marked by the devil and possibly having children who would be similarly marked.

This was a new low for Connor. That was saying a lot.

Patti didn't know if she'd ever felt so humiliated—and angry—all at the same time. "How could you talk to the bishop about my body?"

A flash of embarrassment filled his eyes before he blinked it away. "I had to be sure."

"What if your Internet information is wrong? What if we did get married and have children and one of them was born with something like this? What would you do then?"

"It's unlikely, Patti."

"But possible. What would you do if that happened?" she pressed.

Confusion filled his gaze. "Patti, you're misunderstanding me. I checked. Our children will be fine. They'll be normal."

"Unlike myself, who's abnormal?"

His cheeks heated. "You're putting words in my mouth. I've never called you abnormal."

"Connor, you've been a good friend to me, but I'm upset with you. You need to leave."

"Patti, you aren't listening."

"You aren't either. Don't you hear what you're saying? You've made me feel terrible and ugly and unworthy, when I know I'm none of those things. I would never marry someone who treats me like that."

"You think this Martin will treat you better?"

She had no idea what was going to happen between her and Martin, but she knew without a doubt that he'd never talk about her the way Connor did. "He already has," she said as she opened the door and walked back inside.

Melissa peeked out of her kitchen. She must have noticed Patti's crushed expression because she hurried over to her side. "That talk didn't go well, did it?"

"Not at all." Trying to compose herself, she said, "I was almost done with your ledgers. I'll likely be finished within the hour."

"Come have some tea and cookies with us first." Leading her into the kitchen, Melissa added, "I've learned that these three have a way of brightening one's day."

Patti was about to refuse, then decided that Melissa was right. She needed a moment to regroup. Eating cookies with three smiling toddlers would do that without a doubt.

"*Danke*," she said at last. "I would enjoy that very much."

Chapter 22

Richard didn't have a lot of extra time. He worked a number of odd jobs, attended to his preaching duties, and helped around his mother's house as much as he could. All that left very little time for anything but prayer and sleep.

Even though he hoped to one day marry and have his own family, he hadn't been in too much of a hurry to start courting. The main reason was lack of time, but another had been the fact that he hadn't been interested in any of the women in Walden.

Maybe it was because they'd all grown up together, or maybe it was simply the fact that the Lord had been waiting for the right time to introduce him to his wife. He didn't know. But whatever the reason, for years he'd ignored his family's cajoling about his need for a wife.

Then he met Kelsey Schrock and his world had changed. From the moment she'd smiled at him, he'd been captivated by her. She consumed hours of his thoughts.

Some might even say he was obsessed.

Richard didn't believe he was obsessed, though. That

seemed too strong a word. All he did know was that he wanted her in his life.

Even though she was English.

And didn't know all that much about being Amish.

And wasn't all that good at doing the things expected of an Amish wife.

None of that mattered. Not to him. He thought Kelsey was adorable, no matter what she did. He didn't need perfection. He just wanted her.

Honestly, she was everything he'd ever thought he'd want in a woman—someone smart and kind. She knew her mind and wasn't afraid to have an opinion but didn't hesitate to ask questions or seek advice. And then there were her looks. With her curly blond hair and dark blue eyes, Kelsey was striking. She was also a runner, so she looked lean and strong.

Even though he'd only spent a few hours with her, Richard knew he was smitten. The only problem was that she wasn't Amish.

Not yet anyway.

Riding his bike to her house, he reflected on the conversation he'd had with both his father and brother the evening before. They'd noticed Kelsey at church—and had noticed that his eyes continually sought her out.

After supper, while his brother stood by, his father had cautioned him. "She ain't the first woman I've met who thinks she wants to be Amish," he'd said.

"So, you don't think it's a strange thing?"

"I didn't say that."

"What Daed ain't saying is that the woman he's referring to did become baptized in the Amish faith, promised all of us and our Lord and Savior that she was going to abide by our faith and way of life. And less than a year later, she left."

"She said it was too hard."

"It is a hard way of life," Richard said. "Especially for a woman used to modern conveniences."

"And going out. And flying on airplanes. And speaking her mind."

"Hold on, now. There are plenty of women in our church community who have no trouble speaking their minds."

"Don't I know it," his father muttered. "There have been times I wished your mother would mind her tongue a little bit more often."

"She's said the same thing about you, Daed," Richard's brother said.

"Hmph."

"While I appreciate the story, I think Kelsey is very different from that woman you knew. She's already familiar with the Amish way of life and is extremely close to her grandparents. She knows what she's getting into."

"Everyone thinks they know what is going to happen in the future, but it still can give them a surprise."

"I reckon that's true."

"Don't forget, you're a preacher now."

"I haven't forgotten."

"So, you should spare a thought to how our community will respond if you start courting a woman like that."

"I'm not courting anyone."

"Hmph."

But now, as he turned into the Schrocks' driveway, he wondered if the only person he'd been fooling last night was himself. He couldn't seem to think about anything but Kelsey. If he wasn't courting her, it wasn't because he didn't want to.

Just as he was climbing off his bike, he spied Kelsey standing outside the barn, holding one of her hands.

Was she crying?

"Kelsey?"

Her head popped up. Their eyes met for a split second before she glanced away. "*Mei mommi* is in the *haus*, Richard."

"I came to see you." Stepping closer, he saw that there were tears in her eyes. Concern washed over him. "What's wrong? Did you hurt your hand?"

"Kind of."

"'Kind of'? What does that mean?" he teased.

She didn't return his smile. "It means it's just a finger. And it's not too bad."

She still hadn't let go of her hand. "Let me see it."

"*Nee.*"

"Come on, Kelsey. Don't be stubborn."

"I'm not." When he raised his eyebrows—because she was still holding her hand against her body as if she was shielding it from the world—she sighed. "Fine."

Only then did he notice she'd wrapped part of her hand in a cloth—and there was blood on it. Cradling her hand in his, he gently unwrapped the cloth and saw a small cut on her forefinger. "Ouch," he said. "I bet this hurts."

"It's my pride more than anything."

"Why your pride?"

"Because Anna did this."

"Anna who?" The only Anna he could recall in their congregation was in her sixties and sweet as sugar.

"Anna the chicken. One of my grandparents' hens hates me."

"She pecked at you this morning?"

She nodded. "Mommi says it's because she knows I'm afraid of her."

"Are you?"

Still looking miserable, Kelsey nodded again. "Richard, I hate collecting eggs so much. It smells so bad, plus there are feathers floating in the air." Her voice sped up as it turned more plaintive. "And . . . Anna hates me, and so do the rest of them."

"The rest of the chickens?"

She nodded, as if he should have known that. "Richard, I haven't told my grandmother this, but I also kind of feel like I'm stealing their children when I take their eggs."

She was adorable. Foolish, and a little confused about fertilized eggs, but Richard knew he'd be a fan of Kelsey for the rest of his days. He'd never met another woman like her.

That said, he was having a hard time keeping a straight face. Drawing upon every bit of advice about counseling that he'd gleaned from the bishop, Richard concentrated on not grinning. No way did he want to make her day worse, but Lord in heaven, was it hard not to break out into laughter.

"Richard, what should I do?"

"Let's take you into the kitchen, and I'll help you wash your hand and bandage you up. Then we'll talk and try to figure everything out."

"I can't go in the kitchen. My grandmother is there. If I walk in with my injury, she's going to wonder what happened."

"There's nothing wrong with that. All you have to do is tell her the truth."

"I can't. She's already given me advice." She groaned. "Several times."

"Then only tell her that you cut yourself in the barn."

"You want me to lie?"

"It's just a fib. I reckon God will understand."

Just as she started to nod, she grabbed his arm. "Oh, no. You're the preacher!"

She'd lost him. "What's wrong with that?"

"Are you going to tell Bishop Frank?"

He covered her hand with his own. "That you got pecked by a hen? *Nee.*" The bishop would hate not to hear this story, though. Frank would be just as entertained as he was.

"Richard, listen to me. You can't tell him that I'm bad at

collecting eggs. You really can't tell him that I hate doing it."
Tears filled her eyes as she dropped her hand.

He hated to see her cry. He was still confused about her
concerns, but he decided to tackle one thing at a time.
"Sweetheart, whatever is worrying you, I'll fix it."

"But—"

"I promise. Please don't cry. Everything will get better.
I'll make sure of it. Now, let's get you inside." He curved an
arm around her shoulders. "After your wound is clean, I'll
make us some tea and encourage your grandmother to give
us some privacy."

She didn't move. Instead, she looked up at him with an ac-
cusing glare. "You called me 'sweetheart.'"

Oops. "It was a simple mistake. A slip of the tongue."

"A slip of the tongue?"

She looked slightly scandalized, which was fairly ridiculous
because it was a common enough expression, and she was
English. "Stop worrying so much." His arm was still around
her shoulders, so he gave her a little nudge. "Let's go."

But she still didn't budge. Instead, she looked up at him,
which was bad news for him because now her lips were mere
inches from his own. "And for the record, saying you're
going to shoo my grandmother away so we can sit in private
doesn't sound very preacherlike."

She was maddening. And ridiculous. So why did he want
to kiss her so badly? Sending a few heartfelt prayers heaven-
ward, Richard did his best to look uninterested. And keep
his eyes off her lips. "I promise that I will treat her with the
utmost respect."

"Fine."

"May I help you now, or do you have any other reservations?"

"You may." She shrugged off his arm. "But I can walk on
my own."

"I never had any doubt." He dropped his arm but stayed by her side.

Just before they reached the kitchen door, Kelsey stopped. "I'm, uh, sorry for acting so silly just now."

"You don't have to apologize."

"I feel like I should, though. I'm usually not so prickly."

"I'm pleased about that."

There was a line between her brows. "I'm serious."

"I'm serious, too. I intend for us to have a long relationship. If you were always prickly, it could be exhausting."

"I wouldn't be prickly with a preacher, Richard."

"*Gut.*" As far as he was concerned, she didn't need to know that he hoped there was a chance they would be more to each other than preacher and church member. "Now, open the door."

She did as he bid.

Of course her grandmother was standing on the other side, just waiting for them to enter. For the first time in memory, Sylvia Schrock wasn't looking at him in her usual sweet way. Instead, she was eyeing him with something akin to suspicion . . . right before she spied Kelsey's hand and the bloody rag.

"Kelsey, what happened?"

"Anna."

"The hen got you?"

"I think she bit me, Mommi." Looking mad enough to spit, she added, "That . . . that chicken is a bully."

"And how did you come to be here, Richard?"

"I, uh, came to visit. I saw Kelsey outside the barn and offered to help."

"That is so kind of you." Her voice held a touch of dry sarcasm that wasn't exactly welcome.

"I thought I'd help Kelsey clean her wound and perhaps put a bandage on it."

Up, up, up went Sylvia's eyebrows. "She needs a bandage for a hen peck?"

"*Jah*. Do you have any bandages nearby?" He took care to keep his voice smooth but firm.

"I'll go get them."

"And I'll help myself at the sink," Kelsey said.

"I had no doubt about that."

On went the tap and off went the rag. Even though she knew she was being a baby about something so minor, Kelsey still winced when she ran her finger under the cool water.

"A hen did that?"

Richard sounded rather shocked. Finally looking down at her finger, she felt almost justified. Her finger was not only bruised, there was a tiny gash at the end. It was swelling, too. "At least it's not bleeding anymore."

"That's the only thing to be pleased about."

Mommi approached. "I've got you a bandage, Kelsey, but I must say that I think your fingers might need to get a little tougher."

Before she could respond, Richard waved her grandmother over as he turned off the faucet. "Sylvia, come look at her injury."

"Injury? Now you are . . ." Her voice drifted off as she stared at Kelsey's finger. "I've never seen anything like that, child. No wonder you've been carrying on."

"I'll be okay."

"I have some salve, but I'm not sure if that is all you need."

"What else would I need?"

"When was your last tetanus shot?" Richard asked.

"I don't know. When I was a baby, I guess."

"You don't remember getting one as a teenager?"

She shook her head. "Listen, I know I made a fuss, but I

certainly don't need to go get a shot." She held out her hand. "Hand me a bandage, Mommi."

"Wait until I get you some salve." Turning away, her grandmother hurried down the hall again.

"Boy, I bet this isn't the visit you thought it would be," she joked as Richard guided her to the kitchen table.

"It's not, but I'm glad the Lord brought me here."

Richard sounded so sincere, Kelsey couldn't help but gape at him. "To deal with me crying and carrying on?"

"Yep." He smiled at her. "It's nice to feel useful."

When her grandmother returned, she not only had a tube of antibiotic salve in her hand but a wool shawl around her shoulders. "Here you go," she said to Richard. "Now, Kelsey, you stay put. I'm going to call *mei* friend Stephanie to see if she can run you to urgent care to get that looked at."

What was happening? "Mommi. There's no need. It's just a silly hen peck."

"I'm afraid there is, child. Chickens carry a lot of germs, and if that peck created a wound like that, you could easily get an infection. I would never forgive myself if we ignored it."

"I can go call."

"No need. Richard, here, can help you put on the salve and bandage and then make you a cup of tea. Right, Preacher?"

"Of course. I wouldn't want to do anything else."

His words were perfect and sweet and made her feel protected and cared for.

In short, he was everything she'd ever wanted to find in a man during all the dates she'd had in high school and college. So he was the right man, but at the wrong time.

It seemed God had a sense of humor.

Chapter 23

Martin had been dreading the conversation, but it was soon obvious that Neal had been trying to summon up the nerve to discuss the very same thing with him. The fact of the matter was, Martin Schrock was no carpenter.

They'd been sipping coffee during their break when he'd broached the subject. To his surprise, a hotel manager was sitting nearby and started talking to them. Next thing Martin knew, he was sharing his story, as well as admitting that he had a college degree in business.

That led to his spending the afternoon at the Walden Inn, helping check in guests and getting to know the rest of the staff. It seemed Jackson Weaver had been looking for someone to help out. He thought Martin might be just the person he needed.

As he walked around the quaint building, which looked like a cross between an Amish farmhouse and an advertisement for modern farmhouse interior decorating, Martin felt his entire being relax. Until that moment he hadn't realized just how on edge he'd been. No matter how many people had told him that there was no one way to be Amish, he'd still been attempting to reinvent himself in the image of his grandfather.

Of course that had been a foolish undertaking. Josiah had grown up Amish and grown up on a farm. There was no way Martin could slip into the older man's shoes just because he'd suddenly decided to be baptized in the same faith.

At a quarter to four, Jackson shook his hand. "Martin, what did you think about this afternoon's work?"

"I liked it a lot."

"Do you think you might feel comfortable here?"

"I do. I enjoyed getting to know everyone. It seems like a good fit."

"Ida told me that you started organizing some of the reservations and receipts."

"I didn't do that much. I only filed some things."

"I haven't filed in months, so I'm thinking that was a big deal."

"I hope you don't mind."

"Mind? I'm trying to stop myself from hugging you!" he joked. "How about I offer you a job instead?" He named an hourly amount. "What do you think? Does that seem fair to you?"

It was almost double what he'd been making at the carpentry shop. "More than fair. Thank you."

"When can you start?"

"Tomorrow morning?"

"My wife might get mad at me, say I'm rushing you, but I'm not going to look a gift horse in the mouth." He held out his hand. "See you then."

"Thank you, Jackson. I appreciate it."

"You're welcome. We're real glad you're here, Martin. Real glad. Do you need a ride home?"

"No, I have my bike."

"All right, then. Take care riding home in the dark."

"I will. Thanks again." Walking to the back to get his coat, he was brought up short by a familiar-sounding voice drifting from the front desk.

Turning, he found Jonny standing there. Practically looking like he hung out at the Walden Inn all the time.

"Jonny, what in the world are you doing here?"

"Hey, brother." He hugged him close. "I'm glad you didn't leave yet."

"Why? Hey, is something wrong?"

He shrugged. "I got a call from Mommi about Kelsey needing a visit to urgent care. After she told me, I thought I'd better come out to give her—and you—a ride. That's when I found out you'd come over here. She said you were thinking about a new job."

Martin nodded. "I'll tell you about it later. Like, after you tell me what's going on with our sister. Is she okay?"

"She's good. Both she and Preacher Richard are sitting in the back seat of the Suburban."

Their mother had given it to Jonny after running them all around for years. "How come the preacher is with her? What happened?"

He shrugged. "All I know is it has something to do with someone called Anna."

"I don't know any Annas around here."

"That makes two of us." Looking impatient, Jonny added, "Anything else you need to know before we go to my vehicle, where you can ask Kelsey questions yourself?"

"Nope. Oh, except for the fact that I've got my bike here."

"Good thing I've got the Suburban, then. We'll stick it in the back."

"I'm set." Walking out, he stopped to talk to Jackson. "Thanks again for reaching out to me. I'm grateful to you."

"I think it's going to be a good match. See you tomorrow."

As soon as Martin wheeled his bike to Jonny's SUV, Richard hopped out and helped him and Jonny load it. Then Martin opened Kelsey's door and peeked in. "Kels?"

"Don't look so worried. I'm fine."

Catching sight of the bandage on her hand and the way she was cradling it on her lap, he asked, "Are you sure about that?"

"I'm sure I'm embarrassed. Don't fuss, okay?"

He'd been looking after Kelsey since their parents got divorced. He'd been her constant, and she'd been his little buddy. He'd helped her learn to ride her bike and had glared at some boys when they'd dared to tease her about her braces when she was in sixth grade.

But he knew she was a grown woman now and needed her space. Even though it pinched a bit, he gave it to her. He closed her door and took the passenger seat next to Jonny while the preacher returned to Kelsey's side in the back seat.

When Jonny pulled out after punching the urgent care address into his GPS, Martin turned to look at Richard. "What's wrong and who's Anna?"

"Martin!" Kelsey said.

"You don't get it both ways. If you don't want to tell me what happened, I'll go to another source."

When they heard her sigh, Jonny laughed. "You might be able to get that guy in the back seat to do your bidding, but we're used to your dramatics, Kels."

"Jonny, you watch your mouth," Kelsey said. "This guy in the back seat is Preacher Richard."

Jonny's cheeks flushed as he moved into a left-hand-turn lane. "I meant no disrespect."

"None taken. And for the record, your sister, here, got pecked by a hen named Anna. She got her good. At the very least, she needs a tetanus shot."

"We're all going to the doctor for a hen peck?" Jonny asked.

"I know what it sounds like, but it's bad," Kelsey said.

"I don't know how bad it can be."

"When you see how bad my hand looks, you'll understand, Jonny."

Jonny chuckled. "Doubt it."

"Martin, help me out."

"I believe you, honey," Martin said, but he couldn't help but share a knowing look with Jonny.

His little brother kept his mouth shut but he, too, was obviously trying not to smile or say anything snarky. Martin was impressed. They'd had years and years of Kelsey overreacting to simple things.

After another moment passed, Richard cleared his throat. "Jonny, I understand you're in college?"

"I'm taking two classes, but mostly I work in a restaurant."

"Oh? What type of place?"

"It's a sports bar named Sports Authority. They serve the usual fare: wings, burgers, bar food. I've been working there for years."

"He's a really good server," Kelsey said.

"It's not hard to bring people a couple of cold drinks and a basket of fries."

"It is when it's packed on Sundays," Martin said.

Jonny shrugged. "That's what I do. For now, at least."

"You want to become Amish, too?"

"Yeah. That's the plan anyway." As the GPS called out a final direction, he pulled into a parking lot. "And we're here."

"Great," Kelsey said. "I'll be back out as soon as I can."

"Oh, no. We're all going in," Martin said.

"Martin, no."

"Sorry, but I want to see your hand and hear what they have to say."

"Me too," Jonny added as he opened the door.

Noticing that Richard had also gotten out of the vehicle, Martin grinned. "You're coming in, too?"

"I came along for the ride. I might as well see this through."

"So I'm going into urgent care with three men."

"It seems so. Stop fussing and come on," Jonny said.

Chapter 24

In they went. The urgent care clinic looked like any other one that Martin had visited over the years. The only difference was that there were three Amish families inside, as well as a couple of English people sitting on the plastic chairs.

While Kelsey checked herself in, Martin sat down. Richard sat down on his right, while Jonny stood near their sister. He was listening intently to her conversation with the receptionist. Martin realized he was standing nearby in case Kelsey needed to pay for the visit in advance.

"I like him," Richard said. "He's got a way about him that calms your sister."

"You called it. Jonny is kind of the opposite of how a lot of youngest kids are. In some ways, he's the most responsible instead of the most spoiled."

"I've now met three out of four of you. So far, I haven't seen any of you act recklessly." Richard raised an eyebrow. "Is your missing sister the example of that trait?"

"Beth?" Martin couldn't help but smile at the idea of bossy Beth doing anything without forethought. "Not at all.

Beth's the type of woman who not only decides to organize the cellar in the middle of summer but also cleans the shelves, paints the walls, and makes a list of what to purchase before the first snow."

"Wow."

"Yeah. She's a lot."

Jonny walked over just as Kelsey was called to a treatment room. Martin noticed that Richard, who'd been keeping an eye on Kelsey the whole time they'd been there, tensed. He actually looked ready to get up and accompany her.

"She'll be okay," Martin said.

"You didn't see what her hand looked like. It's swollen."

"Jonny? What did Kelsey say when she checked in?"

"Nothing unusual. Only that she'd been pecked by a chicken, the cut immediately turned angry, and it had been a long time since she'd had a tetanus shot."

"That sounds about right. I guess she'll be okay."

Jonny's eyes narrowed. "Are you this attentive to everyone in your church community . . . or just my sister?"

"I'm attentive to everyone. But I can't seem to help myself with Kelsey."

"Why?"

"I don't know. I guess I get the feeling she could use someone by her side." He turned sheepish. "Or maybe it's me who wants that."

"Or maybe it's you who is feeling the need to dote on my sister. And maybe she does need you right now."

Richard lifted a shoulder, as if to say that his actions were out of his hands and firmly in the Lord's. Martin was tempted to roll his eyes and remind the preacher that his sister was likely feeling out of sorts at the moment.

He knew that, because all four of them were struggling.

That said, he still wanted to protect Kelsey the way he always had. She was a sociable girl with lots of friends. Being apart from them had to be hard. No matter how many letters they exchanged—or how many phone calls she might be able to manage while standing in the shanty—it wasn't the same. His sister needed someone looking out for her right now.

"Kelsey can be a lot," he said.

"Pardon?"

"She's full of drama, even when it's not of her own making. Trouble seems to follow her wherever she goes."

"It's always been like that," Jonny chimed in as he sat down on Martin's other side. "It didn't matter if she was trick-or-treating or out at the movies with her friends; our parents would always get a phone call."

"Or I would," Martin said.

"You've been looking out for her your whole life, haven't you?"

Martin nodded. "It's the way of big brothers, I think."

"I'll do my best not to be the cause of any SOS signals," Richard said.

"Thank you. But it might be inevitable."

"I wonder what's taking so long."

Jonny shrugged. "Everything seems to take a long time around here."

"I reckon that's true." After a couple of minutes passed, Richard eyed Martin curiously. "If Kelsey depends on you, who do you depend on?"

The question caught him off guard. "I don't know," he replied before he thought how it made him sound. "I mean, I depend on our family and friends, too."

"No, I wouldn't agree with that," Jonny said. "Not entirely. You have a habit of keeping everything to yourself. Except for maybe your new neighbor."

"Who did you hear that from?"

"Guess."

"There's nothing going on between me and . . ." Realizing

that Richard was no doubt listening to every word and filing it away, Martin stopped abruptly.

"Wait, are you speaking of Patti?" Richard asked.

"*Jah.*"

When Richard smiled, Martin felt himself tense up. "Why do you think that's funny?"

"I don't think it's funny. I think it's a good thing. Maybe fitting."

"Kelsey says they're a lot alike," Jonny supplied.

"Truly?" He seemed to ponder that thought for a moment. "I suppose that's right. They're both independent sorts."

Though the last thing he wanted was to discuss his personal feelings in the middle of an urgent care clinic, he couldn't resist the opportunity to learn more about Patti. "What do you know about her history, Richard?"

"I've known her most of my life. I can't say it's much of a mystery either."

"I don't remember seeing her when we visited our grandparents for the summer," Jonny said.

"She didn't live there then. She lived in town. Her great-aunt was the one who always liked the country. Patti's parents preferred being involved in the community and keeping busy. And then they decided to move away."

"Why did they move but not take Patti?"

"Will's two brothers live in Kentucky. They have a blacksmith business there. I heard they not only serve the Amish community but have several fancy horse clients, too."

"Fancy horse? Like Thoroughbred racehorses?" Jonny asked.

Richard nodded. "Will and Rachel decided to move, but Patti's great-aunt had been in poor health and Patti didn't want to leave her. They'd always been close. When her aunt Frieda passed on to heaven, she left Patti the house." He kicked out his legs in front of him. "That didn't come as a

surprise to anyone, though a lot of us figured that Patti
would sell the farm and keep the money. Instead, she stayed
and opened her own bookkeeping business."

"She's strong."

"*Jah*, she is." He smiled slowly. "And it looks as if your
sister is all done."

Richard was walking toward Kelsey before Martin even
got to his feet. It didn't escape his notice that Kelsey smiled
at him—without sparing either him or Jonny a glance. When
the preacher leaned down to whisper something to his sister,
Martin narrowed his eyes. Kelsey beamed at Richard,
though.

Martin didn't even need to be there. "I can't believe how
our sister is acting," he said when he noticed that Kelsey was
allowing Richard to cradle her hand in his. "She's never enjoyed being fussed over."

"Until now," Jonny murmured.

"Look at the way he's carrying on. I'm half surprised he
hasn't lifted her into his arms."

His brother laughed. "If he did, she'd probably let him.
Kelsey likes him. A lot."

"Yeah." Watching how she was allowing Richard to stay
by her side as she paid her bill, he sighed.

"Did you mean what you said? That she probably needs
him right now?"

Martin nodded. "I meant it. I just hope there's something
more to it than that, though."

"There is for Kelsey." Jonny chuckled softly. "Look at
the way she's staring at him. There are stars in her eyes."

"I noticed that, too."

"He's eyeing her the same way," Jonny said with a grin.
"Unless he's a really good actor and only hanging around
her out of the goodness of his preacher heart, I'd say he's already counting the days until she can be baptized."

"If he's not serious, she's going to get hurt."

"Yep. She's too old for me to step in, though."

"Besides, you've got your own romance to worry about."

"It's not a romance."

"Maybe you should rethink that, then. I don't think a romance would be a bad thing for you to have right now."

"Come on, let's go see what she needs." Martin didn't want to talk about his own needs.

But he couldn't help thinking that he might be craving someone to look out for him, too. He was independent, but he wasn't as happy to be alone all the time as everyone else seemed to think.

Not at all.

Chapter 25

Needing a break and some companionship, Patti made some potato soup and brought a quart of it to the Schrocks' house. With four of them living there, she figured Sylvia would appreciate a little something to feed either her husband or her grands.

As she'd hoped, Sylvia greeted her with a smile and ushered her in for coffee and conversation. At first, Patti was happy to do most of the talking. She shared a couple of cute stories about her clients and asked Sylvia's advice about a new dress she was sewing.

But it soon became obvious that Sylvia wasn't paying too much attention to her. Actually, she seemed agitated and distracted.

So much so that Patti became worried.

"What's going on, Sylvia? Has something happened that I haven't heard about?"

"*Jah*." She exhaled.

"No one else in your family has shown up wanting to become Amish, have they?" she teased.

Luckily, Sylvia chuckled instead of being offended. "No one has come around lately, but that might have been easier than today's events."

"What happened?" she asked as Sylvia refilled her coffee cup.

"Kelsey got injured while she was collecting eggs."

Patti began to laugh—until she realized her friend was serious—and worried. "How in the world did that happen?"

"You know. The hens know who's an easy target."

"Like Kelsey."

"It would seem so." Sylvia's eyes flashed with amusement before continuing her story. "Ach, Patti. That granddaughter of mine can cook anything, is sweet as sugar and a joy to be around. But she's also a bit too . . . exuberant about everything." She sipped from her cup. "I was in the kitchen when Kelsey came in. She was crying."

"She got pecked."

"*Jah.*" Waving a hand, she lowered her voice. "To be honest, I didn't take her injury too seriously until I saw how worried Preacher Richard was."

"What? Richard was here? How did he get involved?"

"He came calling and discovered Kelsey outside, crying and bleeding."

"My word."

"*Jah.* It's like Saturday morning at a flea market around here. There's never a dull moment."

"I'm sorry."

"Patti, between you and me, I don't know if I'm quite up to the task these grandchildren of mine have asked of Josiah and me."

Patti felt terrible for her. "It is a big burden you didn't ask for, that is true."

"From the moment the four of them asked to live with us for the year, I've been torn. I love each of them dearly and enjoy being with them, too. But trying to teach these young adults how to do even the simplest of chores can try my patience. Josiah's too."

"I think maybe it would try anyone's patience."

"I can only imagine that there's a reason the Lord put the idea of living Amish in my grandchildren's heads, but sometimes I feel like I should let Him know that He's forgotten about Josiah and me."

"I hadn't thought about it that way. Martin and Kelsey did a lot of thinking before showing up on your doorstep. But you two were taken off guard."

"Very off guard." Sylvia pressed both palms to her face. "Please don't think too badly of me for saying all this. I know I sound like a terrible person."

Patti tried to imagine how she would handle the same situation. Would she be as generous with her time? Or would she resent the intrusion? She wasn't sure.

She supposed she would be praying a lot and hoping that the Lord would guide her to do what was right.

"What do you really think about their decision?" she asked after a moment. "Do you think they're making a mistake?"

"Sometimes," she whispered. "It's not that I don't love them or think they could do just fine . . . it's that I think they're running to Amish country so they don't have to deal with their aggravating parents."

"Have you told them your concerns?"

"Not in so many words."

"Maybe you should tell them what's on your mind."

"They need me and Josiah to believe in them."

"You're going to believe in them no matter what, though, right? Just because you don't agree doesn't mean you don't believe in them."

"I hope you're right."

The door opened. Patti was startled to see not only Kelsey

and Martin walk in the door, but also Richard and Jonny. All four of them seemed to be having a conversation about potatoes, of all things.

When they spied Sylvia and her, they stopped.

Patti got to her feet. "Hello, everyone."

"Hiya, Patti, how goes it?" Richard asked.

"Well enough. You?"

He smiled at her. "I've had a bit of an eventful day."

"I heard." Walking over to Kelsey, she said, "How was the urgent care visit?"

"Painful." She rubbed her arm. "I had to get a tetanus shot."

"Your grandmother was just filling me in. I'm so sorry about Anna pecking you."

"*Danke*, but it was my fault. I need to get better at collecting eggs."

"Listen, please don't worry about those chickens anymore. At least not for a while. Tomorrow morning I'll come over and collect eggs with you."

Relief filled Kelsey's expression. "Patti, you are the sweetest person. You'd really do that, wouldn't you?"

"I'm being serious, but don't act as if it's a lot of trouble. I live next door. It won't take me long at all. We can even make a game of it," she added with a smile. "I'll teach you a song I used to sing to the chickens."

Kelsey giggled. "You sang to the hens?"

She nodded. "It did the trick, too. My singing's so bad, I think the hens were happy to give me their eggs without complaint so I'd get out of the henhouse."

"At this point, I'd sing every song I know. Thanks for offering."

"It's my pleasure. You'll get the hang of it in no time."

"As fun as listening to you sing sounds, Kelsey, there's no

need for us to get Patti involved," Martin said. "I'll start collecting the eggs."

"No, I will," Sylvia said. "I feel terrible about this, dear. I
knew you were afraid of those old birds and I didn't lift a
hand. I should've told you that I'd take over egg duty."

"*Nee*, Mommi."

"Why not? I collected eggs before you were here."

Jonny laughed. "There you go, sister. You'll never have to
step in that henhouse again."

"Oh, stop. There's no way I'm going to let Martin, Patti,
or Mommi start collecting eggs. I'm going to work on it."

"Maybe we can come up with a schedule?"

Looking at them all, Richard said, "If you all are devising
schedules for henhouse duty, I think this means it's my time
to leave."

Sylvia chuckled. "We do sound ridiculous, don't we? Will
you stay if we promise to talk about something else?"

"There's no need. I really should be on my way."

"I'll walk you out," Kelsey said.

"Thank you," Richard replied. "Good to meet you,
Jonny. I hope we'll get a chance to visit again soon."

"Me too."

After a round of goodbyes, everyone watched them walk
out the door.

Martin walked to Patti's side. "I don't know what to do
about Richard and Kelsey," he said.

She saw he was concerned but thought he should pick his
battles. "Sorry, but I think their relationship is out of your
hands."

"You sound pretty certain about that."

"She's an adult and so is Richard. Plus, he's a preacher. If
anyone can help Kelsey figure out what to do, it's him."

"I need to give up control, don't I?"

She smiled up at him. "Yes. Especially because I don't

think your sister's relationship with Richard ever was in your control. They'll figure it out. With God's help, I know they will."

"I guess I should remember that."

"I think so. No matter if one is Amish or English, faith is a wonderful thing, Martin."

"*Jah*. It is."

When he smiled at her, Patti felt her heart expand. And realized she needed to take some of her own advice. She needed to stop trying to control so much and give her worries to the Lord.

So far, He'd been managing everything just fine.

Chapter 26

The back of Kelsey's neck fluttered. She knew the minute she walked back inside that both Jonny and Martin would give her the third degree about Richard and her new attachment to him.

Mommi would probably have something to say, too. Her grandmother was wonderful about keeping her opinions to herself, but Kelsey had seen worry in her eyes. She was likely worried about Kelsey hurting Richard in some way.

The truth was that she very well might. She was far from perfect and far from being certain about the right course of her future. She wasn't flighty by nature, but it seemed she had decided to take a vacation from her usual practical self. In her place was a woman who was skittish and constantly changing her mind. One minute she was determined to learn as much Deutsch as quickly as she possibly could. Then the next moment, she was missing her friends, missing her music, her car, and her jeans.

She didn't want it to happen, but there was a chance she

would make promises to Richard and then break them days later.

At the moment, though, she didn't care. She wanted to spend a little more time with Richard without her brothers inserting themselves into the conversation.

"You okay?" he asked in that gentle, patient tone that was becoming so familiar.

"I was just going to ask the same thing of you."

"Me? I'm fine."

"I changed your quick visit into a four-hour ordeal."

"I was able to be by your side and be helpful. I don't think that's a bad thing. I'm glad I was with you."

"Thank you for being so kind. You helped a lot."

"You're welcome." He folded his hands behind his back. His expression was earnest but didn't seem to be judgmental. "And Kelsey, stop worrying and apologizing, okay?"

"Okay. What do you think I should do?"

"I think you should let someone else take over egg duty."

"No, I meant about me becoming Amish. Do you think I'm making a mistake?"

"You know that's not my call."

"You're a preacher, though."

"I'm a preacher, but I don't have a direct link to the Lord. I mean, not anything different from anyone else. You've got a year, right?"

"I thought I would feel at home here. And I do."

"But it's not home, is it?"

She shook her head. "No. Not yet."

"Sometimes even the most comfortable of houses doesn't feel like a home. Not right away."

"And sometimes not ever."

To her surprise, he leaned close and pressed his lips to her forehead. "Don't worry so much."

"What was that kiss for?"

"What do you think?" he asked cryptically before reaching for his bike and pedaling off.

Watching him go, she thought about that chaste brush of his lips on her brow. Thought about how she'd kissed more than one man but hadn't felt the same degree of tenderness.

She wondered why that was.

Chapter 27

Richard might have been chosen for the lot, and the Lord might have believed him to be the right person to be this church community's preacher, but when he wasn't fulfilling those duties, his life was like every other twenty-eight-year-old single man's. He worked on the assembly line in a garage door factory, took on carpentry projects in his community, and lived at home.

His younger sister, Sally, was engaged and worked at the school three days a week, helping the two teachers with their classes. When she wasn't doing that, she was home helping their mother and busy planning every small detail of her wedding.

His younger brother, Ian, was still enjoying the last few months of his *Rumspringa* and courting his longtime girl.

His mother, Sadie, was forty-eight and a force of nature. She'd never had an opinion she didn't feel obligated to share.

His father, Jerome, on the other hand, was easygoing and quiet. Daed was the kind of man who worked hard, kept to himself, and was the perfect fishing partner.

So, all in all, Richard was close to his parents, close to his

family, and embedded in his community. He had many blessings and many things to be thankful for. He hadn't been
looking for love. Not yet. Not until he felt he was settled
enough to ask a woman to be a preacher's wife and the
daughter-in-law of a bossy woman and a retiring sort of man.

But it seemed the Lord had other plans because he was absolutely, without a doubt, completely entranced by Kelsey
Schrock. Sure, the first time they'd met he'd felt sparks. And
their first conversations had been entertaining.

But today's adventure had cemented his regard for her.
Never in his life had he felt such a need to help and care for a
woman. Richard had always thought male protectiveness
was just a cliché. Now he realized that it was a fact. When
Kelsey was upset, his only thought was to make her happier.

He was at peace with it, too. If the Lord felt it right,
Richard was determined to make Kelsey his wife one day. It
might be years from now, but he believed she was his future.

Unfortunately, his family was not on board. Not at all.

Sitting around the dining room table, the other four members of the household stared at him as he told them about his
trip to urgent care with Kelsey.

"She sounds like a complainer," Ian said. "I've never
heard of a woman going so round the bend because of a hen's
antics."

"If you had seen her finger, you would understand. It was
swollen."

"I'm sure whatever was there was nothing that a couple of
ice cubes couldn't solve."

"Ian, you weren't there. You don't understand."

Sally chuckled. "Sorry, but our brother does have a point.
Kelsey does sound rather helpless." Putting down her fork,
she added, "Maybe she was trying to get your attention."

"If she was, it worked," Daed murmured. "You were at
her side most of the day, son."

He hated that his family was reducing Kelsey's injury to

high drama and a ploy to get his attention. "It wasn't like that. She didn't even know I was going to stop by. I found her crying outside the barn."

Sally sniffed. "Richard, I know the Lord wants you to be our community's preacher, but I think you're taking His will a bit too literally, don't you? She isn't Amish."

"She wants to be."

"Sure she does. Until she has to gather more eggs," Ian joked.

"Or worse, make that hen into a Sunday supper."

Sally chuckled. "Kelsey would likely faint."

"Like you go out and chop off chicken's heads, Sally. Don't act like you do such things."

"I could if I had to."

"I'll pass the word on to John that you'd prefer to have your poultry alive when preparing Sunday supper."

Sally looked stunned. "You wouldn't really do that, would you?"

"I bet he would if you aren't nice to Kelsey," Ian teased.

Her eyes widened. "Would you, Richard?"

"Of course not. But you should still be nice to Kelsey, Sally. She's in a vulnerable situation and could use some friends." Richard didn't give her a hard look, but he did hope Sally was reading between the lines. He wanted Kelsey to be happy so she would stay.

Not only did she need to feel at peace with her decision and feel as if the Lord was guiding her to this change, he wanted her to see that she wasn't always going to be a fish out of water. She needed to feel that she could eventually fit in and make a life there.

"Do you think she and her brother really are going to join our community, Richard?" Mamm asked.

"They seem intent on doing so. Plus, I met the youngest member of their family today. Jonny seems just as determined to be Amish as Kelsey and Martin."

His mother frowned. "I'm all for new members, but I don't know what to think about these children suddenly deciding to join their grandparents."

"I don't think their decision was as sudden as you're making it sound."

"How could it be otherwise? She and her brothers and sister went to Josiah and Sylvia out of the blue with their scheme." She waved a hand. "Next thing we knew, the peace and quiet of Sylvia and Josiah's home was disrupted and they found themselves hosting two twenty-year-olds having a midlife crisis."

"That isn't kind of you, Mamm."

"I don't happen to think that these *kinner* are being particularly kind to their elders."

Sally covered her mouth in an obvious attempt to stifle a laugh.

"What do their parents think, Richard?" Daed asked.

"I don't know."

Daed frowned. "How come? Aren't you supposed to be counseling these kids?"

"Their names are Kelsey and Martin, Jonny and Beth. And . . . for the record, I didn't say I was counseling either of them. They're meeting with Bishop Frank once a week and doing their best to live Amish. All I'm doing is trying to be supportive." Okay, that was a lie because his feelings for Kelsey had little to do with supporting her faith-driven journey and much to do with the fact that she was adorable, sweet, and acted as if nothing else but him mattered in the world whenever they were together.

"You like her, don't you?" Ian said.

Their father frowned. "Ian, that ain't none of your business."

"Why not? She could maybe be my sister-in-law."

Sally laughed. "Yeah, right. When pigs fly." She stopped

when she caught sight of his expression. "Hold on. You're not even smiling, Richard."

"I know."

A new tension filled the air, as it was obvious that each one of them was imagining Kelsey Schrock becoming his wife. It was not a shock that none of them seemed to like that idea.

"So Ian's right?" Sally asked. "You do like Kelsey?"

He did. He liked her a lot. His feelings were bordering on love. But did he want to share his feelings with his family at the dinner table? No, he did not.

"Daed is right. How I feel about her ain't none of your business."

"I fear I disagree," Mamm said.

"Does she even know how to cook?" Sally asked.

Richard didn't appreciate the way she was acting—as if she was the authority on being a proper Amish bride. "That doesn't have anything to do with the situation," he said.

But instead of backing down, Sally seemed surer of herself. "Of course it does. Right now, she can't even gather eggs without a trip to urgent care on the preacher's arm. She needs to be able to do something worthwhile."

"Sorry, but Sally has a point," Ian said. "I'm not saying every Amish woman needs to know how to cook and clean but most do."

"And sew. Amish women know how to sew and make their own clothes. And garden and can." Sally raised an eyebrow. "If Kelsey can't do any of that, she is really going to have a tough time living Amish."

"It's a waste of time for you to be sitting around listing things she cannot do. You are setting her up to fail. Instead, you should be looking at the positives, the first of which is her faith. The Lord doesn't wish for us all to be good at cooking and canning. He wants us to honor Him."

Ian groaned. "Can you ever *not* sound like a preacher, Richard?"

"I'm not being a preacher, I'm being a Christian." He glared at his brother and sister. "What about you two? Are you feeling very Christian and kind?"

"He does have a point," Daed said.

"Sally, I must say that I'm fairly shocked at the way you're talking about necessary attributes," Mamm chided. "I have a feeling that if I went around telling you that canning was a necessary skill to be a good wife, you'd give me a mouthful."

Sally's cheeks flushed. "You're right, Mamm."

Empowered by his parents' support, Richard reneged on his decision to stop talking about Kelsey. "Kelsey can do a lot of things. She's really smart and even finished college."

"Which she's leaving to hang out with hens and cry on your shoulder," Ian said. "I'm not sure I get that." Folding his arms over his chest, he added, "Richard, I'm not saying that you don't deserve to fall in love with the woman of your choosing, but I do think you need to seriously consider whether Kelsey is the best woman for you. I know I give you grief about being a preacher, but the fact is you're a good one. You need a helpmate. Not someone who is going to keep you on pins and needles because you have no idea what she's about to do next."

Richard inhaled sharply. Stared at his parents. Waited for one of them to jump in again and chide Ian for being so negative and judgmental.

But this time, neither of them did.

Actually, they almost seemed pleased about the fact that their two youngest children were being jerks so they could just sit quietly.

But he'd had enough.

Rising to his feet, he picked up his plate. "You know

what? I expected better from all of you. I not only expected better, I was counting on it. I might be a preacher, but I'm also a man who likes a girl and is seeking the support of his family." Looking each one of them in the eye, he added, "I'm disappointed that I couldn't get it today."

And with that little speech, he turned, walked into the kitchen, and deposited his dish in the sink. On another day he might have felt bad for not washing his plate and setting it in the rack on the counter.

Tonight, though? As far as he was concerned, Sally could wash his dish and silverware like the good Amish woman she was.

He strode out into the night and kept walking until neither the house nor the barn was in sight. Only then did he take a deep breath, blow out a burst of frustrated air, and lift his head to the heavens. "I need you, *Gott* I need you bad right now."

He hoped the Lord wasn't too busy to respond.

Chapter 28

Patti's morning had started out as it usually did. She woke up at dawn, pulled on her work dress, and set the percolator on the stove to brew a pot of coffee.

Next, just as the sun was peeking over the horizon and the first rays of light danced across the sky, she wrapped a wool shawl around her shoulders and headed out to the barn. There, she fed Arrow and gathered eggs.

When she returned to the house, she pulled off her rubber barn boots, put on her slippers, and poured herself a first cup of coffee. She read a devotional at the kitchen table, gave thanks for her many blessings, and then mentally planned her day.

She didn't have a particularly busy one. She had some bookkeeping work for two women who sold Amish handicrafts to a couple of retail stores in Ashland. Next, she thought she might bake two coffee cakes for a couple in their church district who'd recently had a baby.

And then Kelsey arrived with a panicked knock and a determined expression. "Kelsey, hi."

"Can I come in?"

"Of course." She stepped aside and watched as Kelsey hurried inside. She was wearing a dark gray dress and black leather shoes. Her legs were bare and her blond hair was confined to a ponytail at the back of her neck. "Is everything all right?"

"I don't know."

She looked back out the door, half expecting Martin to be waiting just outside. But of course no one was there. Worry began to churn in her belly as she turned back to Kelsey. "What's going on?"

"I need your help."

"Of course. Anything. What do you need?"

Kelsey took a fortifying breath, exhaled, and then steeled her shoulders. "I need to be more of an Amish woman."

The words had come out in a rush, as if they were a dose of bad medicine she couldn't down fast enough. It took Patti a couple of seconds for the words to sink in.

But they did.

And then she couldn't help but gape. Was Kelsey pulling some kind of prank on her? The notion seemed far-fetched, but so did this request at eight in the morning. "Are you having trouble with Deutsch?"

"Yes, but it's more than that. It's been brought to my attention that I can't do anything Amishy."

Amishy? Patti was going to need more coffee. Picking up her cup, she headed to the stove where the percolator was. "Want a cup of coffee?"

"Um, sure?"

She poured Kelsey a cup, too. "Cream and sugar are next to the toaster."

After Kelsey added a healthy amount of both, she joined Patti at the kitchen table. After a couple of sips, her visitor looked more at ease.

Or maybe it was just that Patti had given herself enough time to come to terms with Kelsey's request. "I'm uncertain what 'Amishy' means."

"You know . . . like being a traditional Amish woman."

Patti hid a smile. She had a feeling if she pulled in ten women of different ages from their church district, each one would have a different opinion about what it meant to be a traditional Amish woman.

The only thing they would all have in common was their faith, but she was fairly sure that was not what Kelsey wanted to hear.

"I don't mean to be difficult, but I'm afraid I'm still not exactly sure what you're after."

Kelsey set down her cup. "Patti, it means I can't sew or can vegetables or plant a good garden." She waved a hand in the air, as if she needed to drive home her point. "I can't do any of that."

"You don't have to."

"There's more. I'm also pretty bad at hanging clothes on a clothesline and hitching a buggy."

"Oh my." She had no idea if there was a bad way to hang clothes but wasn't going to mention that.

"Do you see what I'm getting at now?"

"Kind of." Unable to stop herself, Patti added, "After all, we now know that you can't do anything with hens either."

"I'm useless! I'm a useless Amish woman. I'm never going to find a man to marry me."

Considering that most everyone in the area was aware that Preacher Richard had his eye on Kelsey, Patti knew her concerns were laughable.

But what to say? She needed to somehow both ease Kelsey's mind and give her a reality check.

"I'm not sure what advice I can give you. I'm just a few years older than you and am certainly not perfect."

"I don't need perfect. But is there anything you can teach me now?"

"Now? This morning?" She was torn between telling Kelsey that it wasn't fair of her to think she had nothing better to do than satisfy her whim . . . and trying to come up with a fitting task.

Obviously unaware of Patti's thoughts, Kelsey nodded. "I already asked my grandmother, and she seemed to think you do most of your bookkeeping at home and don't mind taking breaks from your ledgers. Is that correct?"

"*Jah . . .*"

"I know it's spur-of-the-moment, but can't you teach me how to do something useful?"

"Such as what?"

Kelsey waved a hand. "I don't know. Something easy?" She looked around the kitchen and spied a Mason jar of peanut butter spread. "What about this? Everyone loves peanut butter spread, don't they?"

"A lot of people do."

"You must if you've got a half-empty container here."

Patti inwardly squirmed. It was one of the unhealthiest things one could eat—and just happened to be her guilty pleasure.

"*Jah.*" Patti shifted uncomfortably. She had a small addiction to the stuff and ate it on toast almost every morning.

"That's it. Teach me how to make that."

"You want to learn how to make peanut butter spread." To become more Amish.

Kelsey nodded. "Yes. Can we make some now?" She frowned. "Unless it's too hard. Is it really hard?"

"*Nee.*"

"Then, may we? Now?"

"Follow me." They stood up, walked down the hall, down the basement steps, and at last entered her storage room. It was her pride and joy. Not only were there rows of pickled vegetables and canned tomato sauce, apple sauce, and stewed chicken, but a good amount of paper products, root vegetables, and dry goods. When she'd moved in, Patti had decided to honor her aunt by stocking it the way she used to.

"We need light corn syrup, peanut butter, and marshmallow cream." Thank the good Lord, she had all three.

Kelsey picked them up and cradled them in her arms.

Patti grabbed two empty Mason jars along with the lids and led the way back upstairs. When they returned to the kitchen, Kelsey carefully arranged the three jars on the counter while Patti got out her favorite stoneware bowl. It was large and orange. Sturdy enough not to tip over easily, and the glaze made it easy to clean. It was bright and cheerful and made her happy every time she took it out.

In addition, she laid out her favorite stainless-steel spoon. It could stir thick, sticky mixtures like peanut butter spread but also cleaned up easily.

"Here's what you do. Put two cups of light corn syrup, one cup of peanut butter, and one-half cup of marshmallow fluff into the bowl."

"And then?"

"And then you stir it together and put it in the two jars."

Kelsey looked completely deflated. "That's it?"

"I'm afraid so."

"I thought it was a lot harder to make. Are you sure you don't even need to cook the ingredients?"

"I'm sure. But, um, just because something is easy doesn't mean it isn't worthy. Besides, most things we do aren't all that difficult. They just take time and effort."

"And skills."

"But don't forget that we're a community, Kelsey. We care for one another and help one another. No one expects

you or me or Martin or even Richard to be proficient at
everything."

"I'm not sure what I'm proficient at."

"Let's start with peanut butter spread, then." Pointing at
the jars and measuring cups, she said, "Start measuring and
putting everything in the bowl."

"We're really going to pretend that this is my Amish
lesson?"

"I'm not pretending, Kelsey. I started making this when I
was a young girl. You should be able to make it without
complaint."

Kelsey shot her an irritated look but soon concentrated
on the task, opening jars, measuring the sticky substances,
and finally stirring them together.

When she began spooning the mixture into jars, Patti got
out some cinnamon swirl bread she'd made the day before.
With care, she sliced two thick pieces and placed them under
the broiler while Kelsey washed the bowl and measuring
cups. While they were doing all of that, they chatted.

And laughed.

And finally, when everything was clean again and they
were sitting across from each other, they bowed their heads
in silent prayer. Patti gave thanks for the food, for a full
pantry, and for the gift of Kelsey's friendship.

When they lifted their heads, she handed Kelsey a knife.

"What's this for?"

"To put on the peanut butter spread, of course."

"Oh. Of course." With an almost embarrassed look on
her face, Kelsey placed a good spoonful on her plate and
then used the knife to smear it on top of a piece of toast.

And then, after Patti had served herself as well, she took a
bite. "It tastes like it should."

She sounded so surprised, Patti giggled. "You're right. It
tastes exactly like it should. You did a *gut* job."

"I know it's nothing special, but I don't care. I'm kind of pleased with myself."

"You should be. I love peanut butter spread. I'd tell you if it wasn't good." Taking a deep breath, she spoke from her heart. "Listen, I know you came over wanting help, but you gave me something in return."

"I don't know what that could be."

"Laughter and friendship. I know it's nothing special to you, but you should be pleased with yourself."

Some of the lines in Kelsey's face eased as she took another bite. "Are you okay with doing this again?"

"Helping you to become Amish? Oh, yes. Don't hesitate to ask me if you'd like another lesson." She winked. "If we can have more days like today, I'll look forward to helping you be as Amishy as you'd like to be."

Kelsey giggled. "I'm starting to think that everyone in Walden needs to look out."

"I agree," Patti joked. "Before we know it, you'll be putting the rest of us Amish girls to shame with your proficiency at cooking, cleaning, and farm chores."

Kelsey squeezed her hand. "You know, Patti, it's no wonder my brother can't seem to stop singing your praises. You really are special."

Martin had been singing her praises? She felt her cheeks heat but quickly looked away.

It wouldn't do for Kelsey to realize how much her brother was coming to mean to her.

Though she was starting to believe that Kelsey already suspected.

Chapter 29

Patti was still feeling pleased about her morning with Kelsey when Martin stopped by five hours later.

"Are you busy?" he asked when she let him in.

"Kind of." She pointed to the ledgers she was working on in the dining room. "I've been attempting to balance one of my client's statements for the last hour."

He frowned. "Sorry. I'll come back."

"*Nee.* There's no need for that. I need a break."

Closing the door behind him, he said, "I'm still trying to figure out the right way to stop over here."

Was he talking about calling? Certain she was getting that wrong, she studied his face. "I don't understand."

"I'm used to texting people first." She must have still looked puzzled because he continued. "You know, texting something like 'Hey, mind if I stop by in an hour?' Stuff like that."

"Don't worry any more about things like that. I can't think of a reason I would tell you to turn back around."

"Gotcha."

It didn't look like he "got" anything, though. Actually,

Martin looked a bit taken aback by her statement. Just as always, she wished she was able to relay her thoughts a little bit better.

But because it was too late to do anything about that, she headed toward the dining room table instead of the kitchen or living room. For some reason, it felt like the right place for the two of them to be. "Have a seat."

"Thanks." Martin sat down, but he didn't look as if he intended to relax.

Too late, she realized that he could have very well only come over to borrow a cup of milk or something. "I'm sorry, I should have asked if you needed something. Do you need a battery or a cup of milk?"

"Ah, no to both. I'm good."

"Oh. Okay." And . . . now things were awkward. "Well, um, how are you?"

"That's what I came to talk to you about. Patti, I just accepted a new job."

"Who with?"

"The Walden Inn. It's owned by Jackson Weaver. Do you know him?"

"I know of him."

"What do you think of the Inn? And of Jackson?"

"To be honest, I haven't had an occasion to either be in the Inn or speak with Jackson."

"That's too bad."

He looked so disappointed, she tried her best to give him some kind of information. "Everyone likes him, though."

"Do they? Or do people just say that?"

"I'm fairly sure they really do. He's very popular."

"I thought the same thing."

"Why are you concerned?"

"I don't know." Frowning, he added, "Do you think it's unusual for him to have such a popular inn at such a young age?"

"I might think so, except for the fact that his parents used to have a popular bed-and-breakfast when we were young. When the tourists started coming, they sold it and moved to Missouri. Jackson didn't care to go. He apprenticed at one of the more popular hotels in town and just three years ago opened the Inn."

"You know a lot about him, Patti."

She shrugged. "It's common knowledge, for the most part. He has a fine reputation. I would trust him."

"Okay."

He still looked troubled. Taking a chance, she murmured, "Martin, is it really yourself you don't trust?"

He swallowed. "Maybe." He waved a hand. "Patti, part of me feels like I'm pretending when I'm here. I want to embrace Amish life—having no electricity and no phone and no car and no computer . . ."

"But it's hard?"

He nodded. "I've been praying, too. Don't you think if God wanted me to become Amish, he would have given me a sign by now?"

"I don't know."

"That's all you've got to say?"

"Maybe." When he still scowled, she chuckled. "I'm trying hard to listen and be a good friend to you, Martin. I don't want to tell you what I think."

"Patti, I'm asking."

"Fine. I guess I would suggest two things." And boy, she hoped she wasn't making a terrible decision. "First, perhaps you aren't seeing the signs He has been leaving you."

He blinked. "You think He's already told me what he wants."

"I don't know. But I do know that you've had a lot of blessings since you've been here. Including meeting Jackson Weaver." *And me*, she wanted to add. She was Amish, believed in him, and was just next door. It seemed that the Lord had had a big hand in that.

"What's the second thing?"

"I think you need to go back to Cleveland."

"Why?"

"Because you're going to be giving up a lot, Martin." Even though it pained her, she forced herself to say, "If you get home and everything feels right and your heart and mind are more at ease, I think you should maybe reconsider your plans."

"After living with my grandparents and after everyone around here has done so much for me?"

"It's not like that. People care about you. Your grandparents love you no matter what. They don't love you because you want to start driving a buggy. They love you because you're Martin."

"What about you? I think we're becoming close." He swallowed. "You know I like you."

What did he mean by that? Like, as in just friends? Or like, *like*? "I like you, too." She inwardly grimaced. Could she sound any more awkward? It was doubtful.

"What if I leave?"

If he left, she would be hurt. No, if he left and returned to his old life, she would feel devastated.

But she would support him.

"Martin, I care about you, too." After debating about whether or not to say what was on her mind, she blurted, "But—and I'm not saying this because I think we're about to get engaged or anything—I don't want to be wanted because I'm convenient. I don't want to be the best and easiest choice for a partner in a new life. I want a man who wants me because I'm Patti. Whether I'm Amish or not."

"I don't think of you as the easy choice." He looked at her intently. "I think you're pretty special, Patti."

She reached for his hand. "I feel the same about you. But I want you to be sure. Sure about this life you're choosing and sure about me."

"I understand."

Did he? Studying his expression, she wondered if Martin felt more at ease or had become more troubled than he'd been when he arrived.

"Tell me how work is going," he said.

"It's the same. Some days are better than others."

"And?"

"And, nothing. It's just my job."

"Hey, don't say that. You care about it, right?"

"Well, yes."

"And you must be good at it because you have several new clients, right?"

It seemed prideful to admit that. She shrugged.

"Patti, I know you're modest, but there's nothing wrong in knowing that you work hard and try your best."

"I suppose there isn't."

His voice gentled. "So, show me what you do. I wouldn't ask if I wasn't interested."

"All right, then." She pulled over the ledger for Mimi's flower garden and greenhouse. "This here is the customer I've had the longest."

"Show me her account."

Opening the notebook, she showed him what she and Mimi had done together. The five-year plan. The graph showing the progress, the information about her employees and the amount she saved every year.

"You've made a difference in her life, Patti."

She bit her bottom lip. "I don't know if I have or I haven't, really. But I'd like to think I've helped ease her worries."

Linking his fingers through hers, he squeezed gently. "I'd say you have definitely done that. Good for you. I'm impressed."

"*Danke.*"

When they shared another smile, Patti felt as if something new and special had passed between them. He appreciated her skills even though they had little to do with traditional Amish woman's work. He acted as though she was worthy even though she wasn't nearly as pretty as his sister.

Most of all, he was asking her for advice and seemed to value it. Just as she was beginning to relax and trust him.

Was this what falling in love was all about? It didn't hit one like a lightning bolt. Instead, it was a gradual thing, made up of a hundred tiny moments of encouragement and understanding, wrapped up in a fine ribbon of attraction that swirled around one's heart.

If this was love, she was all in. Even if it wasn't easy. Even if it was painful.

What mattered was that it felt real and made her feel alive. Special.

Chapter 30

What had just happened? Walking back to his grandparents' house, Martin looked at his surroundings. The fields, resting after a successful harvest, lay dormant on one side. The trees on the other side were now only half dressed. Many of their bright yellow, red, and orange leaves had fallen, littering the ground below with a covering in various shades of brown.

Up above, the sky was blue and the sun was out. A faint chill was in the air. Someone was burning brush in the distance, its smell making him think of bonfires, s'mores, and chilly nights.

All in all, it was a typical fall day in central Ohio. Just like the day before. No doubt tomorrow would be the same.

So why did he feel so different?

Because you're falling in love, a small voice told him.

It was shocking.

Altogether unexpected, but not unwelcome. As a matter of fact, he liked the feeling. Ever since his parents divorced he'd known he wanted a different life for himself. Though he had no idea what the Lord intended for either him or his future marriage, he did believe in the power of prayer. He vowed to continue to pray for His guidance.

He also wanted to give thanks. He hadn't realized that he'd needed this feeling in his life. He liked the almost giddy, bubbly sensation. It was hope and happiness and nervous jitters all rolled into one.

And it was because of Patti. She was the woman he hadn't realized he needed to know. She was all the things he hadn't known he wanted. There were so many good things about her that she made him want to be a better person.

His footsteps slowed as he realized that he still wasn't 100 percent sure about being Amish.

Just as he got on his grandparents' land, he saw his grandfather on his hands and knees. He was digging holes by the side of the barn.

"Dawdi!"

"Hmm? Oh, hello, Martin. How was your visit with Patti?"

"Illuminating."

He looked up, his eyes bright with amusement. "That's quite a mouthful for a man looking to live without electricity."

Martin laughed. "I guess it is. What are you doing?"

"Well, now, I thought I'd make a special surprise for your grandmother. She loves daffodils, so I'm planting some bulbs out here. I figure if all goes well and the Lord sees fit, one day when she's out walking, she's going to see the lot of them here, all blooming so pretty."

"That will make her smile."

"I hope so."

When he picked up the spade again, Martin took it from him. "I'll dig holes, you put in the bulbs."

"That suits me fine, I think."

Rolling up his sleeves, Martin dug a neat six-inch hole,

then moved a bit to the side and started digging again. Beside him, his grandfather deposited one daffodil bulb in the hole and covered it with dirt. A few minutes later, they both moved to the side again.

"Care to tell me what's on your mind, son? I figure it's either about a certain woman next door or about your future." He grunted. "Or maybe both?"

"You guessed it. Patti gave me some advice. I guess I'm stewing on it."

"What is it?"

"Among other things, she suggested I go back to Cleveland for a spell."

His grandfather had an impressive poker face, but it was evident that this information had shaken him. "Why is that?"

This was it. He could either come completely clean and share his feelings for Patti or keep them to himself for a little while longer. Both options had benefits. On the one hand, he wanted to keep these new feelings private. He also wanted to honor Patti by keeping their conversation to themselves.

On the other hand, he had already asked his grandparents for their help to completely change his life. It was a bit late to decide to take them out of the loop.

Of course there was also the obvious truth that anything he did—whether it was eventually marrying Patti and living next door or returning to his regular life—would have ramifications for them. As much as he might like to pretend he was on his own, he wasn't. His life was intertwined with his siblings and his grandparents.

Put that way, he knew there was no choice.

"Dawdi, I told Patti that I have feelings for her."

His grandfather's carefully blank expression settled into a smile. "Now, isn't that something."

Wariness filled him. "Something good . . . or something bad?"

"Something good, of course." He cleared his throat. "Unless you intend to break Patti's heart."

"I don't intend to break it." Sitting down on the field, he leaned back on his hands. "But I think Patti is worried I might if I think I want this life and then change my mind."

"Hmm."

"What do you think, Dawdi?"

"Well, it ain't unheard of for Englishers to want to try the Amish life but then eventually decide it is too different."

"Do you think that's bad?"

"For a person to change their mind? *Nee*. But deciding to become baptized in the faith is a different thing. It's a solemn vow, Martin. That's why no one gets baptized as a baby or young child. That vow is as binding as a marriage contract, maybe even more solemn, because it is between you and the Lord."

None of his grandfather's words surprised him. But somehow hearing his absolute belief did cause chill bumps to form on his arms.

And it brought back the same feeling of doubt and dissatisfaction he'd felt when he first decided to become Amish. It was as though his heart wanted one thing, but his brain was determined to find any and every flaw in that goal that was humanly possible.

Ah, maybe that was what he needed to stop thinking.

Maybe he needed to stop concentrating on what was humanly possible and start thinking about what would be possible with the Lord's help. Remembering his favorite passage from Matthew 19, he said, "Jesus looked at them and said, 'With man this is impossible, but with God all things are possible.'"

"What do you think I should do?"

"It ain't up to me, Martin."

"I'm asking for your opinion, though."

He pursed his lips. "In that case, I think you should give some thought to Patti's suggestion."

"What if I realize that I love Patti but don't want to be Amish?"

"Then you'll need to talk to her about it, ain't so? After all, love for a woman and love for a way of life don't necessarily go hand in hand. Patti is Patti."

"But what if she doesn't want me if I'm English?"

"Then the Lord is stepping in, even if He's not abiding by your wishes."

A dark knot formed in his stomach. "You make it sound so matter-of-fact."

"It's not. Nothing is ever matter-of-fact when one's feelings are involved." Reaching out, he wrapped a hand around Martin's shoulder. "But son, Patti has her own mind, too. She might choose you over her baptismal vows."

"But she could be shunned."

Dawdi nodded. "But that would be her choice, not yours." He raised an eyebrow. "Just like you choosing to live Amish to be with Patti would be yours."

"I guess it would."

"Just remember this, son. These vows are meant to be offered seriously and to last the rest of your life. That's a long time."

"It would be a long time to live with a mistake."

"*Jah.*" He smiled softly then. "But that is why we have forgiveness, *jah*? It might not be easy, but the Lord knows that we are all filled with flaws. If you realize you made a mistake, you can admit it and ask for forgiveness."

As his grandfather's words sank in, Martin exhaled. "You've given me a lot to think about."

"I imagine I have. But don't fret."

"How can I not?"

"I've always thought moments like this mean that you are

growing. You're choosing not to stay the same. Think about that, okay?" Dawdi asked as they stood up.

"I will." He reached out and hugged his grandfather. When he wrapped his arms around Martin, he realized that his grandfather was smaller and slighter than he remembered. He was getting older. But even though his body might be changing, his mind and his heart were still going strong. He was so wise and loving. He was everything Martin aspired to be.

As he walked back to the house, Martin realized that even if he went back to Cleveland and returned to his old way of life, he would still have that wonderful man as his role model.

No matter what lay in his future, his family would always be part of his life.

That was something to be grateful for.

Chapter 31

You can do this, Kelsey told herself. *You can go back in there, face those old biddies, and give that gal a piece of your mind. At least let her know you're not going to be bossed around anymore.*

Unfortunately, the pep talk wasn't working. She was still standing outside the chicken coop, and all the hens inside were wandering around the pen. She kind of thought they were clucking at each other, too.

No doubt making fun of her inability to collect eggs.

And why wouldn't they? Just twenty minutes ago, when she'd walked into the chicken coop, they'd rushed at her. Even Daisy, the gentlest of all the hens, tried to peck her. She'd turned and run out of there as quickly as she could.

But now, here she was, standing outside the pen once again while her grandmother was working in the kitchen, no doubt waiting for Kelsey to return and help with supper.

The chickens squawked and seemed to strut a bit, as if they were celebrating her departure.

Kelsey didn't blame them. The fact of the matter was that

she was timid around those blasted hens, and they did have the upper hand.

"Kelsey, what are you doing?"

She turned to find her brother standing a few feet behind her. No doubt secretly as amused as Anna and her cohorts. "I'm doing what it looks like I'm doing. Trying to summon the nerve to go inside the coop."

Instead of grinning, he frowned. "How come? I think Mommi already gathered the eggs this morning."

"She did, but the chickens need water and fresh feed. I said I'd take care of it today." She needed to do this chore, too. She already was too much trouble for her grandmother. She and Martin had both vowed that they'd try to help their grandparents while they learned to become Amish. Not make more work for them.

This stupid fear of the chickens was working against that vow. In a big way.

Still in big brother mode, Martin said, "You don't need to go inside the pen now. I'm here." He held out a hand. "I'll take that carton of feed and tend to their water, too."

Let him help you, that weak, oh-so-persuasive voice inside her head whispered in her ear. It would be so easy to push away her responsibility another twenty-four hours. Plus, Martin was such a good guy, he would probably never let on to their grandparents that he'd taken care of the chickens for her.

But she would know.

"No," she blurted out.

Martin let loose a sigh. "Kelsey, we've already talked about this. Don't make it into a big deal."

Again. He hadn't added that word, but she knew it was on the tip of his tongue. Kelsey was torn between wanting to let him know that it actually was a big deal and handing him the container so he could take care of the hens for her.

The latter option was the more tempting.

"I need to do this, Martin."

"So you can be Amish?"

"*Nee.* So I can salvage my pride. No bossy chicken in a henhouse is going to get the better of me."

"Okay, fine." He held out his hand again. "Come on, Kels. I need to talk to you about something, and I don't have all day."

"What is it?"

"It's important enough that I don't want to discuss it inside a smelly chicken coop." He wiggled his fingers. "Come on."

She really had no choice. Taking his hand, she gripped it tightly while grabbing the container of feed with her other hand.

Martin opened the gate and pulled her inside.

The hens squawked and hurried out of the way.

Kelsey felt like rolling her eyes. Those little actors. They were acting as if Martin was the Jolly Green Giant and were running in fear.

Well, all of them except Anna, who'd been sitting in her nest all along, like the queen bee she was.

"Where do you put the feed?"

"All around." Feeling empowered because the hens were moving out of their way instead of rushing at her, she sprinkled the feed the way their grandmother had shown her. "The spigot for the water is in the corner."

"I see it." As Martin dumped out the contents of the water trough on the side of the pen, she squared her shoulders and looked over at Anna.

The hen looked relatively relaxed, but she was watching Kelsey with an expression that could only be described as watchful. Much as she disliked the bird, she couldn't deny that she was intelligent.

Before she could talk herself out of it, she approached the hen. "Good afternoon. I'm pleased you didn't take it upon yourself to attack me today."

Anna tilted her head to one side.

Did that mean she was thinking about it? Kelsey wouldn't put it past her.

Still taking advantage of the fact that Martin was occupied with the other twelve chickens, Kelsey lowered her voice. "You know, I kind of admire your spunkiness. You are a bird who knows her own mind and isn't afraid to show it."

Anna seemed to preen a bit.

"That said, you need to give me a break. You are smart enough to know that there's nothing you can do with your eggs. They ain't fertilized. No matter how much you might wish otherwise, you're never going to get a baby chick from them. That means you might as well let me gather your eggs and pass them on to Sylvia and Josiah. It's only fair. I mean, they're paying for your food and shelter and all."

Anna stared at her for a good, long minute. Then, to Kelsey's amazement, she seemed to relax.

Right there in front of her!

"Everyone's been watered. Do you want some help with these birds?"

"No."

"All right, then. Let's get out of here."

She followed Martin out of the pen, noticing that he seemed to be looking more tense the closer they got to the house. When it seemed as if he was about to start talking several times, she decided to break the silence. "Just tell me."

"I will."

"How about right now?"

"Fine. I think I need to go back to Cleveland for a week. Or two."

"And do what?"

"Live English."

Martin looked so certain, Kelsey gaped at him. Immediately on the heels of her confusion came the realization that this wasn't a spur-of-the-moment decision. He'd been thinking about it for a while. "Why do you want to go back?"

"I need to make sure that becoming Amish is what I want."

"You don't know? You're having that many doubts?"

He nodded. "Some things have happened."

"Such as?"

"Such as things between me and Patti have gotten more serious."

Now she was completely confused. "That's good, right?" When he nodded, she added, "How is living English going to help your relationship?"

He rubbed a hand across his face. "Kelsey, you can be relentless."

"I know. But tell me."

"Sometimes I find myself wondering if I'm falling in love with Patti instead of the lifestyle."

Just as she started to nod, all the repercussions of what he was saying hit her hard. "If you fall in love with Patti but not being Amish, you're stuck. She's already baptized."

"I know that."

"But if you leave, you'll lose her. Or are you thinking of asking her to jump the fence?"

"I don't think anyone would call what I would be asking her to do jumping any fence."

"You're right. It would be more like breaking that fence and burning it."

"*Jah.* I mean, yes."

Her mind kept spinning. What would Beth and Jonny say? What if Martin decided against becoming Amish? Would that influence their decisions? He might not want to believe that he was their leader, but in a lot of ways he was. They all followed his lead. Even Beth.

And what about her? Kelsey was certain she was meant to

be Amish, even though she was equally certain she would never be entirely comfortable doing farm chores. And although she was starting to have very strong feelings for Richard—and she believed he felt the same—she also knew that the hope of having a future with him was not going to determine her decision.

Then, she remembered the person Martin was supposedly doing this for. "What about Patti?" she asked with a gasp. "What is she going to say?"

"It was her idea."

This story of Martin's just kept getting stranger and stranger. "Why?" she asked suspiciously. "Martin, what did you do?"

"Me? I didn't do anything." Looking more worried, he added, "At least, I don't think I did."

"So . . . why?"

"Patti's worried that I might be getting my feelings for her mixed up with my feelings about becoming Amish."

Kelsey wanted to understand what he was saying, she really did. But it didn't make sense to her. Her feelings for Richard were for him, just as her certainty that she should be Amish filled up another part of her heart.

But she supposed what Martin was feeling was possible. Was she reading everything wrong? Had she been doing the same thing and not even realizing it?

"Hey," he said softly. "Don't look like that."

"Like I'm feeling confused?"

"Like you're wondering if you should feel the same way I do. You don't."

"But we're going through the same thing, Martin."

"We are, but we're each our own person."

Kelsey watched his gaze dart around before settling on his clenched hands. It was as if he was searching for help but couldn't find it.

"We should be talking more about everything, Martin. I hate that you've been feeling so alone."

"I haven't been alone at all. I know I can lean on you and our grandparents. I know I have Bishop Frank and Richard, and even Jonny and Beth. I've also been talking things through with Patti. But the Lord has been reminding me that this is my journey, not anyone else's."

"You need to follow your own path."

He nodded. "I really do." After a pause, he added, "I'm pretty sure I'm falling in love with Patti, Kelsey."

Happiness filled her. If that was the case, it was all good. Then the reality of what he was saying hit her like a ton of bricks. "But that doesn't make you happy, does it? Because you aren't sure if you still want to be Amish."

Looking even more stressed, he nodded. "You aren't wrong. I like Patti so much. I can see myself having a good life with her." Running a hand over his face, he shook his head. "No, it's more than that. I think I could make her happy. I'd love to do that."

"I'd love that, too. Patti deserves to have a man like you."

"I don't know if I can be the man she deserves, but I do know that I'm willing to try my best. But not if it ruins her life."

"Which you'll do if you try to be Amish, marry her, and then feel regret."

"That would ruin her."

"Martin, talk to me about your decision. What's holding you back?"

"I fear that I only like the *idea* of being Amish. I love our grandparents, and I love how steady and faithful they are. They're wonderful people." He took a deep breath. "But I'm honestly not sure if I want to leave my former life."

This was where the gap in their ages likely did make a big difference. She'd finished college but hadn't truly started her own, independent life. Martin, on the other hand, had a good job. A *really* good one. He'd gotten several promotions and was respected. He had a group of work friends and another group he'd gone to college with. Leaving all of that had to be hard.

But what could she say to help ease his heart?

Offer support, not advice.

Whether that whisper was from her conscience or the Lord, she knew it was the right direction. She reached for her brother's hands and covered them with her own. "No matter what you decide to do, you'll always be my brother and I'll always support you."

"Even if I break Patti's heart and move back to Cleveland?"

"First, you don't know what Patti will decide to do if you make that choice. She's a grown woman."

"That's true."

"But to answer your question, yes. Even then."

Martin stared at her for a long moment, then leaned back, pulling his hands out from under her grasp. Little by little, his body eased.

It could have been her imagination, but she thought he seemed more at peace.

"Thanks," he said.

"You're welcome."

When they smiled at each other, Kelsey knew that no matter what happened in the future, the two of them were going to be okay. He would always be her big brother, and she would always be his younger sister, looking up to him.

And being so grateful they had each other.

Chapter 32

Martin had walked up to her, right in front of at least half the congregation, and asked to walk her home. He'd been charming and almost bashful-sounding. He'd even smiled in such a way that the elusive dimple in his right cheek appeared. Patti was pretty sure at least two teenagers nearby had sighed.

She was very sure that more than a handful of women sitting nearby had giggled.

"All right," she'd said, just as if it wasn't overcast and damp, with the temperature hovering around the low forties.

Twenty minutes later, he appeared by her side and helped her put on her cloak and mittens. At least she'd dressed for the weather!

Next to her, Martin was wearing dark gray pants, a dark blue shirt, a jacket, and a black wool coat. On his head, instead of the traditional black felt hat, he was wearing the kind of knitted wool cap most of the other men their age preferred. The ends of his blond hair stuck out at the edges. Patti wondered if he was liking the idea of having slightly longer hair, or if he missed his usual short haircut.

When they were out of sight of everyone chatting on the front lawn of the Hochstedlers' house, she smiled at him. "You're acting very Amish this afternoon, Martin."

"*Danke.*" A smile played along the edges of his mouth. Charming her. "I'm trying."

He was succeeding, as far as she was concerned. "How are things going over at the Inn?"

Some of the happiness that had been in his eyes faded. "It's all right."

"That bad?"

"*Nee.* Not that bad."

"Martin, I really do want to know the truth. Not the words you think I need to hear."

"In that case, the truth is that I miss my old job and I don't know how I feel about that."

"How come?" She remembered he'd gone to college and gotten a degree in finance. But she'd thought his old job was part of the problem. Had he changed his mind?

"Back in my cubicle in Cleveland, I only saw the bad things. I was tired and stressed from the projects I'd been given." He waved a hand in the air. "The clients needed a lot of attention. One guy at a company called me at least two or three times a week. Every week." He pursed his lips. "I thought he was second-guessing me too much."

"Maybe he was."

"Yeah. I don't know." Looking a little lost, he added, "I'm starting to think I didn't want just a different job, I wanted a fantasy that wasn't ever going to come true."

"What kind of fantasy was that?"

"One where I loved going to work, I felt fulfilled every day, and people were always appreciative of my efforts." His voice was filled with sarcasm. "Even saying that out loud feels embarrassing. What was I thinking?"

"That you wanted to be happy?"

He chuckled. "I guess so."

"There's nothing wrong with that."

"You're right." He looked down at his feet. "Patti, I love my grandparents. I love visiting with them and helping my grandfather chop wood and my grandma garden or even put clothes on the line. I'm happy at their house. I like the peace and quiet."

"But?"

"But . . . I don't know. The reality of living Amish isn't like my daydreams. I'm trying to come to terms with that. I'm sure I will," he added.

She wasn't so sure if he should.

Chapter 33

His cell phone's alarm beep pulled him out of a deep slumber. Before he even realized he was doing it, he'd reached for his phone, tapped the Snooze button on its screen, and collapsed back on his pillow.

It had taken him a long time to fall asleep last night, and even after he had, he'd woken up several times. Each time he'd opened his eyes, he'd tensed. Both his body and his mind were having a difficult time adjusting to the roomy bed, the dull rush of noise outside, and the slight stale scent of the air.

He'd become used to the fresh air flowing through the crack in his bedroom window and the cozy feel of his room at his grandparents' house.

His bedroom in his twenty-five-square-foot apartment felt vast in comparison.

He couldn't find much wrong with his king-sized bed, though. He loved the space and the luxurious comfort of his Tempur-Pedic mattress and 800 thread count sheets.

When the alarm buzzed again, he was awake enough to

climb out of bed and pad down the hall to the kitchen. Last night, he'd felt a bit out of sorts, but he'd been aware enough to prepare the coffee maker and set the timer.

The scent of brewing coffee made his mouth water. Taking the first sip, he closed his eyes and smiled. His favorite designer blend of bold brew tasted as good as he remembered.

Looking around the space, with its stainless-steel appliances, granite countertops, tile floor, and complicated-looking coffee bar, Martin almost felt as if he was in someone else's home.

Or in a high-end hotel.

Everything was sparkling, modern, and almost unfamiliar. Almost. He'd only been gone for two months, but he already felt different.

Taking another fortifying sip, Martin tried to analyze how that made him feel. Was he pleased to be back? Or did he not fit in anymore?

He wasn't sure.

When he reached for his cup again, he caught sight of the stack of mail on the counter. Beth and Jonny had been taking turns going by the apartment to pick up his mail, make sure nothing unexpected was going on, run the taps, and turn off and on the lights.

When neither of them had called him about his mail, he'd assumed they'd thrown out most of it.

They hadn't. There was a stack of magazines, travel brochures, catalogs on the corner. Next to those was a far smaller pile of cards and letters. Curious, he thumbed through them, putting one or two to one side to read later.

After refilling his cup, he walked through his living room, taking time to contrast the television, speakers, desk, and stack of takeout menus with his former sparse space.

He walked to the bank of windows and looked out at the

view. He was on the west side of downtown, a short drive from Edgewater Park. If he stood in just the right spot and the weather was clear, he could see Lake Erie in the distance.

He'd used to think that was a big deal.

Now he wondered why he'd ever wanted to try so hard to see water in the distance. Had it been a status thing . . . or had it been because he'd been searching for a bit of nature in the middle of a mass of concrete and noise?

Taking another sip of coffee, Martin tried to figure out whether he still appreciated his fancy digs.

He supposed he did, to a certain extent.

Did that mean he couldn't be Amish?

"God, I know with you all things are possible, but I'm sure hoping for some direction. I have no idea what I'm doing right now."

The ringing of his cell phone made him jump.

Realizing he hadn't remembered to take it from his bedside table, Martin strode down the hall and picked it up by the third ring.

"Hello?"

"That's no way to greet your sister."

"Sorry, Beth. I didn't even look to see who was calling."

"You sound out of breath."

"I guess I am." He laughed softly. "I had forgotten my phone in the bedroom. Plus, I kind of feel like I'm in the twilight zone."

"How come?"

"Everything feels the same but different."

"You've only been gone for two months."

"I know. I'm not saying it makes sense—it's just how I feel."

After a pause, she said, "I get it. I mean, I think I will as soon as you explain it to me while we're having breakfast. Buzz me in."

She was there? He might have black coffee, but he was pretty sure there wasn't anything else edible in his condo. "Beth, I'm glad you stopped by, but I'm not ready for company."

"I'm your sister and I've missed you. Buzz me in."

"Fine, but I don't have anything to feed you."

"Don't you think I know that? I brought breakfast."

He buzzed the intercom. "Here."

"Heading up now."

He'd barely had time to run to the bathroom and splash some water on his face when she walked in.

"Hey, you," she said softly. "Look how scruffy you look."

He hugged her tight and kissed her brow before releasing her. "I look okay, right? I mean, I shaved." Two days ago.

Her eyes lit with amusement. "It's not the scruff on your face. It's everything." Her smile widened. "Plus, I'm pretty sure you gained five pounds and maybe even grew a couple of inches, too."

"I might have done that. Mommi's food is so good."

Scanning his face again, she held up a bag. "Well, this can't compare to Mommi's biscuits and gravy, but it used to be a favorite of yours."

Only then did he realize she was holding a paper tote from Hole in One, his favorite bagel place in the area. "Tell me that you got me an everything bagel with chive cream cheese."

"I've brought you an everything bagel with chive cream cheese." She wrinkled her nose. "And I still can't believe you prefer it over the cinnamon crunch."

"*Danke.*"

She smiled as she finally handed him the bag. "You're welcome, brother."

Turning into the kitchen, he pulled out two plates and unpacked the bag. To his surprise, there were six bagels, two tubs of cream cheese, a small carton of orange juice, creamer for coffee, and a plastic container of his favorite soup. "I can't believe you did all this."

"It was nothing. I know when I come back from being on a trip, it's nice not to have to start my day with a visit to the grocery store."

"You read my mind. Honestly, I hadn't even gotten that far yet. I was still trying to get acclimated to the views and my favorite coffee."

She laughed. "You and that crazy, expensive coffee of yours. How was that first sip?"

"Amazing."

Pulling out the toaster from a cabinet, he plugged it in and put his presliced bagel in two of the slots. "Want yours toasted?"

"You know it."

He did the same with hers. When the first hint of the toasted seasoning filled the kitchen, he sighed with pleasure. "You're my favorite sister."

"Only because I'm bringing you all your vices."

"True."

Minutes later, each armed with toasted bagels slathered with flavored cream cheese, they were sitting at his breakfast bar.

"This is so good," Beth said around a too-big bite. "I haven't gotten a bagel from Hole in One since you left."

"How come?" He knew she craved them as much as he did.

"Going there without you wasn't the same. I missed you, Martin."

"I missed you, too." Scanning her face, he knew she was waiting for him to tell her the reason he'd come back to the city, while Kelsey had remained in Walden. Martin knew he owed her an explanation, too. He just wasn't sure if he had the words.

Especially for her, because she hadn't been in Amish country with him for the last eight weeks. It might not be fair of him to think that she wouldn't understand, but he was pretty sure if their places were reversed, he wouldn't.

Of course he probably wouldn't have brought Beth her favorite breakfast and patiently sat next to him while they ate.

He would have been drilling her with a dozen questions the moment he'd walked through the door.

After taking one last sip of coffee, he spoke. "I came back here for two weeks to try to figure out whether I want to stay in Walden."

"I don't understand."

"I don't know if I can fully explain myself. That's why I haven't started talking yet."

"Martin, it's me. Not the board of directors at your company. I don't need perfection. Just some words about how you're doing."

That was it. She cared about him. Period. End of story. Just as Kelsey and Jonny did. Just as he felt about his younger sisters and brother. "You're right." He took a deep breath. "Beth, I wanted to become Amish because I've been dissatisfied with my life. I wasn't sure why I felt that way either."

"I know you've been disenchanted with work." Beth's voice was soft. Almost hesitant.

Martin appreciated that she didn't push too hard for information, though he needed to talk about the jumbled mess in his head. Hearing someone else's perspective could only help.

"I have been," he began, choosing his words with care. "But a lot of things have gotten me down."

"Down? Have you been depressed?"

Worry filled her expression. Martin realized his inclination was to make light of his problems so she would feel better. But he knew Beth wouldn't believe him if he did that. "It's been a lot of things," he finally said. "I have been thinking that I need a simpler life. I thought being Amish might give me that."

"But it hasn't?"

"It has . . . but it hasn't exactly given me what I'd hoped." Before Beth could speak, he rushed on. "I appreciate living Amish, I really do."

"But . . ."

"But by the time I was there about ten days, I started realizing that I wasn't taking to it like our sister was."

"Kelsey is happy, isn't she?"

"Very much so. She's the happiest I've ever seen her."

"I heard she's got a preacher with an eye on her. Is that true?"

"Yep." He grinned. "Beth, you should see them together. Whenever he's around Kels, he gazes at her like she's the best thing he's ever seen."

"Kelsey is okay with that?"

"She seems to be. She hasn't shared too much with me, but she has been talking to Mommi and Jonny and you, and even Patti."

"Patti is your neighbor, right?"

His sister had a glint in her eyes. Obviously, Kelsey wasn't only talking to her sister about herself. "Yep."

She smiled. "Maybe Patti is part of the reason you're feeling so out of sorts."

"She is." As concisely as possible, Martin told Beth about his growing feelings for Patti and how intertwined they were with his feelings about becoming Amish.

To her credit, Beth remained quiet while he talked, only sipping coffee as he rambled. Finally, when he was out of words, she spoke. "That's a lot."

"I think so, too."

She took a deep breath. "Martin, I think you're making everything harder than it needs to be."

"How so?"

"You're asking yourself the wrong questions."

"Beth, I'm struggling here. I'm also in a time crunch. I've got to figure this out. Now is not the moment to become cryptic."

"Fine. The question isn't whether or not you want to be Amish. It's whether or not you want Patti."

"It's not that easy. I need to figure out—"

"No, Martin. You both need to figure out things. She has a say, too."

"Patti's the one who suggested I come back here for two weeks."

"Did you ask her to visit?"

"Of course not."

"Why not?"

"Because there's no reason for her to see my life here."

"Of course there is. Patti needs to know what you're leaving behind. It's a part of you, Martin. And that means she needs to understand your life here. Whether you leave her for it . . . or you leave this life behind you for good. She needs to know about it. And see it."

"You're right."

"I know." Looking far too pleased with herself, Beth folded her arms over her chest.

Martin supposed she had every reason to be pleased with everything she'd said. It had been just what he'd needed to hear.

"While you're dispensing good advice, any suggestions about what to do next?"

She picked up his cell phone. "Yep."

Taking one last bite of his bagel, Martin listened to his sister tell him what to do.

And for maybe the first time in his life, he did exactly what she asked without complaining once.

Chapter 34

Martin's phone call had come out of the blue, but his offer had merit. She'd asked for some time to consider his invitation, but that had only been a formality. The truth was that she was eager to go to Cleveland and finally see what Martin's life was like there. Of course that was going to be a double-edged sword. She wanted to see Martin because she was sure she was in love with him. She wanted to feel his arms around her and bask in the security of his approval and love.

But she knew that going to see him in his condominium, where he was so comfortable in his modern world, was also going to be painful. Much of what was comfortable for him was a mystery to Patti. What if she broke one of his expensive speakers or Alexas or the gadgets in his kitchen? Or worse, what if she realized that she could never live like that . . . and that Martin could never live without all those modern conveniences? Then what would they do?

Her mind had been spinning so much, she barely had been able to sit through the long church service. The moment the last prayer finished, she got to her feet. She needed space and time to prepare for her visit.

But before she did any of that, she needed to say goodbye to Preacher Richard and Bishop Frank.

Unfortunately for her, several other people wanted to speak with them as well.

As patiently as she was able, Patti stood to one side while she waited for her turn.

Just when it seemed the men were finishing up their conversation with Marge and her husband, Connor walked up to her.

He was probably the last person she'd wanted to speak to that afternoon.

"I'm going to walk you home today, Patti," he stated. "Don't leave without me."

She didn't appreciate his bossy tone or his high-handed manner. "I don't need you to walk me home."

"I disagree."

"Why is that?" Not only had he not come calling for several days, but Connor also hadn't acted all that friendly or pleased to see her when their paths crossed in town. His change toward her had been difficult to accept. Even though she didn't want a romantic relationship with him, they'd been friends for years. Good friends. She hated that he could ignore that history so easily.

He clasped his hands behind his back. "I think it's obvious."

It wasn't to her. But what to do? Already several people around them were noting their conversation. If she drew it out any longer, it would attract gossip.

She was prevented from responding because both Richard and Bishop Frank had finally completed their chat with Marge and had turned to her.

"Are you waiting for us, Patti?" Richard asked.

"*Jah.* It won't take long, though."

"It doesn't matter if it does. I always enjoy our conversations," Bishop Frank said in a warm tone.

Richard looked at Connor. "Are you waiting your turn to talk to us as well?"

"Not exactly. I came over to speak to Patti."

"And we finished our conversation." She sent Connor a pointed look.

Connor did not move.

"How are you doing, dear?" the bishop asked.

"I am well," she replied. "I am about to head home and I wanted to thank you for the service today."

"It's *gut* to see you, as always," the bishop said. Lowering his voice, he added, "Just the other day I visited with Elizabeth Brunswick. She relayed what a blessing your bookkeeping services have been to her."

"That makes me happy. Mrs. Brunswick is a nice woman. She's a hard worker, too."

"She is an inspiration to us all," Bishop Frank said. "Not everyone is able to reinvent themselves after a spouse passes away."

"She's told me more than once that her Jimmy would be tickled about her business." She shrugged. "I'm glad I can help her from time to time."

"God is helping you use your fixation with numbers for the greater good," Connor said.

Patti knew that Connor had meant his words in a kind way—at least she thought he had—but it hadn't come out that way. Instead, she felt criticized.

Richard cleared his throat. "I never thought being financially gifted could be classified as being fixated, Connor."

"I'm only saying it's a masculine trait. Most men would not trust a woman to take care of their business ledgers."

"You would not?"

"I have no need." He tapped his head. "It's all in here."

"That is a blessing, isn't it?" Bishop Frank said, with barely a hint of sarcasm in his voice. "I hope you both have a nice afternoon."

"We will. I'm walking her home."

Richard paused. "Patti, when is Martin due to return?"

"Not until the end of the week, at the earliest."

"I'll have to check on Kelsey. I imagine she's missing him."

Patti reckoned she did miss her brother, but that wouldn't be the main reason she would be pleased to have Richard come calling. Anyone could see the two of them were meant to be together.

Keeping her thoughts to herself, however, she simply smiled. "I'm sure she would be glad if you did stop by."

"I'll do that soon."

When she met the bishop's eyes, he winked.

Ah, so she was not the only one to believe Richard and Kelsey were meant to be together!

"Are you ready, Patti?" Connor said. "I'm sure these men have other people to speak to."

She was sure they did but didn't care for the way Connor sounded, as if she should be the least of their concerns. "I'm ready. Good day, Preacher Richard and Bishop Frank."

"Good day to you both," Richard said.

As they walked through the thinning crowd, Patti noticed that Connor seemed to be staying right next to her.

That wasn't how he used to be. He used to sometimes say that she walked too slowly for him to be comfortable by her side. She'd never completely believed him, feeling that he'd been a little embarrassed to be paired with her.

But now that she'd obviously chosen Martin over him, it seemed his opinion of her had changed a bit. His behavior aggravated her, but perhaps that said more about her than him. Had she really expected so little from him?

Or was it that she'd been so lacking in confidence that she didn't expect much from anyone? Martin had changed that, though.

"You seem to be deep in thought," Connor commented as they walked down the Troyers' driveway.

"I'm sorry. I was simply giving thanks that it isn't a long walk to my house."

"You don't feel like walking with me?"

Knowing she needed to be more gracious, she quickly corrected herself. "It's more that it feels like it's already been a busy day. Too busy for a day of rest."

"*Jah*, I can see that. But I suppose when you have a husband and *kinner*, you won't be resting much at all. It's a wife and mother's duty to keep the household running, ain't so?"

"I reckon so."

"But it's also her joy," he added in a meaningful tone.

Which she didn't appreciate. "I didn't know you had much experience being either a wife or a mother." She'd taken care to keep her tone light and teasing, but it hadn't taken the sting out of her words.

It was obvious that Connor had felt that sting, too. "Patti, you seem to be taking offense when there was no malice behind my words."

"Perhaps I am. I apologize." Unfortunately, she didn't feel all that sorry, however. With each step, it was becoming more and more apparent that even if Martin did remain English and there couldn't be anything between them, she would rather be alone than with Connor.

Seeing her house in the distance, Patti realized delaying the question that was on the tip of her tongue was a bad idea. It would certainly not be any easier when they were sitting alone on her front porch.

"Connor, as much as I appreciate your escort, I don't understand why you decided to walk me home."

"I don't think any explanation is needed."

"I disagree. I think it's been obvious for the last couple of weeks that you and I wouldn't be a good match."

"A good match?"

Oh, for Pete's sake. He was going to make her say it. "*Jah.
In marriage.*"

His expression tightened. "That is not your place to say,
Patti."

"I beg to differ." Looking up at him, she said, "Connor,
what is it about me that you love?"

"Love?"

"Well, yes. What is it about me that you greatly admire?"

"I cannot answer that."

Even though his reply had proved her suspicion to be correct, it still hurt. Even when he was trying to show that he
cared, it was obvious that his heart wasn't involved.

She stopped and faced him. "Connor, we've known each
other a long time. I've appreciated your attention and friendship. But I think it's more than obvious we wouldn't suit."

"Do you really think you can do better than me?"

It seemed that Connor's callous attitude knew no bounds.
Though it wasn't usually in her nature to be so direct, she
couldn't help herself in this instance. "If you mean do I
think that I could hope for someone better suited to spend
the rest of my life with, yes, I do."

He looked affronted. "We are suited."

"In what ways? You don't like that I am a bookkeeper,
for example."

He brushed off her statement with a wave of his hand.
"It's not like you would do that when you had a houseful of
kinner anyway."

He was right. If she became a mother, she would certainly
focus on her *kinner*. But she had a feeling she'd also find a
way to continue her business. She'd worked too hard to get
it off the ground. "If I was a mother, I would focus on my
family. I probably would keep my job, though. These
women depend on me."

"So will your husband and children."

Patti wasn't sure why she was still debating their future. She knew she'd rather be alone than be Connor's wife. But her tongue couldn't seem to rest. Almost against her will, she kept debating the pros and cons of a life with him. "I agree, but I know plenty of Amish women who do more than merely cook, clean, and look after their family."

Before he could argue that point, she added softly, "And then there's my looks."

For the first time, Connor appeared wary. "What are you referring to?"

She almost felt like laughing. He'd never been shy about his distaste for the skin discoloration on her neck. "We both know what I'm referring to, Connor. My birthmark."

He stared at her neck for a moment before meeting her eyes again. "Your imperfection is not an issue."

"Really?" It seemed to have been just a couple of weeks ago. "I've gotten used to it."

Even though it shouldn't, his comment hurt. She still hated the idea of him doing research about her birthmark. But more than that, she didn't like that Connor never saw her as just Patti. He saw 'Patti with a birthmark.'

"Martin gets upset when I even hint that my neck isn't pretty," she whispered. "He doesn't see the birthmark as a flaw."

"You didn't think he was being honest, did you?"

"Connor—"

"I know you think I'm being unnecessarily harsh, but I'm being honest with you. Honesty is always the best course of action."

"He was being honest."

"It doesn't matter to me if he was being honest or not. What is true is that we all have things about us that we wish we could change. I, for one, wish I was taller."

Patti felt like rolling her eyes. "I have no desire to be in a relationship in which I'm made to feel lacking." Hearing herself, she felt proud. Especially because she now realized that she'd grown, thanks to Martin's regard. Even if the relationship between the two of them didn't end up working out, she now appreciated herself more than she used to. Sure, she was imperfect, but she was still worthy. Her looks might not be for everyone, but she knew that anyone worth her regard wouldn't see her as flawed or lacking. They'd see her and know that she was a child of God and therefore perfect in His eyes.

There was so much more to her than a mark on her skin. Why had Connor never been able to see that?

Why had she allowed herself to sometimes forget her value as well? She was ashamed of herself. For so long, she'd wished and prayed for other people to look beyond the discoloration on her neck, but she hadn't done that either.

To her surprise, something her great-aunt had once said rang in her ears. "We're all scarred one way or another, child. We live on earth, not heaven. But you mustn't forget that our Lord doesn't make mistakes. You were meant to be special because He sees all of us that way."

Patti swallowed the lump in her throat. When her aunt had spoken those words, she'd been eleven. As a budding young woman, the teasing she got about her birthmark made her bitter. Instead of telling her to stop focusing on things she couldn't change, the way her parents always had, her aunt had held her close and whispered those words.

They'd essentially gone in one ear and out the other.

But her heart had held them close, just waiting for the perfect moment to remind her of the good advice.

Oblivious to everything she was thinking, Connor grunted. "Don't you have anything else to say?"

To him? No, she did not. "I think we've already said everything there is to say."

"So that's it?"

"*Jah.*"

Tension rose between them until he looked away. "You're being stubborn, Patti."

At the moment, she didn't think that was a flaw at all. Doing her best not to smile, she nodded. "Perhaps I am. But so be it. Let's just say that it's yet another reason why we won't suit."

"You know what? You can pretend that Englisher is only interested in your mind and doesn't care about your looks, but I can assure you, Martin is no doubt also imagining his future owning a good piece of farmland."

So that was why Connor had been courting her.

He wanted her land. Not only was he not attracted to her, there wasn't anything else about her he was interested in. All the times he'd acted a little bit possessive over her in front of their community wasn't because he didn't want another man to court her.

He just hadn't wanted another man to get his hands on her property. She'd been so fixated on her flaws and insecurities that she hadn't even realized that. The knowledge made her feel both disappointed and sad for the person she used to be.

"Good day, Connor. I will see myself the rest of the way home."

His light blue eyes flashed with irritation just as he reached out and grabbed her elbow. "Don't walk away from me, Patricia."

Ugh. As if calling her by her full name was going to make her feel any different about him. When his hand tightened, she pulled on her arm. "Let go of me now."

"Not until you listen." He jerked on her arm hard enough to make her gasp. "Stop acting like a fool. You and I both know you have no other choices. Even if this Englisher wants to marry you, he's only after one thing. You might as well stay with me."

She yanked again. "I'd never say yes to you. Not after today. Now, let go. You're hurting me."

"You're fine. At least you're listening."

"I—"

"Connor, I would advise you to release Patti right now!" Josiah called out.

Connor immediately dropped his hand and turned to her neighbor. "Hiya, Josiah. I didn't hear *ya*."

"I reckon not, because you were speaking so horribly to Patti."

"Did you need something, Josiah?" Connor asked abruptly.

As Patti backed away several steps, she felt sick to her stomach. If Martin and Kelsey hadn't appeared in her life and encouraged her to think about her life differently, she might have ended up with Connor. Just imagining a future with such an overbearing, selfish bully made her cringe.

"*Jah*, I need something," Josiah said as he got closer to Connor. "I want you to walk with me. It's obvious we need to talk."

"Sorry, but I'd rather—"

"And me," said Richard, who had just walked up behind them.

Surprised, Patti looked back at him. He must have followed her and Connor from church service.

Richard's expression was a hard mask, though his eyes met hers with a look of compassion. Patti knew right then and there that he, too, had heard much of what Connor had said. She might have been embarrassed, but she was actually glad. She probably would never have told the preacher what Connor had revealed. And based on their conversation, she had a feeling he would have gone after another woman with no one the wiser.

Now, at the very least, the preacher knew what a snake he was.

The men were now standing together, Richard and Josiah facing Connor. Connor looked deflated and wary. Half the man he'd been when it had just been the two of them.

"Richard, what are you doing here?" Connor asked.

"I told Josiah that I didn't feel good about Patti seeing you without a chaperone. And thank the good Lord for giving me those thoughts. It looked like we got here just in time."

"Nothing was happening."

"You're wrong about that," Josiah said. "Patti will likely have bruises on her arm from the way you were gripping her." Crossing his arms in front of his chest, he added, "I'm going to be sure to tell your parents about what I saw."

"I'm a grown man."

"You are at that. Which means you should have been acting far better. I'm ashamed of *ya*."

"It's obvious that we'll need to chat very soon," Richard said.

"Oh, please. You might be a preacher, but you're younger than me. You're in no position to counsel me about anything."

"I disagree, and I believe Bishop Frank will feel the same way."

Connor turned to Patti. "Tell these two that you are fine."

She was going to have bruises on her arm. In addition, she was still shaken by his anger.

"I can tell you a lot of things, but I can't tell you that," she said. "At the moment, I am not fine. Not fine at all."

The last of his bravado faded. "Patti, I'm sorry if I accidentally hurt you. I guess I don't know my own strength."

His apology was a poor one. She turned away from him.

"Come on, now. Don't be like that."

Josiah chortled, a deep, bitter sound. "Hurting a woman isn't a sign of strength, Connor. It's a sign that you're even weaker than I imagined." He held out an arm. "Are you ready to head home, Patti?"

She nodded. When she got close, Josiah surprised her by enfolding her in a warm hug.

Josiah and Sylvia had been like the grandparents she'd never had. Feeling the man's arm around her made her eyes well up with tears. She hadn't realized how much she'd needed his care and concern until that very moment.

"I know you're upset, and you have every reason to be," he whispered. "But don't you give that man the pleasure of seeing it. He's not worth it."

He was right. After allowing herself to rest against him one more moment, she pulled away. "I'm ready to go home now," she said.

Stepping to her other side, Richard smiled at her. "There you go, Patti. That's the woman I know."

She laughed. She wasn't sure if Richard had known that she was strong or not.

It didn't matter.

The important thing was that she had a different future in front of her. No matter whether she was successful or failed at every endeavor, she was going to be the one in charge of her life. Not Connor.

That was something to be very thankful for.

Chapter 35

At last, the moment had come. Patti could hardly wait. "You're really going to do this?" Marge asked. "You're going to let Martin's English sister pick you up in her car and drive you to Cleveland, and then you're going to stay with her while you visit Martin and observe his English ways?"

Patti couldn't help but chuckle at the way Marge was describing Beth and Martin Schrock. "First of all, yes, I really am going to do this. And secondly, stop acting as if they are scary people doing bad things. Martin is still Martin and Beth is his sister."

"I think you should speak to the bishop about this trip of yours."

"Why? Bishop Frank would say the same thing Richard did—which was to be careful with my heart and pray for guidance."

Richard had also told Patti to have a good time, but she didn't think Marge would appreciate that. At the moment, all she seemed to want to do was cast out warnings.

"When is Beth picking you up?"

"In about an hour." Looking at her packed suitcase, her purse, and her stuffed tote bag, she nibbled on her bottom lip. "I sure hope I'm not bringing too much. Does it look like I plan to overstay my welcome?"

"You look like you're planning to stay for at least a month."

"Really?" She mentally went through her suitcase again. "Maybe I don't need—"

"Don't worry about it, Patti. I was only teasing."

It sure didn't sound like it. "Um, okay."

Looking even more concerned, Marge added, "In case you've forgotten, you've already been baptized. You're supposed to be living Plain for the rest of your life."

"I know that." As if she'd forgotten indeed.

"Then what are you thinking? Would you really throw your whole life away on a whim?"

Patti didn't like that her friend was acting as if she hadn't been agonizing over her future for weeks. But in Marge's defense, it wasn't as if Patti had been broadcasting her thoughts to everyone either. "I hear what you're saying and I don't disagree. A lot of what I'm doing doesn't make sense. Not to me or you or Connor or anyone else. But I must do this. I have to visit Martin and see him in his English world."

"What do you want to see?"

"I want to see Martin's life in the city. I want to see if he seems happier there."

"But what if he is?" Marge whispered. "What are *ya* gonna do then?"

That was what she was afraid of. "Then I'll know that as much as he might love his grandparents or wish that the Plain life suited him, his city life in Cleveland is where he belongs."

"And what if it is? Where does that put you?"

"I'm not sure," she whispered. And that was all she was willing to admit to her friend. No way did she want to voice her real thoughts—that she was going to be heartbroken or that it would mean she'd have to break her vows to her community and the Lord.

"I hope for your sake this Martin Schrock tells *ya* that he doesn't want to live in the city and is selling his place and moving to Walden."

"And then declares his love, proposes to me, and we live happily ever after?"

"There's nothing wrong with wanting happiness, Patti."

"I know."

"I hope you do. Sometimes I think you've gotten so used to not expecting too much that you've forgotten to expect anything at all."

Much as she wanted to argue that point, Patti worried it might be true. "*Danke* for stopping by, but I need to finish getting ready."

"I understand. Be safe, Patti."

"Thank you. I will."

"And don't forget to pray."

"I always pray. You might be taken off guard by what I'm doing, but the Lord isn't. He's been aware of my thoughts."

Patti's declaration stayed with her while she swept the floor, dusted furniture that was already clean, and ate a sandwich she wasn't hungry for.

When Beth pulled up in a cream-colored sedan with Kelsey in the passenger seat, Patti's heart lifted. Was Kelsey heading to Cleveland with them, too?

"Kelsey, are you joining us?"

"Oh, *nee*. I just wanted to stop over and wish you well."

"She said she has no desire to return to city life," Beth said as she got out of her car.

"I understand why Martin went, though," Kelsey said quickly. "It just isn't where my heart is now."

"I can understand that, even though you and Anna are still at odds."

"You're talking about that hen, right?" Beth asked.

"Oh, *jah*."

"Anna and I have recently come to an agreement," Kelsey said. "She hasn't tried to peck me in five days."

Beth announced, "I already told Mommi that if that hen gives me as much attitude as she's giving you, I'll be eating her for Sunday supper."

Kelsey shivered. "Not only would that be awful for Anna, but Mommi would make you kill her and take off her feathers."

"You think?" Beth looked at Patti for help.

"I'm afraid Sylvia *would* have you do the hard work. And just warning you, it's most unpleasant."

"Ugh. I guess I'd better start hoping and praying that Anna likes me better than you, Kels."

"She probably will." Looking sheepish, Kelsey walked over to Patti. "I promise, I didn't come over to tell you about Anna. I came to see if you had any questions about either Martin or Cleveland."

"I already told her that you're going to be staying with me and that I can help you with anything you need," Beth said.

"Settle down, Beth."

"Fine."

Patti hid a smile. The two women were talking to each other just as she always imagined sisters did. Once again, Patti marveled at how close the four siblings were. She wished she had the kind of comfortable relationship with someone that they did with one another. Sometimes it seemed as if they could read one another's minds.

Turning to her once again, Kelsey said, "Is there anything you're concerned about?" She lowered her voice. "Even something that you think might be silly to ask?"

"Thanks for coming over, but please don't worry. I'll be fine."

Kelsey still looked worried. "Okay, but don't forget that you can call the phone shanty and leave a message. I'll make sure to check for messages twice a day. If you need a friend, just call and I'll call you back."

"I'll keep that in mind." Patti smiled at her again and hoped that she looked more self-assured than she felt.

Honestly, she wasn't sure if she was going to be just fine or not. Cleveland was a big city, and she was a small-town girl. Then there was Martin. Maybe he'd have forgotten their close bond now that he was back in the city. But if that was the case, she'd deal with it when the time came. She wanted to visit Martin's English world with an open mind.

"I'm also ready," she told Beth with a smile.

"Fantastic. Let's go. Hey, Kels, you want a ride back home?"

"*Nee*. I'm going to take a little walk before I return. I promised Mommi I'd help her with some baking and laundry this afternoon."

Beth hugged her close. "Call me soon."

"I will. You call me, too." Winking at Patti, Kelsey said, "I'm going to be anxious to hear what happens with our brother and a certain neighbor of ours."

After taking one last look at her house, Patti locked the front door and then put her things in the trunk of Beth's car.

They were on their way.

It turned out that any concerns she'd had about being alone with Beth were unwarranted. Beth Schrock was a little more direct and a bit less chatty than Kelsey, but she still had the same caring manner as her siblings.

Soon after leaving Walden, Beth went to a drive-through to get a soda, a burger, and fries and encouraged Patti to order the same. Soon, they were munching on their fries and talking about foods they liked.

The closer they were to Cleveland, the more Beth played tour guide. She pointed out various suburbs of the city and told Patti entertaining stories about each area.

Patti was pretty sure Beth was telling her all those stories so she wouldn't have time to be nervous, but she didn't care whether that was the reason or not. She appreciated that the drive flew by.

When she exited the freeway, Beth became a little more businesslike. "I don't live too far from Martin at all," she said. "Just a fifteen-minute drive."

"Okay."

"Patti, that means if you ever need me or you'd like a break and just want to relax, all you have to do is call."

"Thank you."

She drummed her fingers on the steering wheel. "Of course I'm sure Martin will do whatever you ask him to do. I just didn't want you to think that Kelsey was your only girlfriend. I'd like to be your friend, too."

"*Danke*, Beth."

"And, ah, before I forget, I want to thank you for being so kind to Kelsey. She's told me several times that you've gone out of your way to help her."

"She's easy to help. She tries hard and is delightful. Has she always been that way?"

"Kind of." Looking reflective, Beth added, "I'm not sure how much you know about our family dynamics, but things were a little difficult when we were growing up. When our parents got divorced, all four of us kind of drifted a little." She bit her bottom lip. "It's fair to say our parents did, too."

"Martin said it was hard."

"Yeah, it was." She paused for a moment, then continued. "For a while after, I think all six of us were struggling to find our way. Kelsey leaned on Martin and me a lot."

"She was blessed to have you both."

"We were blessed to have one another." Beth smiled suddenly. "We're here."

"Already? Well, that's great." Patti gulped.

As if she read Patti's mind, Beth wrapped one of her hands around Patti's. "Everything's going to be fine. I promise."

Patti smiled and nodded. And prayed that Beth was right.

Chapter 36

It seemed the sun had left Walden with Patti's departure. Within a couple of hours, the wind had picked up and the temperature had dropped. Folks at the market said they'd heard it was likely to snow over the next few days.

It was now November, so the weather report wasn't exactly a surprise, but Kelsey couldn't help but be depressed by the news. Snow meant wet boots, shoveling, and even more transportation challenges than usual.

"Watching the sky with a glum expression won't change the weather, child," Dawdi said.

"I know. I'm just trying to come to terms with the idea of an early winter."

Under his ancient felt hat, her grandfather scowled. "Pshaw. Folks say things like that all the time, but I think it's all a bunch of worry for nothing. The weather is what it is."

"I suppose." She still stared out at the sky, noticing that it seemed dark and foreboding.

Dawdi studied her for a moment. "You know what? I think it's time you and I took a drive together. Go put on your coat and such."

"You want to go right now?"

"Now's a *gut* time to go, I think." He clapped his hands as if he was attempting to summon a wayward child. "Hurry now, and meet me out in the barn."

"I will." When she opened the back door, she found her grandmother standing at the stove.

"Ready to help me make this stew, Kelsey?"

"I'm sorry, Mommi. I can't. Dawdi asked me to go on a drive."

Her grandmother turned to her. "Did he, now?"

"Why do you think he offered, Mommi?"

"I guess you'll find out when you get in that buggy."

"He told me to hurry and get my cloak."

Her grandmother walked to the mudroom off the kitchen, opened a cabinet, and pulled out a dark navy cloak. The wool was soft and thick. It looked brand-new. "Here you are, child."

"Mommi, did you make this?"

"I did." She smiled softly.

"It's beautiful. *Danke.*"

"It's warm, too. That's what's important, ain't so?" Before Kelsey could answer, she shooed her out the door. "Have a good time."

When Kelsey got to the barn, Leroy, their buggy horse, was hitched up and looked eager to leave. So did her grandfather.

"I was wondering when you were going to come back. Hurrying don't seem to mean much to you."

"Oh, stop. I had to tell Mommi what I was doing. Plus, she gave me this cloak. Isn't it pretty?"

Her grandfather's blue eyes softened. "It is. Hop in, now."

Kelsey did as he asked. When he clicked the reins and Leroy headed down their driveway, she realized that she'd spent a lot of time alone with her grandmother but not as much with Josiah. "I'm glad you asked me to go on a drive."

"Me too."

"Are we going anyplace special?"

"*Jah*. I thought we'd pay a call on Preacher Richard."

"What? Why?"

"Oh, don'tcha start acting all flustered and silly. I know you like the boy, but I thought maybe we'd go for some advice today."

"What about?"

"Being patient, for one."

Kelsey rolled her eyes. "You're a tease, Dawdi."

"You think so?"

She noticed he didn't look too upset by her words. "Maybe."

When he chuckled, she frowned. "Dawdi, that wasn't a compliment."

"Well, I'll still take it. Lord knows I've been called worse."

Though it was on the tip of her tongue to ask him to explain himself, she didn't. Besides, she had enough to dwell on. What in the world were they going to talk to Richard about? Surely not their feelings for each other.

Because she had fallen in love with him! She knew he was feeling the same way—or at least close to it.

"Ah, here we are."

Richard's house was a neat, two-story white building on a gently sloping hill. A splendid-looking blue spruce stood in the front corner of the property, and there were multiple flower beds scattered around the house's perimeter. "It's lovely."

"I always thought so. Before Jerome and Sadie bought it, a Mennonite couple lived there for forty years." Dawdi frowned. "When they got on in years, the family decided to sell just as Richard's father was ready to relocate from Indiana."

"So they haven't lived here long."

"Not by a lot of folks' standards." He winked. "Only about seven years."

Kelsey was just about to ask her grandfather some more questions about Richard's family when the door opened.

"Ah. There he is." Having already set the brake, her grandfather practically bounded out of the buggy. "Hiya, Richard!"

"Hello, Josiah," he called back. "And Kelsey, too."

Dawdi held out his hand. "Come along, child. I ain't got all day to stand here."

Just as she was about to roll her eyes, Kelsey noticed her grandfather's expression was soft. He was telling her without words that everything would be okay. "*Danke*, Dawdi," she murmured.

After a small nod, he turned to Richard, who had walked out to greet them. "Richard, Kelsey and I came to visit with you. We have some things to discuss."

Richard caught her eye. When Kelsey shrugged, he turned back to her grandfather. "This sounds serious."

"It is. A bit, I think."

"Oh?"

"I think Kelsey might be feeling a little worried about her future. On account of Martin being back in Cleveland, you know."

Kelsey pursed her lips. That wasn't exactly how she'd put things, but she supposed it was close enough. She hadn't realized her grandparents had noticed she was feeling anxious, though.

"What are you worried about?" Richard asked as he guided them into the house.

Kelsey only had time to take a quick glance around the house's entryway before Richard ushered them into a study and closed the door. Her grandfather crossed the room and sat down on the couch with a sigh.

Richard remained where he was. When he folded his hands behind him, obviously waiting for her answer, Kelsey

knew she had to be completely honest. With him, her grandfather, and herself. "I'm afraid that I might be the only one
in my family to actually decide to get baptized."

"Ah." Richard gestured for her to take a seat before he sat
down in a brown leather chair. "That would be hard. Do
you think it's a possibility?"

"Sometimes." She paused, wanting to explain herself as
best she could. "We all know that Martin has been missing
his job back in Cleveland."

"He's there to see how he feels."

"And now Patti is there visiting him. And my sister Beth
drove her."

A line formed between Richard's brows. "Does that upset
you? Do you wish you were there, too?"

"No! Not at all. I just thought . . . well, I thought we'd all
do this together."

"What about Jonny?" Richard asked.

She glanced at her grandfather. Dawdi was practically re-
clining on the couch, but it was obvious he was soaking in
every word.

Instead of sharing his two cents, he only motioned for her
to keep talking.

"Jonny is a junior in college," she began. "He's having a
good time and making good grades, too. I don't know if he's
going to want to quit before he graduates."

"And you fear that afterward he might choose to take a
job and use his degree?"

Kelsey nodded as she leaned back against her chair's cush-
ion. "He might still want to come live here and get baptized,
but he might not."

"That's true."

Kelsey stared at Richard. As always, his dark eyes seemed
to hold a wealth of emotion. Today, instead of making her
feel warm, he was making her feel calmer. She realized then
and there that God really had known what He was doing

when He'd guided Richard to be a preacher at such a young age. She might be falling in love with the man that he was, but she respected the preacher he'd become.

"Kelsey, would you like to share more of your feelings?"

"I'd like you to tell me what you think."

"All right, then." Richard straightened a bit, then finally rested his elbows on his knees. "Kelsey, as hard as it is, I think each of us is on his or her own journey through life. We can support each other and help guide loved ones, if they wish that. But at the end of the day, every decision is between each of us and God."

"You want me to just worry about myself?"

Richard smiled softly. "I think it's in your nature to worry over everyone you care about. But I think you maybe need to remember that Martin, Jonny, and Beth are on their own paths. Only the Lord knows what will happen, right?"

"Right."

"So, let me ask you this. Will you still consider Martin, Jonny, and Beth to be your siblings even if they remain English?"

"Of course."

"Why is that?"

"Because I love them and . . . and they're my brothers and my sister." Her eyes widened. She had no doubt about her love for them.

Reaching out for her hands, he squeezed both gently. "I happen to know they all feel the same way about you, Kelsey. They're going to love you no matter what."

She looked at their joined hands. Richard's were so tan and firm. She felt she could hand all of her burdens to him and he'd carry them without faltering. "*Danke*," she whispered.

He leaned close. "I'd kiss you if your grandfather wasn't sitting across the room watching us like a hawk."

"I'd let you," she whispered back. "Perhaps that means you'll call on me this evening?"

"I'll be there at seven."

"That's enough of that, you two," her grandfather said as he surged to his feet and headed to the door. "Kelsey, let's go now. Leroy is probably anxious to return to the warmth of the barn."

"*Jah*, Dawdi."

Richard wrapped a hand around her shoulders as they followed her grandfather out of the room. "You're sounding almost Amish, Kelsey."

She smiled up at him. "*Gut.*"

She was sure she heard his laughter even as she walked onto the front porch.

Chapter 37

It was obvious that something had happened between Patti and Beth during the short drive from Walden to Cleveland. Martin was sure of it.

Unfortunately, he was not sure what exactly had taken place. All he did know was that his sister and Patti seemed to have come to some sort of understanding. Beth was now acting like a mother hen and practically bristling at everything he said.

Martin wasn't sure if Patti sensed it as well. The tentativeness that had dissipated over the last few weeks in Walden had returned. He wanted, no, he *needed* to know what was on her mind, but he wasn't going to find out with Beth hanging on every word of their conversation.

When Patti excused herself to go to the bathroom, Martin handed Beth her purse.

"I need you to go and leave us alone for a while."

She didn't take it from his hand. "No."

"Beth, I haven't seen Patti in days. She's looking at me like I'm a stranger. I need to figure out what's going on with her, but I can't with you being a pest."

"I'm not being a pest!"

"You are and you know it." After darting a glance at the bathroom door, he said, "When Patti comes out, tell her that you've got to go run some errands or something. We'll meet you later for dinner, and then you can take her back to your place."

"I think she needs a chaperone."

"You've got to be kidding."

"I'm not. She's a sheltered girl."

"She's sheltered, but she's not naïve. She's also not a young girl. She's a woman the same age as you."

"Martin."

"Do you really want to start this with me? Now? Don't forget that I was around when you were dating Charlie your senior year of high school." The guy was a jerk, but Beth had begged Martin to give them space.

Hurt—and maybe a bit of embarrassment—filled her expression. "I don't know what Charlie has to do with anything."

"I'm just saying that if you don't give me some time alone with Patti, I'm going to go full Amish chaperone on you when you're living at our grandparents' house."

"You wouldn't dare."

"Sure I would. And every time you complain, I'm going to remind you of this moment."

"Fine," she said as Patti walked out of the bathroom. "Give me my purse."

Patti's footsteps slowed. "What's going on with the two of you?"

"Um, I was just telling Martin that I'd forgotten to go to the . . . dry cleaners."

"The dry cleaners?"

"Yeah. I have a dress there that I need to pick up. So, I'm going to go."

"Oh. Okay." Turning to Martin, Patti looked regretful. "I guess I'll see you—"

"You're staying. We're going to meet Beth for supper, and then she's going to take you back to her place afterward."

He was pleased to see a look of relief cross her features.

"Are you okay with me leaving, Patti?" Beth asked.

"Of course. Why?"

He tried his best not to look smug, but he was pretty sure he failed miserably.

Patti might not have caught his smirk, but his sister sure did.

Beth coughed, then gathered herself together. "No reason. I'll see you later. Unless you'd like my cell phone number?"

"I don't have a phone. Plus, I'll be with Martin."

Yep, Beth was surely digging herself into a deep hole. "You'd best get going before the cleaners closes," he said.

"Don't make me regret this," she whispered as she walked out the door. At last.

When they were alone, he exhaled. "I thought she'd never leave," he joked.

"I started wondering if you were going to walk her to the door."

"So . . . you caught what was going on?"

"I don't have to be a fisherman to know that's there's fish in the ocean, Martin. I think I would have to have been blind and deaf not to realize you were shooing your sister out the door."

"Yeah. I guess I was hoping for some privacy. Are you upset?"

She shook her head. "I am just curious about why you needed her to leave."

That felt like a loaded question if there ever was one. Glancing into her pretty brown eyes, so warm and caring, Martin felt himself melt a little bit. He never would've imagined that he would be the type of man to get so sentimental and soppy, but it seemed he was.

"Want to have a seat? I'll get you something to drink, too." Opening his refrigerator, he scanned the contents. "I have water, orange juice, a quart of apple cider, and a couple of cans of Sprite and Coke. Or I could make a fresh pot of coffee."

"What are you having?"

He smiled. "Whatever you are, Patti."

"May I have a Sprite?"

"Of course. Have a seat, okay?"

Instead of just handing her a can, he pulled out two glasses, filled them with ice, and then divided the can's contents between the two. When the drinks were ready, he flicked the switch on his gas fireplace and sat down on the couch.

Patti joined him there. She looked relaxed and comfortable in his apartment. She didn't look out of place either. Somehow, she even made her *kapp* and forest-green dress look perfect in the modern space.

"I know why Beth went down to get you. But what I'm not sure about is why you took her up on the invitation."

After taking a fortifying sip of soda, she looked at him directly. "Your sister said something that made a lot of sense to me. She said I should probably know what your life is like here, in case . . ."

"In case?"

"In case you decide to stay." Taking another breath, she blurted out, "or in case you decide to leave and return to Walden."

He didn't like the feeling that she seemed to have made peace with whatever he decided. The selfish part of him wanted her to fight for him. No, fight for a future for the two of them together. On the heels of that thought came the realization that she was scared of depending on him. Unlike him, with his grandparents and the solid support of his brother and sisters, Patti was alone in the world.

Of course she was going to guard her heart. Or, at the very least, her thoughts.

"I guess that makes sense," he finally said.

"I don't know if it does or it doesn't." She took another sip of her drink. After placing it on the table, she added, "When I look around, I can't help but feel that you fit in here. Maybe more than you do in Walden." She smiled softly. "Even seeing you in jeans and a sweater and tennis shoes makes me feel like I'm seeing the real you."

He looked down at his faded Levi's and the dark gray thermal shirt. When he'd put them on, he'd felt like himself again. "These clothes do feel more comfortable. I'm not sure if that means anything, though. It could be that I'm just not used to dressing Amish."

"Maybe, or it might mean that you already are the person you are meant to be."

Was the Lord's will that easy to discern? He'd never thought so. "Have you ever dressed English, Patti?" When she frowned, he explained, "You know, like during your *Rumspringa?*" His parents had told them tons of stories about the different ways Amish kids experimented in all things English.

She averted her eyes. "*Nee.*"

He was surprised. "I thought all Amish kids put on English clothes from time to time."

"Not me. I never felt the need to imagine being a different sort of person than I was."

"You're comfortable with who you are."

Her cheeks pinkened. "I don't know if it's that exactly. I mean, there have been many, many times when I prayed for the Lord to make my birthmark go away. I even used to ask my mother if there was a scarf or something I could wear around my neck so it wouldn't show."

"Patti." He hated to hear that. He hated that she'd grown up feeling unhappy and insecure about her body, and that she still wasn't at ease with her looks.

"What I'm trying to say is that I've had lots of moments when I wasn't exactly comfortable with myself . . . but I've never yearned to be English or Mennonite. I never wanted to be different inside. I guess you've felt differently?"

He nodded.

"I'm sorry for that. Between the two, I think I'd choose being dissatisfied with my looks instead of my faith."

"There's nothing to be sorry about. Would you be willing for us to just have a good time for the next couple of days instead of constantly trying to figure out our future?"

She looked relieved. "I'd like that very much."

"Let's finish our drinks, then, and head out."

"Where are you going to take me?"

"I've thought a lot about it. I think we'll start with University Circle, Severance Hall, and the art museum."

She frowned. "You're going to take me to the art museum?"

"Yeah. Why? Do you not like art?"

"I do. I mean, I suppose I do. I'm just surprised that you do."

"I like art. I like the building and how peaceful it is. I want to take you places that are different from anything you might have seen before. They're favorite tourist spots."

"I'm looking forward to it."

Standing up, he reached for her hand. When Patti slipped it into his, he pulled her to her feet. For a moment, he was tempted to bend down and brush his lips against hers. But it still didn't seem like the right time. Not when he was still so confused about his future.

Releasing her hand, he bent down to collect their glasses. "I'll put these in the sink and grab my phone and jacket. Do you need a sweater?"

"You know, I guess I do. I was wearing a cardigan, but I left it in Beth's car."

"You can wear one of my sweatshirts over your dress. It will be big, but I think it will do. Is that okay?"

She smiled at him again. "I think it will do just fine."

Chapter 38

Richard had barely been able to think about anything other than Kelsey's visit to his house that afternoon. He'd watched the clock all day, practically wishing his afternoon would go faster.

At six o'clock, right after they'd eaten supper, he took a shower and put on clean clothes. Then he paced in his room for a while.

Finally, he was at the Schrock house. He was clean, he was prepared to speak to Kelsey about their future, and he was even ready to talk to Josiah.

It was just too bad his palms were sweating and his chest felt tight. He felt as if he was on the verge of having a panic attack.

Standing on the front porch next to him, Josiah Schrock noticed. "You've got to get a hold on yourself, man."

"I'm trying."

He frowned. "Try harder. What's got you so in knots anyway?"

"Kelsey."

"I'm afraid you're gonna have to be a bit more specific, Preacher."

Richard grunted. Josiah was a good man, but he did enjoy playing mental games from time to time. They both knew exactly why Richard was a nervous wreck. "I can't do that. It's between Kelsey and me."

"Is that right? You've already talked to her brother?"

"*Nee.*"

"Her father?"

"You know I have not." He was pretty sure Kelsey hadn't talked to either of her parents in weeks.

Josiah folded his arms over his chest. "It looks like I'm your best option, then." He raised one eyebrow. "Start talking."

"She's an adult. She doesn't need her grandfather's permission to do anything."

"She doesn't need me to do most things. But you need me right now." He stepped to the right. Essentially blocking the path to the front door.

"I can't believe you."

"Believe it." Triumph gleamed in his eyes.

"Josiah, you know my intentions are true. I would never hurt Kelsey."

"Do you love her?"

"I . . . *jah.*"

Josiah's lips pinched. "Richard, you know I like you very much. I think you're a good person and a halfway decent preacher."

"*Danke*, Josiah."

The older man waved an impatient hand. "Oh, don't go getting your feelings hurt. I'm being honest with *ya*. And what I honestly think is that your profession of love doesn't sound too convincing to me."

"That's because you aren't Kelsey. I'm not going to pour my heart out to you."

"You've got to do better than that, son."

Worried that the girl had caught sight of him out the window, he added, "I know you mean well and I respect your need to look out for Kelsey. But I'm not sure how she feels about me. And no offense, but this isn't ever going to be a family meeting. Kelsey and I need to talk and come to an agreement before we involve anyone else."

"Hmph."

"I'm not joking, Josiah. As much as I respect you, Kelsey needs to hear what I have to say first."

"I see."

Richard hoped he did. He really did. But he honestly wasn't too concerned about Josiah at the moment. What he did care about was the fact that the man was keeping him from his mission. Didn't the fellow realize that this was hard enough without his interference?

"I'd like to see Kelsey now."

For a second, Josiah looked as if he was about to erupt and tell him exactly what he thought of Richard's behavior, but he nodded. "Please come inside."

The living room was spotlessly clean. So different from the way it had looked some of the past times Richard had visited. Oh, Sylvia kept things tidy, but the living room usually looked lived in. Comfortable. Today the atmosphere was different. Almost more formal, though he couldn't see how.

And then Kelsey walked down the steps, and he didn't think much about anything at all.

Truly, his mind had gone blank.

Kelsey was dressed Amish. From head to toe. Crisp, white *kapp* covering neatly arranged hair, dark blue dress with matching blue apron, black stockings, and simple black, lace-up shoes. She didn't have a bit of makeup on.

Her face was a little bit pale. It was obvious she was nervous about her appearance. Richard knew it was his job as a preacher to say something reassuring and kind. Maybe tease a bit to coax a smile from her.

But at the moment, he couldn't seem to be anything but a man, and this man was thunderstruck by how beautiful she was. No, it was more than that. He'd always thought her pretty because she *was* pretty. But at this moment, he could honestly see the two of them together. He could imagine that she could be happy with him.

The changes she was willing to make hit him hard in the center of his chest. Even though she wasn't making the change for him, he was the recipient of her sacrifice. It was humbling.

And made his head go blank.

One minute turned to two.

Kelsey licked her bottom lip. He noticed. And to his shame, he allowed his gaze to linger on her lips.

When he heard a not-so-discreet cough behind him, Richard knew he had to say something or Josiah would interfere yet again.

"Hi, Kelsey." Inwardly, he groaned. That was the best he could do? No wonder Josiah was practically standing sentry. He was a foolish, tongue-tied idiot.

Kelsey's blue eyes widened before she regained her composure. "Good evening, Richard. How are you?"

"Well, I'm currently wishing I was a better man."

"That's how you're feeling?"

She looked surprised, and who could blame her?

"Not exactly. Mostly, I'm feeling sorry that I'm standing here like a fool. It's just—"

"That I look so different?"

He nodded but knew that didn't do his feelings justice. "*Nee.* It's just that you look so beautiful. Perfect." He stepped forward, not daring to look behind him because he didn't care who was there. The bishop, or Kelsey's entire family, or even the entire population of Walden could be there.

Her right hand was curved around the edge of her apron. She was gripping the fabric tightly. "You really think so?" Her voice was a whisper.

"Oh, yes."

If there were other witnesses, so be it. He just hoped they would stay quiet long enough so he could do this moment right.

Stepping forward, he reached for her hands. "I know so. Kelsey, I don't know if you did this for you, or for me, or just on a whim. But whatever the reason, I want you to know that I think you are the prettiest thing I've ever seen. I didn't know what to say at first . . . you took me off guard. My mind went blank."

The hesitant smile that had been teasing the corners of her lips expanded into a full-fledged smile.

Not taking his eyes from Kelsey's, he said, "Josiah, we need you to leave."

"I'm here, too, Preacher," Sylvia called out.

Kelsey's eyes lit with amusement. One of her eyebrows rose.

Obviously, she was giving him leeway to clear the room. He was up to the challenge. "Sylvia, please escort your husband out of the room so I may speak to Kelsey alone."

"Oh. You want both of us to leave?"

"I want that more than anything else in the world."

Kelsey bit her bottom lip, obviously in a futile effort to stop laughing.

"Come on, Sylvia," Josiah said around a chuckle. "The boy has a plan. We should probably get to it before he passes out."

Sylvia didn't move. "What kind of plan is that?"

"I'll tell you in the kitchen."

"Do you want coffee, Richard?"

"*Danke*, but no, Sylvia."

"Fine."

He was pretty sure they walked off, but he had no idea because he was afraid to turn around. "Are they still here?"

Kelsey's eyes were bright. "No. They've left."

"Thank the good Lord." Looking down at their joined hands, he prayed for the Lord's help.

Only then did he feel a warmth surge through him. He wasn't sure if his nerves were making him warm, the fire burning across the room, or God really was holding him close and giving him support.

But at last, he had the words he'd been looking for.

"Kelsey, the first time I saw you, I knew that you were the woman for me. Ever since then, I've been drawn to you in a way I've never felt before. I can't seem to think about anyone but you. I don't want to think about anyone but you, because all I see is you."

"Richard." Her voice sounded a little breathless.

"I know you still have a lot to go through. I know you have a family to care for and that you care about, but I felt this need . . ." He shook his head. "*Nee*, I knew this was the right thing to do."

"What, Richard?"

"To tell you I love you. I am certain about it. It's strong in my heart, and there isn't an ounce of doubt in my mind. I want you, Kelsey. One day I want to stand in front of your family and mine and promise you everything I can."

"Are you asking me to marry you?"

"I wish I could, but it's too soon."

"How do you know?"

"Well—"

"I mean, is it a rule? Does one have to be officially Amish to be officially engaged?"

"I have no idea. I'd have to ask Bishop Frank."

"He's not here."

Her eyes were warm. He looked down at their joined hands. Sometime during their convoluted conversation, their hands had rearranged themselves and their fingers had linked together. Their hands were joined.

"What are you saying?"

"I'm saying, just once, could you not be Richard the Amish preacher and just be Richard the man and say what you want to say? What is your problem?"

The problem was that Richard the man was imperfect, full of thoughts he shouldn't be thinking and very human. Though he'd never felt saintlike, Richard was trying to be the best version of himself with Kelsey. "I don't know if you want to hear the words."

"Try me. What do you want, Richard?"

He knew what he wanted. Of that, there was no doubt. "Kelsey Schrock, I want to marry you. I want you to be mine for the rest of my life. I also want to hold you in my arms and kiss you senseless."

"You want to kiss me right now?"

He was relieved that she didn't look shocked. Not one bit. He grinned. "More than you can imagine."

"If I say yes, will you finally kiss me?"

"Yes?"

"Yes, Richard Miller, I will be your wife. I will be yours for the rest of my life." She lowered her voice. "But I also would very much like to be kissed senseless right this minute."

He was imperfect but no fool. Pulling her close with one hand, he held her face with the other. Thought about how precious she was. Thought about how just a warm look or a smile could turn his day around.

Thought about how the Lord was so good because He had known that this woman who practically every man in the world would see as lovely and sweet had chosen him to be hers.

And then, as he ran his fingertips along her spine, he thought about how no other woman could ever feel so perfect in his arms.

Tired of thinking, he brushed his lips against hers and felt as if he'd at last experienced heaven on earth. "Kelsey," he whispered.

Her eyes heated. "I know. I feel the same way."

Richard needed no other encouragement. He pulled her closer, cradled her in his arms, and plundered. Kissed her deeply, giving her every ounce of his longing for her. Holding nothing back.

Kelsey lifted herself up on her tiptoes as she pressed against him.

And stars seemed to erupt as their kiss continued, until he realized he needed to stop before they completely lost sight of where they were.

When he finally lifted his head, Richard knew he was breathing hard. "I love you, Kelsey, and am glad you are going to be my wife."

"I'm glad you're glad." Kelsey's happy laughter floated through the room, filled his heart, and, in his imagination, flowed all the way to heaven.

Few moments in life could compare.

No, nothing in his life needed to compare. Because this was perfect.

Chapter 39

"What did you think?" Martin asked as they sat down in the museum's lobby café with cappuccinos. Each had come with a pair of delicate-looking almond biscotti cookies on the saucer.

Both were delicious.

Looking at Martin, appearing so relaxed and confident, Patti saw a whole new side of him that had been hidden in Walden. He was still the same Martin, but all day she'd been thinking he was something more.

More outgoing. Quicker to smile and laugh. Even more attentive. She could only equate it to the behavior of a caged animal that was released into its native habitat. Although it had survived in its other surroundings, it flourished when it was back in its home.

Martin might feel different, but it sure seemed that he was meant to live in the city among the English.

"About the coffee or the museum?" she teased.

"About both."

"I am enjoying both." Thinking her comment was far too generic, she added, "I've never had coffee this way. It's deli-

cious. And the artwork is lovely, though I think this building is just as beautiful as some of the famous paintings you
showed me."

"I feel the same way."

He was looking at her intently. Patti wasn't sure if he
was looking for a specific phrase or comment or not. She
hoped not, because she had no idea what he was hoping to
hear her say.

"Where are we going next?"

"I thought maybe we'd hit the grocery store and pick out
something for supper. I could grill on the back patio."

"That sounds like fun." She sipped her drink again and
nibbled on the corner of her second biscuit.

"Patti, I have a feeling you're pretty confused about me."

"Not about you." Realizing there was no point in keeping
all of her feelings to herself, she added, "I am a little confused about our future."

"That makes two of us."

"You seem more at home here. Is it because it's more familiar or that you feel like you fit in better here?"

"I don't know. It feels like a bit of both." He grunted, ob-
viously irritated with himself. "I enjoy being in Walden.
When I'm with you and Sylvia and Josiah and even Richard,
I'm happy."

"Everyone likes you."

He smiled at her. "I'm very glad you do, Patti. But I . . . I
just don't know if the Lord means for me to be Amish."

"Have you talked to Bishop Frank about your feelings?"

"I have."

"And?"

"And he wasn't as helpful as I'd hoped." He laughed
softly. "I think I was hoping he would tell me what to do,
but all he kept saying was that he felt certain that God and I
would make the right decision."

"That wasn't very helpful."

He laughed. "I thought the same thing." He shrugged. "But I guess he was right. Just as you were right to suggest that I come here for two weeks."

"I'm glad Kelsey and Beth encouraged me to visit you here. Of course, I know a lot of English. I've been to some of my English friends' houses, too. But all that was in Walden. Not in a big city like this. It's very different." Thinking of his job, she said, "Have you gone by the company where you worked?"

"No. I quit, and they've already hired a replacement."

"I guess you could find a different company to hire you?"

"I could, if that's what I choose to do."

They stared at each other. Patti was fairly sure that he felt the same thing she did. There were a lot of unanswered questions between them, but it sure seemed as if all the signs were pointing toward Martin returning to his modern apartment and finding a job in the world of finance, while she simply became the Amish neighbor of his grandparents.

Standing up, he reached for their empty china cups. "Are you ready to leave?"

"*Jah.*"

"I'll take these inside."

When he disappeared, Patti turned to look at the expansive museum lobby. It was so large and airy-looking, she felt as if she was outdoors.

Then she noticed a pair of schoolchildren staring at her. They appeared to be brother and sister, perhaps around ten or twelve? The brother was whispering to his younger sister.

Her first reaction was to cover her neck with her hand, but then she realized they weren't staring at the skin discoloration but her Amish clothing.

That she could deal with!

She smiled at them.

The girl smiled back. Then, much to her brother's obvious discomfort, she sauntered over to Patti.

"Hi."

"Hello."

"My brother said I'm not supposed to talk to you."

"I am a stranger."

"No, it's because you're Amish."

The girl was pronouncing "Amish" with a long "A." Patti thought it sounded rather amusing, especially because the little girl had a slight lisp. "I am Amish, but I don't mind talking to you."

"Where's the rest of your family?"

"Pardon?"

"My teacher said you Amish always go places with your families and your horse and buggy. Is your horse outside?"

"No, I didn't bring it to the museum. And my family didn't travel with me." She figured that was the truth, though maybe not in the way the little girl imagined.

"You know how to speak English," the brother said.

"I do. We Amish learn English when we're in school. Sometimes even before."

"Oh."

"Everything okay?" Martin asked as he joined them.

"*Jah*. These *kinner* were just curious about me." She smiled at him. "They were wondering if my horse was parked outside."

He chuckled. "Not today, right?"

"*Jah*. Not today."

"Lane? Michelle?"

"We're over here, Mom!" the girl said as a woman hurried toward them.

"I hope you aren't bothering this lady?"

"They weren't," Patti said quickly. "We were just getting acquainted."

"She speaks English, Mommy. Plus, she doesn't have a horse here."

Their mother released a put-upon sigh as she faced Patti again. "I hope we haven't offended you."

"*Nee*. I'm used to people being curious about living Amish."

"Well, thank you for being so kind to them." Turning to her children, she said, "We need to go home and let the dog out."

"We have a golden retriever named Jack," the girl said with a smile.

"That's a *gut* name, *jah*?"

"Uh-huh." She smiled again before hurrying to catch up with her mother and brother.

Martin wrapped an arm around her shoulders. "Everything okay?"

Still smiling at the innocent exchange, she nodded. "Like I told the kids, this isn't exactly an unusual occurrence."

Noticing that Martin looked bemused, she said, "Are you thinking that this could be your future?"

"Actually, I was thinking that it's the first time I've noticed you being so comfortable with who you are."

She didn't know what he meant. "Martin, obviously I'm used to being Amish."

"I was referring to the fact that you didn't seem worried about your birthmark."

She had forgotten all about that. "I guess it's because the children weren't asking me about it, and I can't fault them for their curiosity. I haven't seen too many Amish having cappuccinos in here," she joked. Actually, she'd only seen one Amish person: herself in the mirror.

"I might be wrong, but I think the Lord was teaching us a lesson here."

She wasn't sure if the Lord was, or if Martin was simply attempting to make a point.

But she couldn't deny that no one had stared at her rudely or asked her questions about her disfigurement.

Was it because they were more concerned about her *kapp* and dress?

Or because there was a variety of people out and about and her birthmark seemed insignificant?

Or was the difference in her? She wasn't acting as if she was carrying extra baggage or actively attempting to hide the birthmark, and because of that, no one took notice of it either?

She wasn't sure, but it was something to think about.

Yet another item to consider.

She wondered what was going to happen with the two of them.

If there ever was going to be a "two of them."

Chapter 40

It was late at night when Kelsey decided she had to do something. Even knowing that both her grandparents and Richard would be upset with her for walking down to the phone shanty in the dark, she went anyway.

She needed to speak to her siblings, and she wasn't going to be able to sleep if she didn't talk to at least one of them. She armed herself with a cozy sweater and her best flashlight, went downstairs, and finally crept out the front door.

Hopefully, she'd been stealthy enough that neither of her grandparents would know what she was doing.

As she walked down the quiet road, listening for the squawking of birds or the rustling of some kind of woodland creature, she concentrated on her grandparents' reactions to her news.

Mommi had burst into tears and hugged her tightly. Even Dawdi had looked shaken—in the very best way.

Richard, too, had seemed almost surprised by her acceptance. Obviously, she was going to need to finish her talks with the bishop and agree to become baptized, but there was a definite change. They now had a future.

All that was wonderful.

Realizing that she'd just chosen to move away from every-thing she knew—possibly without her brothers or sister—had shaken her to the core.

After weighing the pros and cons of calling Beth or Jonny, she decided on Beth. Beth was the one most likely to be home and still awake. She loved to watch whole series on Netflix or some other channel late into the evening because her work hours were her own.

Sometimes one just needed an older sister's advice or, at the very least, her understanding ear.

Beth picked up the phone on the second ring. "Hello? Kelsey?"

"*Jah.* I guess it wasn't hard to figure out it was me, huh?"

"Well, Martin is here in Cleveland, so you're right. There weren't a lot of options. I can't imagine either of our grand-parents calling this late unless there was an emergency. There isn't an emergency, is there?"

"Not that I'm aware of," she said with a laugh. "What are you doing?"

"Want to take a guess?"

"It's a toss-up between reading or watching a new series on Netflix. My vote is the series."

"You'd win, though it's on Hulu."

"Is it good?" She didn't bother to ask what it was about. TV shows didn't interest her anymore.

"So-so." Beth shuffled and adjusted the phone to her ear. "I'd rather talk to you, Kels. Want to tell me why you're out at the phone shanty at a quarter to eleven at night?"

"I couldn't sleep."

"No? What happened?"

Taking a deep breath, she blurted out, "Richard asked me to marry him tonight."

"Whoa. Hold on a sec."

Kelsey could hear the phone drop on the couch, followed

by some shuffling of pillows and the click of the remote control.

"Sorry," Beth said when she got back on the line. "You caught me off guard. But Kelsey, I'm shocked!"

"I know. I knew you would be."

"What did you tell him? No, wait. You obviously left some things out. What made him want to ask?"

"We've gotten close."

"How close?"

"Richard says he loves me, Beth." Even thinking about Richard loving her made her entire being fill with happiness.

Her sister chuckled. "That's awfully quick, don't you think?"

"Actually, no. Because I think I love him, too."

"What are you saying?"

"I said yes, Beth. I'm going to marry Richard sometime in the next year." She heard a swift intake of breath. "I know it sounds sudden—"

"Because it is."

"But I've never felt anything like this before." Still feeling swoony, she attempted to put her feelings into words. "He's so amazing, Beth. You wouldn't believe how much responsibility he has as a preacher. Everyone depends on him. Then there's his carpentry work. He's either working at the garage, the door factory, or repairing a table or chair or refurbishing something in someone's house."

"So he's really busy."

"He is. I'm so proud of him."

"What about you?"

"What about me?"

"Well, what are his expectations of you? Does he want you to help him with his preaching responsibilities? Or just wait at home for him?"

The questions stung, and not just because she didn't have

the answers. "Beth, do you hear what you're saying? I called you up to tell you that I got engaged tonight, but you haven't even congratulated me."

"Congratulations."

"Thanks." Sure, sarcasm was thick in her voice, but she had every right to feel miffed, didn't she? "Beth, this is a good thing."

"Honey, I'm sure it is. I'm sorry if I'm not more excited, but you caught me off guard. You have to remember that we haven't talked all that much."

"You have a point."

"Even when I drove down to pick up Patti, we didn't talk about anything more than your struggle with those hens."

"I know."

"Does Richard know you aren't very good at farm chores?"

"He does. He doesn't care about that, Beth. He knows that I'm going to struggle for a while, but he says that He thinks I'm strong. And what's funny is that when I'm here, doing my thing and helping Mommi and Dawdi and seeing Richard, I feel strong. No, better than that. I feel complete."

"He really is your one, isn't he?"

"Yes. I'm really happy, Beth."

"Then I'm happy, too."

"Really?" Pure relief filled her. She'd feared Beth was going to berate her for not being more cautious.

"Really and truly. Have you told Jonny yet?"

"No, I wanted to call you first. Martin doesn't know either."

"What about our grandparents? Do they know?"

"Oh, yes. I told them. They were in the next room trying not to eavesdrop when Richard proposed."

Beth's voice warmed. "And what did they say?"

"They were happy, Beth." Unable to help all the mixed-up emotion in her voice, she added, "They seemed almost as happy as I am."

"Oh, Kelsey. I'm crying right now. I wish I was there to give you a hug."

"I wish you were, too, but this is a close second. Thanks for understanding how I feel."

"You don't ever need to thank me for caring about you, little sister. All I've ever wanted is for you to be happy."

Remembering her talk with Richard about how they were each destined to walk on their own path toward the future, Kelsey said, "I hope you find happiness, too. Soon."

"I will. One day, I know I'm going to be as happy as you are. That's good enough for me."

"I'll pray for you."

"You do that. But don't worry about me. You've got a wedding to plan."

Standing alone in the darkness of the phone shanty, Kelsey grinned. "You're right. I sure do."

"Go back home and get some rest. I'll come see you soon, and we can celebrate in person."

"Thanks, Beth. I love you."

"I love you, too. Now go on home and be careful!"

"I will."

Turning on her flashlight, Kelsey walked back in the dark, Beth's warm words keeping her company.

Chapter 41

Martin hadn't always believed in God's plans for him. Oh, he had faith, and he truly believed in the Lord and the power of prayer. But if he was being truly honest with himself, he would have to admit that sometimes he was in charge of his destiny.

He hadn't thought that was a bad thing, and maybe God didn't either. It was because of these feelings that he'd looked after his younger siblings so much. And the reason he'd worked so hard in school and at his part-time jobs to get the scholarships he'd needed to go to college.

It also was one of the reasons he'd been so sure it was possible to decide to become Amish in his late twenties. In his mind, anything was possible if he put his mind to it, and he was really good at that.

But now he realized that he'd been so very wrong. He might have believed it would be hard to learn Pennsylvania Dutch, go without electricity, and drive a buggy, but he'd never imagined that he would fall in love with an Amish woman.

Or that it would be so hard not to be everything she needed.

The Lord really was in charge after all.

As he drove his SUV down the winding, hilly roads into Walden, his heart felt as if it were being broken into a dozen pieces.

To make matters worse, Patti looked as though she felt the same way.

They'd been on the road for almost an hour. There were only about thirty minutes remaining until he pulled into Patti's driveway. For the first time ever, he wished they were stuck behind an accident or something. Anything to postpone their saying goodbye.

"You doing okay?" he asked. It was a useless question, but he felt the need to break the silence. They'd barely talked and hadn't even had the radio on.

"*Jah*. I'm *gut*."

"Good." He drummed his fingertips on the steering wheel. "I hope everything at your house will be in good order."

"I imagine it will be. Kelsey, your grandparents, and even Preacher Richard said they'd stop by from time to time. Besides, I've only been gone four days."

"Yeah. I guess it wasn't that long. It did go by fast."

"I thought so, too. Plus, it was nice to get to know your other sister. And Jonny, too. Everyone was so kind to me."

"Everyone in my family likes you." Especially him. Glad when the light turned green again, he stepped on the gas. "I mean that, Patti. Um, no matter what happens between you and me, Beth, Kelsey, and Jonny want to keep in touch."

"*Jah*. It will be easy to do that because I live next to your grandparents."

That was the ironic part of it all. Here he'd been on a quest to become Amish because of how much he adored and respected his grandparents, but Patti was the one who was like them. Not him.

The lump that had formed in his throat was threatening to choke him. "That's good," he muttered.

After another five or so minutes, Patti spoke again. "Martin, I've been struggling over how to tell you something this whole way home. I just realized that if I wait much longer, I won't have the opportunity." She glanced his way.

"I'm listening." He hoped he sounded encouraging and not as stressed out as he felt.

"All right. Well, um, I just want you to know that I'm glad we met. I'm also really glad I got to go to the city and see your condominium and how you live. It made today easier."

"How?"

"Before you and I got to know each other, I'd been in a rut. I'd focused on things about myself that I considered to be flaws and let those negative feelings take hold of me. I didn't expect to fall in love or be loved in return."

Their conversation was breaking his heart. "Patti, you are a wonderful person. I think you're beautiful, too. I've never lied to you about that. Those brown eyes, framed by the thickest eyelashes I've ever seen, just about kill me, they're so pretty. And the rest of you . . . well, I'm not going to embarrass you by admitting the things I've noticed. I'm just going to say that there is not one thing about you that I'd change. But listen, the best part about you is your sweetness. You are kind and patient with just about anything." He grinned. "Then, to top it off, you've got a crazy-smart brain when it comes to math and figures. Please believe me when I tell you that you don't need to settle for anyone. Not even me," he said in a whisper.

Feeling awful, he added, "Patti, I'm really sorry. I want to be the person you need me to be. I . . . I just don't know if I can."

"I know. I know and I understand."

"If you do, I don't know how."

"Well, first of all, I believe in love, and second of all, I believe in us. And we're only in our twenties. Maybe something will change for one of us."

"Maybe so." He didn't believe it, though. He'd never ask her to leave her community, and he was almost 100 percent certain he could never be comfortable being Amish.

"Look, we're almost there."

She was right. He'd been so focused on their conversation that he'd practically been driving on autopilot.

After he pulled into the driveway, he popped the back hatch of his vehicle. "I'll help you take everything inside."

"*Danke.*" She got out on her side of the car, clutching her jacket, purse, and the tote bag she'd put in the back seat, full of the items she'd bought at the supercenter the day before.

He went around the back, unloaded her suitcase, and then wheeled it to her door. When she unlocked the front door, he pulled it in.

The house was dark and quiet. A small pile of mail was on the table in the living room, as was a sealed envelope with her name on it.

"Would you like me to walk around the place and make sure everything is okay?" The offer was a bit of a stretch because it was obvious that everything in her house was in good order.

"*Nee,*" she said. "I'll be fine, Martin."

Her statement hit him hard. It was as if those three words were referring to a whole lot more than just the state of her house.

"I understand." He faced her. Gazed into her eyes once again. Allowed himself to look at her lips and remember what it had felt like to kiss them.

Wished that things had been different.

"May I hug you one more time?"

Patti's eyes filled with tears, but she nodded.

He couldn't stand to see her cry. "Shh," he whispered,

though it didn't mean anything. How could he ask her to be quiet when his heart felt like it was breaking as well?

Instead, he wrapped his arms around her, felt her body curve into his, closed his eyes, and inhaled the hint of vanilla and cherries that had always fascinated him so much.

He wanted to tell her that he'd miss her. That he still loved her. But she knew both.

Instead, after pressing his lips to the curve of her neck, he pulled back and released her.

"Bye for now, Patti."

"*Jah*. Bye for now." She smiled.

And showed Martin that she was not only beautiful and smart but braver than he. Because tears were falling down her cheeks unabated.

She wasn't afraid for him to see how she felt.

It was too much to take.

He turned around and walked out the door. Got in his vehicle and turned on the ignition. And after he backed out, he bypassed his grandparents' house.

It might be wrong, but he couldn't face them. Couldn't face any of them. His emotions were too high, and he didn't trust himself not to change his mind.

And so he turned right instead of left and headed back to the highway. In an hour and a half, he'd be back at his condo.

He wasn't sure that was where he belonged, but he had nowhere else to go.

Not yet.

Chapter 42

It had been two weeks since Martin had taken Patti home and then left again without stopping by to see her or their grandparents.

Kelsey had been so mad when she found that out, she'd given him a call at work, where he'd been rehired, and had given him a piece of her mind. But instead of arguing with her the way he usually did, or trying to get her to understand, he'd apologized for not taking time to see her before hanging up.

Which made her feel worse.

For all her life, Martin had been her compass. He'd reminded her about doing good deeds, given her perspective when she'd been upset with her friends, and provided the love and support she'd been so desperate for when they'd been shuttled back and forth between their parents.

She'd thought the two of them were especially close to each other. She'd even thought they were meant to become Amish together. She'd been wrong.

She didn't fault his decision, though. She knew enough

about this journey they were on to realize each person needed to do it at their own speed. So she didn't blame him for his choice one bit.

But she was having a very difficult time now that he was essentially out of her life.

"Ah, there you are," Richard said when he found her sitting next to the henhouse. "Your grandmother said she thought you might be out here."

"I seem to be out here any time I have extra time." Standing up, she showed him the simple white stool she'd been sitting on. "Dawdi made me this."

He grinned. "Not every woman in Walden is blessed enough to have her own special white stool so she can chat with her chickens."

She laughed. "I agree. My grandfather is the best." Embarrassed that she'd become so close to the very hen she'd once prayed would be Sunday supper, she smoothed out the skirts of her eggplant-colored dress. "Here, we can go in. It's a little chilly out here."

"I have on a coat, and you've got on both a sweatshirt and a shawl. We can stay out here for a spell if you'd like." He waggled his eyebrows. "We'll have some privacy."

"That's true. Dawdi went over to Mount Hope for the auction today, and Mommi is sewing in the living room."

"Stay here a moment. I have an idea." He disappeared into the barn and came out with a blanket. Sometimes they put it on the horses, but most of the time her grandfather kept it on hand for moments like this. He always said that one never knew when a thick blanket would come in handy.

Kelsey watched him smooth it on the ground beside the barn. They would be near the hens but in their own space. Most of the hens seemed to be napping, so it was fairly quiet, too.

"My lady?"

Shaking her head at his silliness, she sat down on the blanket. When Richard joined her, he wrapped an arm around her shoulders and pulled her close against him.

"That's better, *jah*?" he murmured.

"Much."

"So, how are you doing? Feeling any better?"

"Leave it to you not to shy away from the hard stuff."

"I've got some practice talking about hard stuff. Besides, I'm worried about you."

She shrugged. "I guess I'm better—I don't know. I should be. Poor Patti still looks like her world ended." She sighed. "Maybe that's part of my problem, Richard. I'm so happy for the two of us but sad for both Martin and Patti."

"I know you are. There's nothing wrong with feeling both happy and sad at the same time, by the way."

"It doesn't seem to make sense, though."

"I like to think that our hearts are big enough to be able to handle both things."

"I suppose." She looked up at him. "I want them to be happy, though. And Richard, you might think I'm being awful, but I think they need to be together no matter what."

"I know." Reaching for her hand, he threaded his fingers through hers. "And for the record, I don't think you're being awful."

"But you don't agree."

"I take my baptismal vows seriously, Kelsey. Even if I wasn't a preacher, I'd expect everyone else to take them seriously, too."

"So you think Martin should become Amish."

"I think it's up to him and God. Not me." Looking down at her, he continued, "Besides, I'd rather talk about you and me and our future."

"Your sister told me that there's been talk at your house about building a *dawdi haus*."

"There has been. My *mamm* and *daed* have said they'd

be happy in their own little place and will leave the big house to you."

"What do you think about that?"

"I think I'd like to sleep next to you without my parents' being in the room next to ours."

She could feel her cheeks heat. "You can't say things like that."

"Sure I can." He laughed. "Seriously, I think that would be a good thing. It's how a lot of families do things anyway."

Kelsey nodded. Thinking about being Richard's wife. Taking care of him and his brother and sister and parents and the house. And doing it all without the dozen modern conveniences she was so used to. "It scares me a little. All that responsibility."

"I know, but you'll have help."

"Do you think I'll be able to handle it? Our wedding is in six months."

"Yes."

"Just like that? You sound so sure."

Just as he was about to answer her, something caught his eye. Without a word, he opened the henhouse door. Anna walked out, her head high. Acting as if she owned the place. "Richard—"

"Wait. And talk to your friend, Kelsey."

He knew that silly hen had become her confidante. "Hi, Anna. Have you been listening to our conversation and decided to weigh in?"

Anna pecked at the ground, glanced at Richard, then walked toward her.

Before Kelsey could stop herself, she was holding that chicken as if it was a favorite pup.

"Relax, Kelsey. Let her sit on your lap."

"My lap?" When Richard just raised an eyebrow, she situated the stout hen on her lap and then let herself relax.

To her surprise, Anna tucked her beak under a wing and went to sleep.

"Richard!" she whispered. "Look what she did. I can't believe it."

"I can. The two of you have become fast friends. I think that chicken likes you."

"It's a mira—" she stopped herself just in time. Smiling up at him, she said, "Did you know Anna was going to do this?"

"*Nee.*"

"But?"

"But I thought it was a possibility." Lowering his voice, he said, "I figured anything could happen because I'm engaged to you."

"You're right." Who would've ever imagined that she would accompany her brother to Amish country, follow his lead, and then become the one better suited to this new life?

And never would she have imagined she would meet Richard right away and they'd practically fall head over heels in love instantly?

"Faith means expecting the unexpected," she murmured. "Don't you think?"

"*Jah.*" Dipping his head, he kissed her.

She raised her hands around his neck, enjoying his passion. Loving the sweet words he was murmuring, reveling in how perfect the moment was.

All while holding a sleeping hen on her lap.

He was right. If all this was possible, anything could happen for Martin. And for Beth and Jonny, too.

When at last they parted, her pulse racing and her body feeling comfortably languid, she smiled.

She'd take one thing at a time and let the Lord do the rest. And the first step was knowing she wanted to be Amish.

She was sure of that.

Chapter 43

It was June. How had that happened? After all these days of helping Sylvia and Kelsey plan and organize and cook, the wedding day had arrived.

He looked as handsome as ever. No, Patti decided, Martin Schrock looked even more handsome than she remembered. And she'd thought it wasn't possible to forget one single thing about him.

She'd sure tried, though.

"Patti, would you like another cup of kaffi?" Sylvia asked. "It's decaf, you know."

"*Danke*, but I think not. I'm going to head home soon."

Dear Sylvia's expression faded a bit. "Are you okay?"

"*Jah.*" She smiled brightly and kept that smile on her lips until Sylvia turned away to offer another guest some decaf.

When she did at last, Patti admitted the truth to herself. Which was that she wasn't okay. Not at all.

There was no way she would ever admit it, though. Most especially not to Sylvia.

Not when she and Josiah had been celebrating their granddaughter's wedding all day. Their granddaughter's Amish wedding to the community's preacher at that. It had been a wonderful-*gut* day for the older couple, who had lived through many hardships, both when their son had jumped the fence, then later divorced, and then still later had essentially turned his back on all four of his children.

Now, all this time later, they had one of their grandchildren baptized in their faith and another one moving in with every intention of being baptized as well.

Yes, there was much to be celebrated in the Schrock family. No reason at all for any of them to dwell on Patti's heartache.

As laughter broke out, Patti watched Richard clasp Kelsey's hand and raise her knuckles to his lips. Kelsey's expression, illuminated by the bonfire, was filled with love and longing.

There had been more than one whispered joke about how eager the couple looked for their wedding night. One woman in the kitchen had even cackled that she would be surprised if Richard allowed Kelsey to stay at the reception a full hour.

The joke had been shocking, but many of the other women had smiled at one another knowingly. Passion and marriage went hand in hand, it seemed. Especially with a couple as in love as Richard and Kelsey.

Getting to her feet, Patti decided to sneak out while she could. Her spirits were plummeting, and she was embarrassed about how selfish that was. She really would have thought she could push aside her sadness for at least one day.

Standing up, she headed toward the house, then, at the last minute, detoured toward the barn. Just beyond it was the well-worn path to her land and house. The evening was cool even though they were in the midst of summer. In no time the walk would be a noisy and brighter one, thanks to the crickets chirping and the fireflies dancing in the dark.

Now, though, her only company was the half-moon and the stars. There hadn't been a cloud in the sky, which made for a particularly sparkly night.

"Patti, were you really going to leave without telling me goodbye?"

He'd come after her. Glad that they were on the other side of Josiah's barn so no one could see them, Patti stopped. "Martin, you know there was no point."

"No point in telling me goodbye?" His voice, husky and warm, sent chill bumps down the back of her neck.

Or maybe that was because of the way his breath felt against her bare skin. She closed her eyes and reminded herself not to turn around.

He spoke again. "I told you I was leaving early tomorrow morning."

"I remember."

"Then?"

"Martin, there's nothing to say."

"Are you going to turn around?"

Her hands fisted. Did she want to face him? Yes. Was it a wise decision? No. No, it was not. "Martin, I need to go home, not stand here and talk to you."

He paused. For a second, Patti was sure he'd been about to run a finger down the side of her throat. Along her birthmark. Just as he had the last night she'd been in Cleveland. When they'd ordered in and pretended to watch a movie.

Her pulse quickened as she remembered how his touch had felt. Slightly rough. Perfectly masculine.

Beautifully right.

Over the part of her she'd been once so embarrassed about but now only viewed as another part of her body. Maybe it was her prayers that had stopped his hand.

Maybe it was Martin's own.

"I miss you so much. Have you given any more thought to what I said?" he asked urgently.

Oh yes, she had. But could she tell him that? She didn't think so.

The truth was that she missed Martin. She missed him so badly, she'd been sure nothing in her life was going to have any color in it again. He'd given her so much but then had taken it all away when he'd asked her to make an impossible choice.

"*Nee,*" she said.

Martin inhaled sharply. Turned around and started walking back to the party. Back to his life.

She remained where she was. It was impossible to move. Even if she tried, she didn't think her feet would take her anywhere. Tears pricked her eyes. And because there was no one to see them, Patti allowed them to fall.

What had she done? Had she made the wrong choice? When her body was racked with sobs, she pressed a hand to her mouth to stifle them. Her body froze. For a second, it felt as if she couldn't breathe. Had her heart stopped?

"I'm not giving up," Martin called out. "In a couple of weeks, I'm going to be back, Patti. Don't you dare act surprised when I show up at your door."

As his voice faded, she drew in a deep breath. At last, the paralysis that had seemed to take over her body lifted.

Maybe it was because her heart had started beating again.

He was coming back? Giving thanks, Patti continued her journey home. No one needed to know that her steps already felt a little lighter.